MASTERS OF DARKNESS

MASTERS OF DARKNESS

MURRAY LEINSTER

INTRODUCTION BY
SAM MOSKOWITZ

COVER BY
HOWARD V. BROWN

ILLUSTRATED BY
ROGER B. MORRISON
VIRGIL FINLAY

POPULAR PUBLICATIONS · 2021

TABLE OF CONTENTS

Introduction by Sam Moskowitz i

The Darkness on Fifth Avenue 1

The City of the Blind 83

The Storm That Had to be Stopped 141

The Man Who Put Out the Sun 219

About the Author 294

INTRODUCTION BY
SAM MOSKOWITZ

THE YEAR 1929 was a boom year for science fiction. Hugo Gernsback, who had fathered *Amazing Stories*, lost control of the magazine but not his interest in science fiction. He came back with the first competition the field had yet seen, producing under one banner *Science Wonder Stories, Air Wonder Stories* and *Science Wonder Quarterly* all in the same year as well as a group of pamphlets called the *Science Fiction Series*. It was a year when the weird-fantasy magazine, *Weird Tales*, aware of the stepped up tempo was offering "The Dunwich Horror" and "The Silver Key" by H.P. Lovecraft as just two of many stellar performances from a team that included Robert E. Howard, Clark Ashton Smith, Henry S. Whitehead, S. Fowler Wright, Gaston Leroux, Seabury Quinn and Otis Adelbert Kline.

In the general periodicals such as *Blue Book*, Edgar Rice Burroughs followed quickly on the heels of "Tanar of Pellucidar" by showing "Tarzan at the Earth's Core." Somehow, in an argosy magazine that had just completed science fiction attractions by Otis Adelbert Kline, Erle Stanley Gardner, Ralph Milne Farley, F.V.W. Mason, Garrett Smith and Ray Cummings, a veteran named Murray Leinster managed to score powerfully enough with "The Darkness on Fifth Avenue" to rate three sequels and a "welcome back!" from devoted science fiction readers who had seen only a few things by him in the previous eight years.

Murray Leinster was to remain a "regular irregular" in science fiction from that point on. "The Darkness on Fifth Avenue," published when S.S. van Dine was all the rage in detective stories and scientific sleuthing was very much the vogue, forcibly reminded the reader ship that science was not the exclusive property of the forces of law and order, that brilliant minds could ally criminal ingenuity with science and that a scientist might well have to be the strong right arm of the law if sanity were to survive.

—Sam Moskowitz

THE DARKNESS ON FIFTH AVENUE

*An Amazing And Baffling New Weapon
Of The Underworld Puts New York At
Crime's Mercy And Leaves The City's Police
Blindly Groping In A Topsy-Turvy World*

1

BLOTTED OUT

THE MOON WAS shining brightly in Central Park as Police Lieutenant Hines went at a leisurely pace toward his home. He'd been at a party, and it had been a tiresome one, as far as he was concerned.

The gravel under his feet crunched and crackled. He pulled a cigar out of his pocket and lighted it. The path curved and recurved. It came out at the edge of the lake and followed along its shore. And the moon was rising high above the tall apartments that line Fifth Avenue. Its light flickered and shimmered on the water in small, irregularly-shaped lambent flames.

Hines slowed down and stopped, to look at it. Shrubbery on every hand, silvered by the moonlight. The rising shores of the farther side of the lake were made queerly glamorous. The throbbing, rumbling murmur of the city all about him came as a curious incongruity. It seemed particularly odd because the wavelets of the lake were running up on the shore edge with small lapping noises, and it seemed that the city should be thousands of miles away. And Hines could hear the heavy, rather monotonous plashing of the huge fountain at the end of the Mall, but it sounded like a waterfall.

"It is pretty, isn't it?" said a girl's voice behind him.

Hines turned around. A girl was sitting on a bench, quite alone. She couldn't have been speaking to any one else.

She lifted her hand as if in a gesture for him to sit down beside her. He couldn't make out her face, but the slim silken legs were shapely in the moonlight, and the dress was fresh and cool.

Police Lieutenant Hines smiled to himself. Being attached to the detective bureau, he never wore a uniform, and he was off duty anyhow. He said unreproachfully:

"Sister, I'm a cop. You ought to be careful."

But the girl chuckled. She clasped her hands together and laughed; and then she chuckled again.

"But, Mr. Hines, it isn't against police regulations to speak to an acquaintance in the park, is it? Or do you deny my acquaintance?"

Hines stared and suddenly flushed.

"I'm Kathryn Bush," said the girl on the bench, still amusedly. "Remember me, now?"

"Oh, Lord, yes!" said Hines.

"I'm not hunting copy to-night," she assured him, with a bare trace of malice. "I came out to be by myself and look at the moon and be stupid and romantic. The combination's necessary, isn't it—stupidity and romance?"

HINES PUFFED AT his cigar.

"I was wondering myself," he admitted ruefully. "I just came from a party. The girls were pretty and stupid, and the music was stupid and pretty. And I didn't have a good time. I've been enjoying myself more, just looking at the moonlight, than I did at the party."

*He fired blindly
into that sudden,
mysterious black void.*

There was a little pause.

" 'Sentiment on the Police Force,'" murmured a soft voice. " 'Police Lieutenant Hines Discovered Moon-Gazing. Famous Vamp-Proof Detective Prefers Chaste Luna to Chasing Flappers. Special to the *Star!*' "

Hines stiffened and groaned. That was the exact method Kathryn Bush used in her column in the *Star.* She could make any man ridiculous; and she could twist her column to the bitterest and most sardonic tragedy when she chose.

"Don't!" said Hines desperately. "Please! I'd—"

"I wouldn't," said the girl. But she chuckled. "It wasn't even a temptation. Don't worry. I like you much too well. You do play fair, Mr. Hines, and you get fair play in the city rooms. I was sorry, afterward, that I treated you as I did."

She'd served him up to her delighted readers after the

Paulson murder case, which he'd handled. On the whole she'd let him off easily. He knew it. She'd been no worse than gently malicious about one or two of his personal traits—enough to let people who knew him rag him.

There was another pause.

"I fibbed when I said I came out here to be alone," she said suddenly. "I had a sort of hunch that something was going to happen. Intuition, if you like. I don't know—I get hunches sometimes. When I saw you, I knew I was right. You generally manage to be where things are happening, too. What's going to happen?"

"Nothing that I know of," said Hines. He was relieved by her promise not to use him again in her column. "I was just walking home. That's all."

"Then," she said comfortably, "you'd better sit down. Something is going to happen. It always does."

Hines sat down. The waves were lapping almost at their feet, on the other side of the path. A park light glowed perhaps twenty yards away. Now and again the soft purring of a motor car on one of the automobile roads came to their ears.

"What do you think will happen?" asked Hines, mildly amused.

"I don't know," she admitted. "It's just a feeling."

The purring of a car came near. It was a heavy, powerful car, and the singing of its tires was as loud as the noise of its motor. It was moving slowly—very slowly. It went by the bench hardly more than fifty feet away, on the other side of a planting of shrubbery. A voice came suddenly from it, a trifle muted by the distance and the car's movement.

"Hell! How long's it goin' t' take yuh?"

Hines stiffened. He knew that voice, but couldn't place it. Some one he'd had dealings with some time. A crook's voice.

"I'm ready now."

This second voice was clipped and precise. Hines frowned to himself. He didn't know the second voice at all. But the first was—was—somebody he knew, and somebody who was wanted.

"Jam on the brakes, Pete," ordered the voice he knew. "He's goin' to try it now."

BRAKES SQUEALED, THIRTY or forty yards away. The park was very quiet indeed. It seemed as if the two on the bench could even hear movements within the softly purring car.

Hines felt the girl looking up at him. He was listening, while he racked his brains for a name.

"I think it must be happening," she said detachedly. "My hunches do work out sometimes."

The harsh, precise voice reached them:

"Look at the moon."

Involuntarily the girl raised her eyes. The full moon was swimming in a sea of stars. It was big and bright and smiling—

It went out.

Pitch darkness fell instantly. Hines was on his feet in a second. He felt the girl's hand tighten convulsively on his arm. He unbuttoned his coat unobtrusively, seized his service revolver.

But he was staring about into a blackness which was exactly that of a moonless night with a sky full of thunder-clouds. The suddenness of the fallen darkness was

horrible. Its completeness was terrifying. The silence all
about became ghastly.

There was no noise except the lapping water and the
sound of a powerful motor idling at low speed a little way
off, and a tiny sound which was not even a whisper—the
vagrant night breeze stirring the leaves of the trees and
shrubbery.

The silvery moonlight was cut off, absolutely. The moon
had gone out. The stars had ceased to exist. Yet, dimly—
very dimly—the opposite shore of the lake was visible.
Its outline was sharp. And flickers of what could only be
moonlight came from there, bright and vivid and scintil-
lating. Hines flung his head back once more. The sky was
blotted out exactly as if some one had suddenly placed a
roof over a part of Central Park.

Then a voice came from forty or fifty yards away. The
clipped, precise voice of the second man in the car.

"Satisfied?" It was almost a snarl of triumph.

"Yeah!" came the first voice again. It was awed, and it
was exultant. "Plenty! If y' c'n do the rest y' say, it's a cinch!"

The darkness lifted, exactly as if some one had turned
on soft lights with a switch. The moon shone down again,
round and benign and placid, swimming in a sea of stars.
There was the minor roaring of a heavy car going into first
speed, second, and away.

Hines suddenly uttered an exclamation.

"Lefty Dunn!"

The girl beside him was shaken. Her grip on his sleeve
showed that. The abrupt and complete darkness and its
equally complete and abrupt removal, had unnerved her.

But she shook herself a little and became the newspaper woman again.

"It happened," she said coolly, in a voice that quavered only a little. "But what was it?"

"That voice was Lefty Dunn," said Hines grimly. "I thought he was in Chicago. He's wanted—for murder, among other things. If he'd known I was sitting here, he'd have taken a chance on trying to plug me, with a good car for a get-away. He has no particular reason to love me."

"But the darkness!" said the girt sharply. "What was that? And why was it done?"

Hines looked at her blankly for an instant. Then he searched the sky. From horizon to horizon the stars shone out through the smoky haze which the city itself interposes between itself and heaven. There was no trace of cloud, no trace of any mistiness which was not of the city's own production.

"I THOUGHT—" HINES knitted his brows, and then said impatiently:

"I don't know what it was, but I've got to get word in that Lefty Dunn's in town. He's— Good Lord!" He stared at her. "Did you hear those voices in that car, and what they said?"

"Of course!"

He took her elbow and began to march her along the path at a rate that forced her to trot a little.

"Lefty said, 'When are you going to be ready?' and some one said they were ready then. And that second voice said to look at the moon, and the moon went out. And then somebody, the same voice, asked if Lefty was satisfied."

Hines was talking almost feverishly and increasing his pace toward the Mall. "Do you see what it means?"

"I see," said the girl practically, "that to-morrow afternoon I have a headline, 'Moon Turned Off in Central Park,' and some wise-cracks about cruelty to petters in the city's recreation spaces."

Hines was hastening his pace almost to a run. The path they were following branched. One branch led out to the smooth automobile roadway. The other meandered on about the lake. Hines fairly dragged the girl down the shorter branch, toward the nearest police phone.

"Please don't!" he said sharply. "It is too serious for that— much too serious! Lefty Dunn's a dangerous man. He's one of the very few men who can organize criminals into coop-eration. Don't you see that if we aren't crazy, both of us—"

Lights swept the ground before him. A horn honked in a startled fashion. There was a swoop and a rush and a humming noise, and Hines jerked the girl with him as he flung himself backward.

A huge car flashed by so swiftly that its back mudguard flicked at the girl's sheer skirt.

A voice came back from it. "Get t' hell outer the way!"

The car was gone, and Hines was staring after it and reaching into his pocket, his lips compressed.

"Things are happening," said the slightly shaky voice of the girl beside him. "Thanks. They weren't a bit careful, were they?"

"That's Lefty Dunn's car again," said Hines grimly, "and I got its license number, which may mean nothing at all."

The car was speeding away, smoothly and silently, its headlight beams visible through mist and dust-swirls.

Hines began to write swiftly; but the girl caught at his arm again.

"Look! Oh, look!" she gasped.

The automobile roadway branched, ahead, and there were two cars with gleaming headlights coming down toward the intersection. Each one was perhaps twenty yards from the point where they would be visible to each other.

Lefty Dunn's car slowed down; and suddenly, before it there poured out a dense cloud of blackness. It was not smoke. It was not dust. The headlights of Lefty Dunn's own car bored into it and were smothered instantly, without being dissipated or reflected. It did not waver, as a mass of smoke or vapor would have done.

Dunn's car was going ahead still swiftly, though at less than its former rate, and it did not run into the darkness. The darkness kept on ahead! It seemed even to have a definite cone-shaped form.

Now the intersection of roads, and the traffic policeman at that intersection, and the tall hillock of earth behind it which had been brilliantly illuminated a moment before—everything was blotted out utterly.

From that incredible oblivion came a terrific crashing noise. Instantly thereafter the darkness vanished. The headlights of Lefty Dunn's car shone pitilessly upon the scene. One car had its nose halfway into the chauffeur's compartment of the other. Both of them had been slued around by the shock.

A woman began to scream shrilly in one of the cars. A man dragged himself out of the other. The traffic policeman ran to the spot, blowing on his whistle.

Lefty Dunn's car swerved to avoid the wreckage, took the right-hand road, and swept on out of sight.

THERE WAS NOTHING in the least peculiar about the rest of it. It was merely an automobile accident, and an ambulance arrived and administered first aid, and a long time later two derrick-cars arrived and towed the crippled machines away; and there was only a puddle of oil and a few splinters of glass left to show that anything had happened. The only thing at all odd was that the traffic cop and all the occupants of both cars insisted that they had simultaneously been stricken blind for a few seconds before the crash, and that that blindness had been the cause of the collision.

2

A TERRIBLE WEAPON

HINES LEFT THE office of the commissioner of police next morning with his jaw tightly set. In his own car, on the way back to his office, he swore softly but luridly; and he went into his office with an expression in which impatience was the least disagreeable ingredient. The commissioner of police had been incredulous and at the last impatient himself. The corroboration of the traffic cop had been dismissed as a very clumsy alibi for carelessness. Even the park policeman who had seen the moon go out for two minutes withered under the commissioner's sarcasm. Hines sat down at his desk and swore steadily, getting madder the longer he thought about it. He knew what he had seen. Two other members of the police force backed-him up. A total of seven people in two cars which had been smashed up made exactly the same statements. And the whole thing was dismissed as a pipe dream.

It was only when disgust began to take the place of wrath that he noticed a report on his desk. He'd given orders that the license number he had noted down should be traced. The report was laconic, in the usual form. The license had been traced to Oliver Wetmore of —— Central Park West. Mr. Wetmore was in Europe, and the car, a Pierce-Arrow, was in storage. The reporting officer had examined the car in the storage garage and found the license plates missing.

"Stolen," said Hines grimly. "Anybody who went to put a car in storage or take one out could have taken them. Somebody did. It's a dead end; but it proves, anyhow, that whoever was using 'em last night is crooked."

He called headquarters and succinctly repeated the report, asking that all officers on beat be ordered to look out for the number and report it by police phone. Within half an hour every uniformed man on the streets of New York would be watching for it, among other things. Those other things would include twenty-seven small lost children; five runaway girls, with descriptions attached; seventeen stolen cars—license numbers given; anywhere from four to fifteen fugitives from justice; and a philosophical anarchist.

It did not look especially promising. Hines knew it. But he also knew that the famous police dragnet sometimes has its inexplicable successes. Meantime he made some telephone calls.

The Museum of Natural History referred him to the research bureau of the American Electric Company. After twenty minutes of more or less patient waiting he had an anonymous specialist in research physics on the wire, who listened with amused patience to his account and then told him tolerantly that what he had seen was impossible. Light could be neutralized, to be sure. Monochromatic light could be altered by another monochromatic wavelength to a non-visible color. And interference would neutralize even sunlight, but only by the use of partial reflection, which was only practicable under laboratory conditions.

Hines thanked him politely and hung up.

"But, dammit, I saw it!" he growled.

The phone rang as he prepared to make still another call. It was Kathryn Bush.

"Good morning." She seemed to be amused. "Have you been told you're crazy?"

"I have!" said Hines grimly.

"So have I," she laughed. "But I have a news item for you. It wasn't used anywhere, but it's news. Get a pencil and write it down."

Hines pulled a memo pad into place. "Ready."

SHE READ SLOWLY. There is a vast amount of news that goes into newspaper offices, and more especially into the press associations, which is either unimportant or improbable and never sees print.

" 'Edginton, New York. This town has heard a lot about freak weather, but Elias Rowe, of Stony Mountain, makes the latest contribution. Mr. Rowe drove over from Stony Mountain to-day to ship two calves and buy supplies. He reports that Stony Mountain is getting the fanciest brand of summer weather yet. He first noticed it a month ago, when as he was plowing his north twenty field he noticed a grateful shade. He looked up and saw the sun shining brightly, but with most of its heat missing, and the sky much darker than usual. He went home and put on his coat.

"Nearly every day since then he's been getting fancier weather. He reports that yesterday it was pitch-dark for over half an hour in his barnyard, so dark that even with a lantern he couldn't see to water his horses at dinner time. He was inquiring how long these here eclipses were going to keep up, but when assured that nothing of the sort had been seen in Edginton, he drove home muttering about city wisecrackers. Local wits assert that Stony Mountain has either an inferior brand of sunshine or a very superior brand of moonshine."

"Got it," said Hines laconically. "What about it?"

"It's about a month old," came the voice over the wire.

"I was wondering if it didn't refer to some experiments with apparatus that might—er—turn out the moon."

Hines stared. Then:

"It sounds like it," he admitted. "I'll look up Edginton—"

"I have," said the voice in the receiver, comfortably. "It's a little hamlet of about three hundred people, away upstate. Stony Mountain isn't a village. It's a mountain, with no more than two or three houses within miles. A splendid place to do experiments of this sort in."

"Thanks. You ought to be on the force."

She laughed once more.

"Oh, this stuff is a bribe. I expect to be given the inside, when you find out what's up."

"Something's up, all right," agreed Hines grimly. "Lefty Dunn had those two cars smashed up just to see if he could, I'm thinking. The moon business was a test, the wreck was an experiment."

She rang off, and Hines read the clipping over again. It did look foolish in one way, and it looked important in another.

This clipping had been discarded from the news because it was impossible. And what Hines had seen had been termed impossible by a scientific authority. And yet, if Hines wasn't crazy, he'd heard Lefty Dunn ask somebody to give a demonstration of some sort, and the demonstration had been the putting out of the moon.

Considering what had happened later, it seemed probable that some piece of apparatus had been pointed upward into the air, from the car in which Lefty Dunn was riding. Later the same car had shot out a beam of darkness straight ahead of it instead of upward, and that beam had blotted out its own headlights, the headlights of two other cars, and a park light just over a traffic officer's head. It was at least conceivable that the production of an accident had been another demonstration.

But the question before Hines was, why had Lefty Dunn been chosen as the person to be convinced that a certain apparatus could throw a beam of darkness in any chosen direction from a car? What had he meant when he said, "If y' can do the rest y' say, it's a cinch?" What else had the man with the clipped, precise voice claimed he could do? Was the beam of darkness ahead of the car the thing in question— Was—

THE PHONE RANG sharply.

"Hello!"

"Lieutenant Hines, a report on the license number you queried." Clickings, and the fainter voice of a patrolman on beat, making his regular report at the box telephone. "The car with license J 41166, sir, is parked just on Madison Avenue on Fifty-Eighth Street, sir. It's been there two hours, sir, and I tied a ticket to the steering-wheel and made a note of the number and recognized it as one to look out for."

"Still there, eh?" asked Hines.

"Yes, sir," said the faint and faraway voice. Hines could

hear the rumbling of traffic in the police telephone transmitter.

"Keep an eye on it. Lefty Dunn was riding in it last night," said Hines briskly. "I'll be there in fifteen minutes."

He hung up and instinctively felt beneath his coat for the regulation revolver. Lefty Dunn would be a dangerous man to arrest. If the street was crowded it wouldn't be wise to try it unless they could jump him so he wouldn't have a chance to pull a gun.

The little police runabout had no outward indication of its official status. But there is, if you have noticed it, a certain sequence of numbers that you never see on any but police cars. Neither the first numbers nor the last ones are involved, but if a car breaks all traffic rules and the traffic cop ignores it, and you can discover no sign about it anywhere that explains its exemption, why the letter designation on the license plates is "C," and the next to the last two figures are three and six.

Honking impatiently, the little runabout threaded traffic, crossed against traffic lights with a certain confident impunity, and went streaking up Madison Avenue. Hines was driving, and he was in civilian clothes, of course. His companion smoked languidly as the car darted northward.

Its horn blew impatiently as the patrolman on beat dawdled past. He looked unhurriedly, and made an inconspicuous motion with his hand. Hines drew up to the curb, stepped out, and stopped the patrolman with exactly the air of one asking for information.

"In front of the Blowbar Building, sir," said the uniformed man. "Been there about two hours, now. The tag's on the steering-wheel."

"Right. Thanks."

Hines went leisurely to the corner. He saw it at once. The car of the night before, powerful and gleaming and insolent, standing before one of those incredibly slender eighteen-story buildings that spring up on narrow frontages in New York. The building was new. Next to it an old-fashioned, sedate brownstone house still stood blowsily, with a "Furnished Rooms" sign visible in the front parlor window. There were three other houses just like it, and then a massive building of six or seven stories that went on to the end of the block and Park Avenue.

Hines went briskly across the street, turned into the office building, and scrutinized the floor directory carefully, as if he were looking for a name and was puzzled at its absence. Nothing. The lobby was merely a golden-marble entryway to the building, and a means of communication with its two elevators, both now aloft. There was no one in sight at all. From inside, however, Hines could look the car over thoroughly. It was a Packard, not a Pierce-Arrow, and he was justified in making an arrest on account of the false license plates alone. The street, too, was by no means crowded, and while gunplay would not be desirable, it could be risked.

HE WENT OUT of the building and saw his companion from the roadster strolling toward the corner. The patrolman idled negligently near by. And then, quite suddenly, there was the clashing of elevator-doors from the building he had just left, and four men came out. Hines looked at them swiftly, recognized two of them. He thought he recognized a third. The fourth was Lefty Dunn.

He signaled with his hand. His companion and the

patrolman drifted his way as the four men moved to the car and stood a moment, talking, beside it. The door of the blowsy brownstone house opened and a man came out of it. He was a tall, blond individual with flowing yellow whiskers. He came down the steps to the pavement.

Hines saw a nod pass among the men beside the car. One of them climbed into the chauffeur's seat and pressed on the starter. Hines unbuttoned his coat. And suddenly his whistle shrilled.

It was not quite quick enough. He blew it instead of opening fire, but even a shot would not have been quick enough. The three men beside the car had jerked glittering things out of their pockets. The sharp barking of automatic pistols cut through the shrilling of the whistle, and the tall man shuddered suddenly and began to collapse slowly to the pavement. The automatics barked.

Suddenly everything went dark. One instant Hines had been hurtling himself toward the huddled group of three men who were pumping lead at an evidently intended victim. The next instant he was careering through a blackness that was utterly opaque. He could not see the ground below him, or the sides of the street, or the sky. He felt the pavement striking the soles of his feet, but otherwise he might have been lost in the abyss of nothingness.

The whistle went on shrilling eerily in the darkness. In that absolute opacity before him a man cursed, and some one began to shoot at random. A bullet stung the skin of Hines's arm. He shot savagely at the sound. There was no flash to shoot at. He stumbled on the curbstone as some one squealed. A voice was roaring orders, and the exhaust of the big Packard boomed. Caroming wildly on, Hines struck a man. He fell on him savagely, striking viciously as the man collapsed, twisting an automatic from the unseen fingers and flinging it away. The man writhed and was still.

The voices were almost on top of him. Hines shot furiously at the space below them. Then a clash of gears, so near that he put out his hand. Something brushed against it and was gone. He knew the feel. He had reached out and touched the moving tire of the car at the curbing. He had been so close that but for the blackness he could have leaped into it. It roared away, sharply, swiftly—

There was silence except for the traffic noises, and startled, excited exclamations. The patrolman was blundering about.

"Lieutenant! Lieutenant Hines!"

"Here!" snapped Hines. "See how far this damned darkness extends. I've killed a man, I think, and they killed another one first."

"It stopped at the corner," said the plain-clothes man dazedly, blundering toward Hines in the blackness. "I came into it because I heard you shooting, sir. What—"

Hines swore again. He'd struck a match, which had not seemed to light, and he'd burned his finger on the invisible flame. He struck another, now, and held it carefully closer and closer to his eyes. At four inches he could just distinguish it. At two inches its flame was clear. He thought he could see his finger in the light.

But he began to feel the man underneath him. His victim, no doubt. A sickish feeling came over him as he felt something warm and wet on his fingers. He felt unspeakably ghoulish, squatting there in the darkness. The hair rose at the back of his neck.

WITH AN INFINITELY slight sensation of flickering, the darkness vanished. The street, the sky, the buildings on every hand flashed into view. There was a dead man under him, and his hand was stained red, and there was another man lying quite still on the pavement a few yards away, and the patrolman was in the act of blundering against a brick wall. The plain-clothes man was fumbling his way with outstretched hands through broad daylight.

Hines stood up. He wanted to be sick, and he was filled with a vast and incredible rage. Two other uniformed men were running toward the spot.

"Get an ambulance," snapped Hines savagely. He looked in the direction in which the big car had disappeared. It was no longer in sight, of course. It had turned into Park Avenue and was mingled indistinguishably with the other traffic. "Take a look at that man there. See who he is. I'm going to look in this building."

He turned into the office building. An elevator was coming down. The doors slid open as he reached out his hand to touch the summonsing button. A broad-shouldered man with a professional Vandyke and a professional-looking bag in one hand and suitcase in the other, stepped out.

"Can you tell me what that shooting was?" he asked harshly. "I'm a doctor, and I thought I might be needed. You're hurt! Here, let me fix it."

"It's not my blood," snapped Hines. There are two men out in the street who need looking after. I'm a police officer."

He dismissed the elevator-passenger summarily and fixed the colored elevator-boy with his eye. Hines should have been more tactful. He should have been less official and much more pleasant. But he was human, and he was wild with rage at the knowledge that he had been squatting on the pavement within a yard of a car into which murderers were fumbling their way, and while they shot ahead, out of the arbitrary zone of darkness, and so to an accomplished escape.

"Y-yes, suh!" gasped the elevator-boy. He turned several shades lighter when he saw a glistening reddish stain on the hand that pointed a grim finger at him. "Y-yass, suh!"

"You know the clients of this building. How many offices have been rented lately—within a week or two, or a day or so?"

"A-ain't but one, suh."

"Take me there, in a hurry," said Hines savagely. "Speed!"

It was clear enough. The four men who had come out of the building had timed their exit for the emergence of the man they'd shot. They must have been in some office in the building from which they could see the brownstone rooming house, and possibly even into, say, a skylight room. When the man they intended to kill put on his hat and approached his door, they had started for the street.

Moreover, Hines had been able to look into the Packard fairly thoroughly, and it had contained nothing but the cushions. There was no sign of any complicated apparatus for the production or a direction of a beam of any sort. The darkness must have been sent down from some point in this building.

The elevator-boy was trembling visibly, but the doors swept shut with a swift hissing sound and the car abruptly shot upward. If the stopping-point of the elevator had not been automatically controlled, it is certain that the operator could never have made a reasonably accurate landing. The glass doors slid aside.

"Th-there y' are, suh."

"Which door? Wait here!"

THE PEBBLED GLASS of the indicated door was unmarked and plain. Hines tried it, standing behind the solid wall. No sign. The door was unlocked. He flung it wide and stepped within.

The office was small and empty of all furniture, and was dusty as if it had been left unoccupied for a long time. One or two nails in the wall, and a few untidy smudges upon the paint were evidences of some previous occupant, but the only sign of its last inhabitant was a half dozen radio B batteries near the window with wire terminals still affixed. The red sealing-compound tops were bright and shiny and untouched by the dust which lay heavily upon the floor. And there was a smell of tobacco in the air. More, it was tobacco which had not had time to stale.

Hines jumped to a conclusion. He put his head out of the window. A short blast on his whistle made the patrolman's head swing back. Two other uniformed men had arrived at the spot where shots and a police-whistle blowing indicated something wrong.

"Nobody to leave this building!" shouted Hines through cupped hands. "Hold the doors until I get down!"

He went swiftly back to the elevator. The operator trembled again.

"Who rented that office?" he snapped, "and how long had he had it?"

"M-mistuh Preston, suh," said the trembling colored

man. "He—uh—he rented it las' week, suh, Sayd he was a doctuh, suh, but his furniture ain't come in yet. He was in heah a coupla hours to-day, suh, an' some frien's of hisn, suh, jus' went out 'bout five minutes ago."

The elevator began to sink rapidly toward the ground floor.

"What does he look like?" demanded Hines. "When did you see him last?"

"Uh—you, suh," quavered the operator, "you seen him, suh. He got outer the car an' spoke t' you, suh, when you got in."

Hines clenched his hands and ground his teeth. Memory came to him enragingly. The voice that had asked what had caused the shooting, and that had offered to bind up his supposed wound—it had been the same voice that had spoken in the car with Lefty Dunn the night before.

The instant the elevator doors opened, he knew the futility of pursuit. The shots had been fired all of three or four minutes before. A crowd had already gathered and was surging closer and closer about the uniformed men who now struggled to keep the two dead men from being trampled on by the merely curious crowd. The square-shouldered young man with the Vandyke and suitcase had walked out into that crowd and vanished. There were plenty of taxicabs about. He was undoubtedly sitting comfortably in one of them and being driven to a destination which might be any of the million homes in Greater New York.

Hines nodded despairingly to the plain-clothes man who had essayed to guard the door and keep the occupants of the building from leaving until Hines's arrival.

"That darkness was made by a man in an office on the

fourth floor," said Hines bitterly. "He was working with Lefty Dunn to kill that other man, and he's got away. Oh, my God! What a fool I am!"

3

BOLDNESS WINS

HINES'S SELF-DISGUST HELD until the ambulance left and the crowd had dwindled to a mere sprinkling of sightseers who pointed out to each other where the two men had been standing when shot, and other argumentative persons who debated with much vehemence and no information whatever on whether or not the reported cloud of darkness had actually been present.

The man with the yellow whiskers was breathing, but that was all. He needed surgical attention in a hurry. He was rushed to a hospital. The same ambulance took away a huddled figure in very natty clothing and a sporty cap to whom surgical attention would be of no use at all.

There would be only commendation for Hines for shooting that second man. In the case of a felony any policeman or private citizen has the right to shoot if it is necessary to prevent a crime. And Hines, as a police official, was relieved of the citizen's dilemma of being a criminal if he possessed the means to shoot.

The dead man was Micky the Dope, wanted by several States and by the Federal government in addition. Decidedly, Hines had come out of the affair with credit.

But he was bitterly disgusted with himself. He had more

than a hunch, now, that there was much more at stake than merely the shooting down of a still unidentified man. There was, it was very clear to Hines, more involved than the capture of Lefty Dunn.

Hines was the only man in New York who saw the possibilities inherent in the settlement of darkness down upon parts of Central Park the night before. He was the only man in New York who could have nipped those possibilities in the bud. And he had let the man with the clipped, precise voice walk right past him after speaking to him.

"There's going to be hell to pay before we get him," he groaned, "if I know Lefty Dunn and if I guess right what that man's got."

He waited impatiently for the fingerprint wagon and rushed the photographer and the finger-print technician up to the deserted office with the radio batteries on the floor.

"There'll be finger-prints on those batteries," he announced. "At least two sets—the man who sold them and the man who handled them in here. I want to know which is which, and the best set of prints you can cook up of that second man. And here, by the window." He pointed. "Here on the sill, and right here where a man'd steady himself when he looked out to get a good sight of that house next door. There were five men up here, I think, and they were watching for a man to get ready to go out. I figure they were all here waiting for him."

"Yes?" said the finger-print man. He yawned. The detective bureau was always demanding improbable things, and sometimes its members got mad when the finger-print bureau upset all their ideas. "Anything else you want?"

Hines managed to grin.

"Plenty," he admitted. "The commissioner thinks I'm crazy. If he finds out I dragged you up here—when the shooting happened down in the street—he'll be sure of it. I want proof that Lefty Dunn was here this morning, and Micky the Dope—that's the man I plugged—and Joe the Greek, and I think Pete Lazzarini. The last two have records, but they aren't being looked for. Lefty and Micky were supposed to be out of town. Now, will you find those prints for me?"

"If they're there," said the fingerprint man.

HE YAWNED AGAIN. But he would work a good deal harder because of the appeal. There is no man on the force who does not enjoy setting the commissioner—whoever he may be—gently and respectfully in his place. He is the head of the Police Department, to be sure. But he is a political appointee, and in the last analysis he is a civilian. And it pleases a man in the department to let him discover it.

The finger-print man dusted a little of his grayish powder about the B batteries and blew very gently. He surveyed the result with satisfaction.

"Pretty," he said pleasantly. He went over to the window and went through a slightly more involved process on a small area.

"Plenty of prints here," he said boredly. "All right, lieutenant. These prints are new ones, and some of them are very nice ones. I'll have photos ready in two or three hours, but I can't promise they'll be untangled right away. That'll take time."

With a sigh of relief, Hines left. He debated an instant down in the lobby of the building. He ought to— But the man in hospital might recover consciousness. It was most important of all that he tell who had wanted him out of the way.

Trace down the man with the motive, and sooner or later Hines would trace down the gunmen themselves. And if he traced down the gunmen, sooner or later he'd find out who had flung on a curtain of darkness at a remarkably convenient moment. And if he caught that man, he'd have forestalled a number of undesirable happenings he began to feel more and more sure were in the wind.

It wasn't very imaginative, perhaps. It would be extremely laborious. But it was common sense. And nine-tenths of the success in this world is gained by using common sense and plenty of work.

At the hospital the blond man was still unconscious and Hines was impatient.

"But he may come to any moment," the surgeon told him comfortably, peeling off rubber gloves that went up to his elbows. "I took a chance. Unconscious, no response to stimuli, severe shock. No need to give him anaesthetic shock besides. I had an ether-cone handy, but he didn't murmur while I worked on him. Much better off. He can talk as soon as he comes to, instead of your having to wait an hour."

Hines was thinking busily. His eyes hardened.

"Any chance of his living a few days?" he demanded. "Long enough to do some identifying if I catch a man I'm looking for?"

The surgeon chuckled comfortably.

"He should live ten years," he said placidly. "A bullet glanced off his skull, and there's not even concussion.

Another went through the fleshy part of his shoulder. A third just missed his knee-tendons—a narrow thing, that. He'll be able to walk out of here in three or four days, most likely. He was lucky. Why was he shot at?"

"That's what I want to find out," said Hines.

"Go up to his bed, then," said the surgeon. He slipped out of his operating gown. "Thank Heavens, I'm off duty now. Somebody else adjusts the mangled ones from now on."

Hines was pacing impatiently up and down the corridor outside the ward when an idea struck him. He examined it warily. Then he called a nurse. In five minutes the still unconscious man was shifted to a private room, and his clothes were brought in.

Hines was going busily through the pockets and frowning savagely at the lack of identifying data when there was a knock on the door. A nurse put her head in and said:

"The young lady you were expecting."

HINES'S FACE WAS blank when Kathryn Bush came in.

"You're not playing fair!" she said, her eyes stormy. "I had to fib to get in. But the press must be served. I told them you were expecting me. I guessed you'd be here. How is he?"

"Knocked cold," said Hines. "That's all." Then he added exasperatingly, "But look here—"

"Look here?" she echoed reproachfully. "I'm responsible for your getting the leads in this affair from the beginning. If I hadn't had a hunch and gone to the park, and if I hadn't risked arrest by speaking to a police officer who happened to be moon-gazing, and if I hadn't kept him talking to me, he'd never have known a darned thing was out of the way! And I gave you some important stuff this morning. It wasn't fair to hedge."

"Good Lord!" said Hines irritably. "It came too fast. I didn't have time to do anything. Certainly not to telephone you—"

"Oh!" She seemed mollified. "You would have phoned me if you could? That's all right. Now, what happened? A wild account of mysterious shootings, and darkness in broad daylight, was phoned in, and I grabbed the assignment. Threatened to weep all over the city editor's desk if he didn't give it to me. So I'm handling this for the *Star*. It sounded too insane to be true, but I knew better, especially when I heard you were in it. What really did happen?"

Hines went back to his investigation of the clothing, while he told her jerkily about the whole thing. She listened tranquilly.

"The city editor wouldn't believe it," she said placidly. "As an assignment it is a dud. I told him about the moon and the accident last night and he looked at me as if he expected me to say I was Mary, Queen of Scots in one minute more. I blushed. Actually, I blushed! I felt proud of that blush afterward. Something of youth has survived even the city room."

Kathryn was possibly twenty-two or three, but whatever Hines might have intended to say, it was interrupted by a nurse. She came in, bent over the bed, and glanced up.

"He's conscious."

Hines moved swiftly to the bedside. Bland, clear blue eyes looked up at him above the rather incredible yellow whiskers. A booming voice said without emotion:

"I have been conscious for some time. Verdamm! Is that what happened?"

There was a distinct accent in his speech, but his sentence-structure was the careful accuracy of the educated European, tinged, presently, with exotic colloquialisms.

"If you heard me talking," said Hines, "you heard what happened. Yes. I'm Police Lieutenant Hines, and I want to know some things. Please try to tell me who you are and who you think wanted to have you killed, and why."

"In spite of the very deffil of a headache," said the booming voice from the bed, "I have been trying to think of the answers to those questions for at least fife minutes. I saw the gentlemen who shot at me, yes. You, Herr Hines, were running toward them when I fell. But I nefer saw any of them before at any time. And I am *verdammt* if I know why they should shoot me. I am being calm, howefer. I shall give it my attention. Maybe I shall think it out. How much am I hurt?"

"Not badly," Hines assured him. He was biting at his lips and frowning in thought.

"TELL ME," SAID Kathryn suddenly, smiling down at the bandaged man on the bed. "Were you ever in a place called Edginton, New York, or a place called Stony Mountain?"

The candid blue eyes turned to her, but they were wide with astonishment.

"Young lady," said the booming voice plaintively, "as a scientist I haff refused to admit magic into my considerations. But how in der name of forty-sefen deffils do you know that I came from there only a short time ago?"

Kathryn was twinkling, triumphantly at Hines. He grunted.

"You win," he said briefly. "Go on."

"Who worked with you up there?" she asked. "I think he had you shot."

"Breston? No. He is a scoundrel in his way, and I do not like him. But he is a good scientist, and I haff no quarrel with him."

Hines grunted at the name. "Preston: he's about thirty-five," the detective said shortly, "very broad-shouldered, and he affects a Vandyke beard. His voice is rather harsh, and he speaks very precisely."

The wide blue eyes swung blankly to him.

"I think I will haff to call on more than forty-sefen deffils," the booming voice said more plaintively still. *"Himmel!* You know eferything. That is him. Do I need to say that my name is Schaaf—"

Kathryn looked up.

"Oh! You made the direct measurements of the size of a molecule."

The yellow-bearded man blinked.

"I nearly starff to death," he observed, "because there is in America no way for a theoretic physicist to earn a lifing. Nobody has efer heard of me. And I am shot at by utter strangers, I wake up in hospital—I must be in a hospital— and a young lady tells me where I haff been, a gentleman describes to me a man I most prifately dislike, and then I am reminded of a relatifely unimportant mistake I made six years ago."

Hines grunted impatiently.

"Preston's the man who had you shot, all right. And I think I know why. Professor Schaaf, it all works down to this. Up in Edginton you were working on the production of darkness, the neutralization of light—"

"No. Not I. I merely did measurements for Breston. He offered to gife me passage-money back to Europe if I did them. He got them cheap. Measurements of der mass and dimensions of der atmospheric ion, and changes in der mass and volume of der molecule when der allotropy of ionization took place."

"Well, then, Breston, or Preston, he was working on the neutralization of light—"

"*Ach*, no! On der production of fluorescence in ionized bodies under der influence of short Hertzian wafes. Wait—yes, I suppose you could say that. It is not scientific, but you might say that. When his apparatus finally got working it gafe off darkness that was like der bottom of hell."

Hines emitted a grunt that was almost explosive.

"Ha! Now we're getting somewhere! He has an outfit that makes darkness. It was used to help his gunmen escape when you were shot at, and I have excellent reason to think it's going to be used for more criminal purposes still."

"Criminal? It was pure science. Theoretic science. Der fluorescence of ionized substances under der influence of short Hertzian wafes. Does that sound like a help to safe-blowers?"

HINES DREW A deep breath and began to talk. When he mentioned the shutting off of moonlight in Central Park, Schaaf nodded rapidly. He seemed to have lost surprisingly little strength.

"Yes. He could do that. He was working on a beam apparatus when I left, so that der darkness would be gifen off on one side only. He could not read der instruments before."

The account of the automobile accident that seemed to have been deliberately produced made the yellow-bearded man frown angrily. When Hines had given a succinct account of Lefty Dunn's police record and the ambitions he might be expected to cherish, Schaaf was rumbling in his beard.

"Hm—I see. I see. Maybe I can help you. Maybe I can't. I try, anyhow. I did not like Breston. He made me mad. When I saw der success of his experiments come about I said, 'Breston, I congratulate you. Der Atchison medal is der same as yours. If you carry on your work as splendidly as this, it may be efen that I shall yet read of you as a Nobel Prize man. You haff der disposition of a dyspeptic crab, but you are a great scientist and I congratulate you from der bottom of my heart.' I said that to him, in spite of der fact that he had made me mad. And he laughed at me. 'Atchison medal?' he said in a sneering sort of way, 'Nobel Prize' Schaaf, you are a damned fool. I am for bigger things than that.' And I turned around and left him. I thought he must be crazy."

Hines said curtly:

"With Lefty Dunn's organizing ability, he might pick up anywhere from a hundred thousand dollars to half a million within the next week, in New York City alone."

Schaaf blinked.

"Maybe, then, he is not crazy. You tell me, anyhow, he tried to get me killed. Hm—Lieutenant Hines, you send somebody to my room at that abominable house where I liff. Get eferything out of it. Eferything. I have papers of my own, and there are some memoranda of his that I took by mistake. I had intended to send them back to him. It was by accident that I took them. We will begin to see what we see. I haff an idea, maybe. A small idea, but it is an idea. And I will need all that I can findt about his figures."

Hines looked at the girl. She had been listening. But a good reporter, these days, does not go about with a pencil and a pad of paper. With soft shirts and soft cuffs in vogue, he does not even write on his cuffs. And Kathryn had no cuffs, anyhow.

"I'll go myself," said Hines briefly. "I'm going to post a guard at your door in case anybody has heard that you're still alive. My own opinion is that it would be wisest for you to die."

Schaaf blinked, and then smiled wryly.

"*Ach*, yes. It is better that I die. For der sake of my health, let us say. Fery well, I haff expired, and while you go get der things from my room I will think der wise deep thoughts of der defunct."

Kathryn smiled at the man in the bed and followed Hines from the room.

"I'm coming, too, if you don't mind," she announced, in the hall outside. "As a news story, this is a dud. Even if the *Star* printed it, the other papers would laugh. But I want to follow up what happens, because if Lefty Dunn and his friend Preston do use that darkness, I'll have the whole story for the *Star* while the other papers are just guessing. You see?"

"I do," said Hines, relieved. "It shouldn't be printed just now. I was trying to think of some way to persuade you to kill it, as far as publication is concerned."

IT TOOK LESS than five minutes to get two uniformed men on guard outside the yellow-bearded man's door, but it took ten to arrange that if any inquiries were made, by telephone or otherwise, the answer would be given that the bearded man shot on Fifty-Eighth Street had died without regaining consciousness.

"Schaaf knows too much about what Preston has developed," said Hines dryly. "Of course Preston wants him killed."

Then the little police runabout went sliding through traffic down town again. The finger-print car had vanished from before the Blowbar Building. Hines let his mind linger hopefully on the possibilities finger-prints might offer if they turned out well. He went up the steps of the blowsy brownstone house. An angular woman with her head in a towel opened the door.

"I'm Police Lieutenant Hines," said Hines briefly. "A lodger here was shot about two hours ago and taken to hospital. I've come to take charge of his effects."

He displayed his badge. The woman wiped her hands nervously.

"O' course you can go up," she said uneasily. "O' course! But his things have been took. A friend of his came an' said he'd helped put Mr. Schaaf in the ambulance, an' Mr. Schaaf was very likely hurt bad, an' he paid the room rent that was due an' packed the things up, an' 'bout half an hour ago he sent a taxi for the things that were left. He said Mr. Schaaf would be in the hospital for a long time an' he'd take care of them for him."

Hines's jaws snapped shut.

"He was a broad-shouldered man," he said grimly, "with a beard like a doctor."

The woman nodded, relieved.

"Yes, sir. He'd been to see Mr. Schaaf before, sir, but he missed him."

"When did he come in, to-day?" demanded Hines.

"Why, right after the ambulance left, sir."

Hines ground his teeth.

"I'll look at the room," he said savagely, "but it's no use."

It was very clearly useless to look in the room. It had been stripped clean of everything but the furnishings plainly provided by the house itself. The bureau drawers were emptied. The suitcases one would expect any transient to possess were gone.

"That was Preston," said Hines to Kathryn Bush with a savage calmness. "He was in here, packing up papers and such things, while I was in the building next door. He was probably in this room when I stopped on the sidewalk, not certain whether to come here or go first to the hospital. Nerve? That man has it!"

"And you think—" said Kathryn.

"He'll bleed New York dry," snapped Hines. "He'll make the police force a laughing-stock."

4

BLACK HORROR

THE SHOOTING OF an unknown man who died without regaining consciousness was not big-time news. The curtain of sheer darkness which eye-witnesses swore had blocked the whole of Fifty-Eighth Street for nearly five minutes would have been big-time news had anybody believed in it.

Reporters who questioned Hines got noncommittal answers, found out that of the two men killed one was a well-known gunman previously supposed to be in Chicago, and let it go at that.

The finger-prints satisfied Hines completely and convinced the commissioner finally, but that bit of evidence was not made public. So the killing got an average of a quarter-column on an inside page in that afternoon's papers; the curtain of darkness was either not mentioned or was referred to as a smoke screen left behind by the fleeing car, and the whole affair was summed up as a New York reflection of a probable Chicago gang-war.

Schaaf grimaced when he reread the accounts three days later. Hines had moved him from the hospital to his own apartment, and the big German was recovering rapidly.

And as his strength came back a certain grimness came with it.

"Breston," he explained firmly, "is a scoundrel. He stole my records, which I had intended to publish. Those records are important. *Himmel!* I had an entirely new method of measuring. Der amplitude of der Brownian mofement in a dilute electrolyte enabled me to calculate der ion-masses perfectly. I had proof of der multiatomic nature of der molecule of six supposedly simple substances, by der demonstrable extra weight of der ions. Sooner or later I shall find Breston, and I shall exterminate him! I haff all my work to do ofer again, and right now if somebody offered to sell me der whole city of New York for six cents, I couldn't buy enough dirt to stop a watch."

Kathryn chuckled.

"I've an idea, Professor Schaaf," she said encouragingly. "When this thing breaks, you're going to get publicity. You're dead right now, of course, but when you're resurrected you'll be famous. And when you are famous—"

"When you are famous, efen if you are a fake," said Schaaf pessimistically, "der laboratories fall ofer themselfs to offer you a salary. All right. You make me famous, Miss Bush, and you, Mr. Hines, giff me a chance to practice *Schrecklichkeit* on that *verdammt* Breston."

He retired behind a cloud of smoke with every appearance of gloom. But presently he was explaining, in answer to Kathryn's questions:

"Breston does not make darkness. Not directly. He has found that ionized particles are fluorescent under der influence of certain short Hertzian wafes. And there are ionized particles eferywhere. Especially where there is dust. Fluorescence is der property of absorbing light of one wafe-length—one color—and radiating out light of a longer wafe-length, another color.

"You take rhodamine dye, for instance. You throw ultra-violet rays upon it. Der ultra-violet rays are a color so far past der blue end of der spectrum that it is infisible. But when they strike der rhodamine, they are absorbed and radiated away again as light of der most fifid of scarlet. Well, under der influence of Breston's short Hertzian wafes, der ions on dust-particles and in der air absorb all der colors of fisible light. And they radiate it away again as infisible colors we call heat, which is so far past der red end of der spectrum that you can't see it.

"Ordinary air contains enough ions to cause der absorption of practically all der light in der room. A laboratory with Breston's apparatus in it gets as dark as der bottom of hell, and after awhile it is as hot as hell's chimney."

KATHRYN ROSE.

"I'll call on you," she said soberly, though her eyes had devils of mischief in them, "to give me a special interview. 'Thermometry in Hades. Famous Savant Measures Ultimates in Heat and Discusses Refrigerating Rooms for Red-Hot Mammas.'"

"Laugh," said Schaaf pessimistically, "but laugh in print, Miss Bush, and I won't complain."

He lapsed into a depressed silence as Hines and Kathryn went out.

"He takes the loss of his notes pretty seriously," said Hines, frowning. "So do I. He might have been able to work out something to neutralize the infernal thing."

"It's still hanging fire?"

Hines opened the car door for her. "Still," he said grimly. "We can't locate Lefty Dunn, but we do know that half a dozen of our most prominent gunmen and gangster-leaders have met him. We offered one of them, in particular, to forget about two of his most useful murderers if he'd come across with information that would enable us to nab Preston and Dunn. But he insisted he didn't know what we were talking about. The commissioner soft-pedaled the newspapers, but he's convinced. There were too many eye-witnesses to the last stunt."

"And so?"

"We're passing out word to all the big jewelers to put paste in their shop windows, and the banks especially have been warned to take extra care."

The little runabout was running swiftly down upper Broadway. The parked center-spaces with the air-ducts for the subway beneath were flowing by at an even, regular rate. Columbus Circle appeared dead. The facade and canopy of an uptown motion-picture palace swept by to the right.

A heavy gray car jerked suddenly out into the traffic and came purring up to a space no more than ten yards behind the runabout.

Quite silently and quite suddenly everything was blotted out. One instant the runabout was speeding along with Hines frowning abstractedly at the wheel; the next it was rolling through an opaque blackness that was so sudden that it stung the eyes. The girl gasped in her seat beside Hines. All the world was obliterated. The girl beside him ceased to exist; the wheel in his hands and his hands themselves could not be seen.

For perhaps three seconds there was stunned silence

everywhere; then a multitudinous squealing of brakes, a scared squawking of horns.

The runabout shuddered as Hines jammed his foot down hard on the accelerator. It shot ahead through nothingness. There was a peculiar little lurch. He had swung imperceptibly to the left, and his left-hand tire had just slipped down the tiny drop of the surface-car rail that parallels the parked spaces on upper Broadway.

"We're all right for a block or more," he snapped into the blackness all about him. "I'm following the car track, and all's clear for at least that distance."

He drove on and on. Brayings and bellowings arose on every hand. Every car in motion had stopped stockstill and its driver was sounding his horn desperately. Every man, it may be, believed he had been stricken blind. Certainly no man dared attempt to drive.

Hines eased the car to a stop.

"Get down in the bottom of the car," he said quietly into the nothingness that surrounded him. "I don't think they'll risk coming this far in the dark, but get down."

He felt the little car responding to her movement. Then there was a wait of seconds—minutes. Then, with a sudden flickering, the light went on again.

PEDESTRIANS, GROPING HYSTERICALLY for something solid to hold on to in their inexplicable blindness, grew dizzy and dazed at the sudden restoration of their sight. Drivers of many cars burst into speech which varied from the ludicrously prayerful to the grotesquely profane.

But Hines had whirled about in his seat and his service revolver was out and ready. The sudden return of light dazzled his eyes for a moment, but he saw a big gray car

that had not quite stopped turn abruptly and dart off into
a side street. It was crowded with men. It was the car that
had pulled out from the curb and followed along some ten
yards behind him.

With a grimace that was not in the least mirthful, Hines
put his revolver away.

"Fooled 'em," he said harshly. "But I think hell's to pay to-day. This was half an accident."

Kathryn scrambled to her seat.

"I was s-scared," she said quietly. "Very much. But I only got down there because you told me to, and so you could shoot anywhere you wanted to. I didn't get down there because I was s-scared."

"They saw me drive by," said Hines grimly. "Lefty Dunn has reason to dislike me. And I killed one of his men the other day, when they shot Professor Schaaf. So when they saw me they pulled out into the traffic behind me. They figured I'd do what everybody else would do when the blackness fell—jam on my brakes and blow my horn. And they'd come up to the car, turn off the darkness, fill me full of holes, and turn on the darkness again when they moved to a corner and turned down it. They could have sighted their way easily enough in two seconds of brightness. But I stepped on the accelerator instead."

The traffic was a nerve-racked, hopelessly disorganized mass of shaky drivers. Drug stores were being packed with clamorous people demanding a doctor's attention. Women had either fainted or were fainting all about. Because of the incredibility and consequent non-publication of the three previous uses of the darkness-producing device, every person who had been in the darkness considered that he had suddenly gone blind.

Hines jammed on his brakes again and fought his way into a drug store. He made two calls—using his police badge to force a way into the phone booths—and fought his way out again. The first strictly individual panic began to give way to a stunned amazement as people discovered that not only themselves but every one else had been blinded at the same instant.

The runabout circled Columbus's statue and went streaking down Seventh Avenue.

"I called headquarters," said Hines savagely, "and reported that I thought the whole works would come off within an hour or so. I admitted it was a guess, but Dunn and Preston are in a car fitted up to make darkness, and they aren't taking chances for fun."

"Please!" said Kathryn imploringly. "Please don't put me out of the car to make room for a detective. Please don't! If you're right I'm going to realize my life's ambition and scoop the town. The first things I learned in newspaper work were that there isn't any Santa Claus, and scoops don't happen any more. But please let me stay in this car!"

Hines shot on down town.

"Headquarters said the Merchants' National is moving three-quarters of a million in currency some time this morning. That will be Lefty Dunn's meat, if he can make it. When I stop the car you find a place to take cover."

A small, firm hand closed over his arm ecstatically.

"You're a darling!"

HINES DODGED A truck which an unshaved driver seemed to think had a divinely bestowed right of way over such trivial vehicles as police cars, private autos, and street cars. The runabout swung east at Thirty-Ninth Street.

"I phoned Schaaf, too," said Hines jerkily. "Told him I thought the darkness just now was intended to get me, but that I didn't believe it was planned. Just that they'd caught sight of me. He agreed, and said if things went dark there he'd crawl under a bed. They'd have to turn off the darkness to find him, and he'd have a chance to get some of them. He's enthusiastic and hopeful."

"He's rather a dear," said Kathryn exuberantly.

There were a series of staccato poppings to right and left. Half a dozen motorcycle police dived through the traffic and shot ahead, weaving in and out, in a dead run for Fifth Avenue.

"There's proof the commissioner's convinced," said Hines dryly. "He's afraid not to be."

He grunted in annoyance and swung in to the curb again.

"What's the matter?"

"I proposed that patrols of four or five men be put at strategic points down town, wherever being able to turn on the darkness would offer a killing. The darkness is shot out in a beam ahead of the car. The back part of the car that makes the darkness will be visible, as we saw in the park. And if we have a patrol closing in on the edge of darkness, wherever it may be, they'll spot that car."

He had dived out of the runabout and was plunging in to use a telephone again. Kathryn remained seated, her eyes shining. She began to visualize headlines, a by-line on the first page, photographs.

Then, quite suddenly, she realized that the headlines she had imagined were hopelessly bad, from a newspaper standpoint. Police Lieutenant Hines would be featured in the story, of course, but his name and title would not—would definitely not by any chance be set in hundred-and-twenty-point type across eight columns.

He came out, frowning.

"They'd forgotten it. It seems certain to be Fifth Avenue. They're going to post men now."

He shoved in the clutch and put the car in first. Fifth Avenue was only half a block away.

And there was a sudden flickering in the air, and then an obscure duskiness everywhere, and suddenly Thirty-Ninth Street ceased to exist about a hundred feet ahead of the car. There was a huge, thick wall of darkness that rose out of the earth and towered upward. For three seconds it loomed far above the tiny vehicles in the street, and suddenly it broke, and for three seconds more the light showed again, and then the cylinder of darkness abruptly formed once more and held.

Hines jammed on the brakes, and the car stopped with a jerk. He stared at the impalpable barrier of opacity that rose a hundred feet in the air.

"It's turned on," he said grimly.

Kathryn stared. The blackness looked almost exactly like the section of a monster cylinder of black velvet. There was not a particle of flickering or wavering about it. It was steady enough to seem tangible. A touring car with the top down was exactly halfway into it, and a woman in the back seat began to scream. The car began to back, slowly, and emerged from the apparently solid mass of darkness. The chauffeur stared up at it, his face a sickly gray. He backed and backed, senselessly, until his car crashed into a parked car behind him.

The back cylinder curved gently, and up aloft it could be seen to have a less definite edge. Four stories up on the Lord & Taylor Building one could see a cobwebby darkness begin at the edge of a window, and deepen to the complete opaqueness of a solid barrier only at the other side of the glass.

THEN A MONSTROUS, muffled uproar began on Fifth Avenue. It was the horns of many, many thousand cars being sounded by panic-stricken drivers to prevent their being run into while they could not see to drive. That moaning, discordant uproar began far down town. It extended far uptown again. It seemed to reach from one horizon to the other. And a vast column of implacable darkness lay athwart the city. It seemed to grow in size as it went uptown. At Forty-Second Street it was definitely over a hundred feet in height. At Fifty-Seventh it was two hundred, but seemed less tangible. It was thinner at the edges. In the Eighties it seemed hardly more than a thick, dense smoke that made all drivers slow down to a crawl and careful drivers stop altogether. At One Hundred and Twenty-Fifth Street it was a shadow only. Beyond the Bronx it was not noticed.

But from Madison Square to the Sixties a deep, discordant bedlam rose to the skies. The horns of thousands of helpless, stationary cars arose in a vast bellowing sound that seemed like a million-tongued cry of agony.

5

WOLVES TO THE HUNT

FIFTEEN MINUTES BEFORE, Fifth Avenue had been entirely normal, which is to say that it was crowded and picturesque. From curb to curb the asphalt was a solid stream of vehicles, going swiftly north and south in parallel lines, then halting abruptly for a space, and darting into swift motion again. The sidewalks contained their diverse populations.

About Madison Square, north of that small and isolated parking space the city fathers permit, there were openings in the wheeled traffic. And people could walk comfortably on the sidewalks, pausing to gaze into windows without being jostled, or they could hasten if they chose without jostling others.

Whistling young men in their later teens pushed wheeled boxes with a self-admiring dexterity from the location of one wholesale firm to the location of another wholesale firm. The occupants of the sidewalks were mostly men going from one place to another place.

Around Thirty-Fourth Street the character of the pedestrians had changed entirely. At least half the crowds on the sidewalks were women, and in consequence there was vast confusion and more than a little obstruction to anybody who had a definite destination. The wheeled traffic was a solid mass of gleaming vehicles, and a swift mechanical purring came from the space between the curbings whenever certain colored lights showed appropriate tints in suitable directions.

At Thirty-Ninth Street the pedestrian traffic was almost exclusively female, and most men moved west to Sixth Avenue if they were in a hurry. And a surging, solid mass of motors rolled north and south in mechanical obedience to lights and whistles in their five-block units.

This was fifteen minutes before the event that made women who could afford it have nervous breakdowns, and gave other women less luxurious nightmares for weeks afterward.

At about that time taxicabs began to appear here and there on the side streets leading to the avenue. The taxis stopped anywhere within a block of Fifth Avenue and disgorged their fares.

Most of those passengers were youngish men, and nearly all were impeccably dressed, and a few of them had that curious bluntness of features that comes of many batterings in many battles. Some, however, were distinctly shabby and furtive-eyed. And there were a few figures who were not young at all, but old and bent and broken. But in all these anomalous newcomers to the avenue one common feature could be observed. All were eagerly expectant, and all were more or less uneasy, or at least in doubt.

But for the most part the arrivals passed unnoticed. A patrolman at Thirty-Seventh Street widened his eyes at sight of one little group of amiably chattering young men who smiled and talked and very curiously did not move their lips at all. That patrolman turned deliberately about and strolled in their wake, swinging his night-stick and privately cursing the fact that so many women had not stayed at home that day, and that a policeman has so many duties entirely unconnected with the basic duty of his profession, and that he might lose sight of those young men if some fool woman stopped him to ask an idiotic question.

A traffic cop stepped over to a motorcycle patrolman resting on a still but chugging mount beside the curb.

"Better keep an eye on that car, Pete. I think I know the guy that's drivin' it."

And the motorcycle sputtered loudly and drifted off into the stream of vehicles.

A doorman outside a particularly exclusive store cocked a wise eye at a bent, white-bewhiskered figure trudging rather pathetically through the crowd, buffeted about by chattering women. The doorman was an ex-cop, and reflected inaudibly:

"There's old Schmeel, out of stir again. He'll be gettin' in trouble if he tries his old dip tricks in this crowd."

THESE OBSERVATIONS WERE made, it is true. But the vast majority of the new arrivals slipped unnoticed into the throng. Even the fact that a great many of them looked now and then at their watches passed without comment.

Of course, no one could have been expected to observe a gentleman who had rented desk-space three days before, in a front office overlooking the facade of the Merchants' National Bank. He was gazing intently out of the front office window, and he held an office telephone in his hand.

No one could have guessed that he was talking to a man

in another office fronting on Madison Square. Nor would any one guess that the man next to him with another telephone instrument in his hand was similarly connected with a telephone booth in a confectionery store just around the corner from Fifth Avenue.

A big gray car parked in the triangular parking space where Broadway crosses Fifth; it was not particularly observed, even though it was not empty of people like the other parked cars. And nobody at all noticed that the man at the driver's wheel was a broad-shouldered man with a professional-looking Vandyke beard, or that he was looking intently up at a window in which a man stood with a desk telephone in his hand.

Fifth Avenue for its whole length was a picture of swift and colorful movement in the bright sunshine. From the sidewalks where women predominated a babble of voices arose with the shuffling sound of many feet in movement. From the roadway came the booming, purring noise of many motors and the singing of innumerable tires. It was a highly picturesque and wholly normal sight.

But suddenly, one of the two men in the office facing the Merchants' National Bank said sharply:

"It's in sight."

The other man spoke into his transmitter. A clumsy gray object had appeared in the flood of wheeled things flowing below. New Yorkers gave it no second glance. Armored cars, equipped with bullet-proof walls and tires, and armed with machine guns and hand-grenades, move regularly through the streets of New York. It is, you see, the most civilized city in the world, and therefore land battleships are necessary for the movement of valuables about its thoroughfares.

"Get movin'," snapped the man whose phone communicated with the phone-booth around the corner. "The cops are comin' out now. They' goin' to rush it."

He listened, hung up the receiver, and lit a cigarette. His hands trembled a little. Four policemen were issuing suddenly from the bank. But six young men were rounding the corner, five of them having just ceased a cordial conversation in a candy store lobby on having been joined by the sixth from within. The policemen more or less efficiently checked the flow of pedestrians. They had a clear path made from the bank doorway to the curbing at the exact instant that the armored car came to a complete stop. It was excellent, neatly timed work.

"It's stopped. Get set!" The man at the telephone to Madison Square was tense. He'd seen, too, the six young men among the milling, curious crowd that had been checked by the police guard.

The door of the armored car opened. Simultaneously, two men appeared in the doorway of the bank, carrying apparently heavy bags. They came quickly down the steps.

"Shoot the works!" snapped the man at the telephone. His voice was strained to the breaking point.

THERE WAS A breath-taking pause, just about long enough for a man in a window on Madison Square to make a signal with his hand, and for that signal to be acted upon by a man in a parked car. Then, quite suddenly, darkness—tangible, blank, and absolute—fell upon the earth. All visible objects were blotted out.

It held for three seconds. Then unbearable and unbelievable daylight flooded the world once more. A shot, two, three— Then darkness fell again in the same incredible quietness and with the same unbelievable intensity.

From the darkness there arose the sound of firearms crashing savagely. There were screams. And then from south to north, as far as the ear could range, came the discordant, throaty bellowing of automobile horns. Men, struck blind, jammed on their brakes and set their horns to bellowing. The tumult that arose was horrible and insane; it was insistent and terrifying.

The crashing of guns ceased. The crowded, stunned mass of people before the Merchants' National heard panting snarls, heard a voice gasp triumphahtly, "Got it!" and then many of the blinded, staggered people were hurled aside.

The bellowing horns of the cars were enough for orientation. Men and women who had stopped stock-still with their hearts in their throats at the sudden feeling of hopeless blindness upon them, were hurled to the ground.

A compact group of panting figures was heading swiftly and ruthlessly northward, and battered its way through the dazed crowd until a shrill whistling sound was audible through the deeper toned bellowing of the horns. Those figures turned in their savage progress, then, and clutched at the man who blew that whistle. He chuckled. A blind man is a good guide in darkness. He went before them, tapping, down a side street.

Unbelieving people who stared from bright sunlight at a monster cylinder of darkness that seemed to have engulfed Fifth Avenue saw six hatless young men come panting out of that darkness, dragging two heavy bags, saw them pile themselves into a waiting car, and saw that car plunge madly away from the darkness and the uproar that issued from it. And a blind man chuckled and went tapping his way back into the darkness.

That, though, was not the only occurrence which later showed that the darkness had not been unexpected. An old, bent blind man, returned from guiding panting gangsters to the light, went zestfully about his ancient trade. A dip, of all men, needs his eyesight second only to his nimble fingers. But here all men were blind.

There was the cushioned tapping of a stick amid all the tumult of blaring horns, and figures felt one brush accustomedly against them, and were too dazed to feel gentle but nimble old fingers abstracting here a wallet, there a watch.

Proprietors and clerks in jewelry stores fronting on the avenue heard the tremendous crashings of their plate-glass windows, and burglar alarms rang resoundingly, clanging clamorously even through the bedlam from without. Those clerks and those proprietors were entirely helpless to stop the clutching fingers that reached in and groped, and left empty traps where treasures had been on view before.

One man was found dead with a knife wound in his back, when the darkness lifted, and he was known to be a person who had acquired a certain amount of wealth by very dubious means, but nobody ever found out who had preferred the opportunity of a safe revenge to the chance of robbing with impunity.

For fifteen minutes Fifth Avenue was in darkness, darkness that was tangible and blank and absolute, and in that fifteen minutes forewarned persons of the underworld reaped a harvest. Each to his specialty, they sprang like wolves in the blackness whose duration they foreknew.

The list of thefts alone filled two columns in the next morning's papers, and there were some persons badly hurt—mostly women, who clutched hysterically at hands that groped about them. The list of smashed cars and traffic accidents was impressive. There had been three or four drivers who lost their heads and plunged madly through the blackness until brought up by insurmountable obstacles.

And since the underworld is the resort of people of all grades of mental distortion, there were one or two crimes that were quite too horrible to be reported in full.

But at the end of that fifteen minutes, with the barest possible trace of flickering, the darkness vanished as suddenly and as silently as it had come. The sunlight shone again upon hordes of motors, blaring frantically, and upon streets full of people who abruptly charged frenziedly here and there the instant they could see to flee. There were small crumpled figures which were women who had fainted, and who were, quite frequently, inconspicuously robbed of purses and trinkets while the hysteria of the light returned still held.

In all this uproar a gray car moved quietly out of the parking space the city fathers still permit in that vast triangle of asphalt where Broadway crosses Fifth Avenue. The columnar—later it was proved to be the cone-shaped—beam of darkness that had been sent north from Madison Square had widened out at that spot.

For nearly two blocks in every direction the darkness had held about Madison Square. So that the gray car moved undisturbedly out of the parking space, and turned, and went down the nearly emptied lower Fifth Avenue to Ninth Street, and there turned east and vanished.

And nobody seemed to notice that it was driven by a broad-shouldered man with a Vandyke beard.

6

WAITING IN THE DARK

THE STREET LAMPS glowed with a peculiar glitter upon pavements still wet from a recent rain. The rumbling of the city, which never ceases, had died down to that partially discordant muttering which is the city's voice in the small hours.

Kathryn came out of the doorway and shivered a little at the damp chilliness of the night air. But she smiled warmly when Hines held open the car door for her.

"It's decent of you," she said gratefully, as she stepped in and when the car started off. "I almost refused to get up when the telephone call came, but I'm glad I didn't. You think something's going to happen?"

Hines nodded. The little car was purring toward Broadway and swung into the nearly deserted but brilliantly lighted way. It began to shoot on down town with a singing of tires.

"Either we get him," he said tiredly, "or we'll have to throw up the sponge. I've never worked so hard in my life as I've done this last two weeks."

It was two weeks since a cone of darkness had lain along Fifth Avenue's length for fifteen minutes and left New York panic-stricken. In those two weeks Hines had been doing the work of at least six men. He was the only man in New York, aside from Schaaf, who would recognize the man Preston. And Preston had to be found.

"Crooks are fools," said Hines drearily. "You'd think those yeggs that were tipped off about the darkness would have known how to take advantage of it. But we picked up six more men to-day that we'll be able to send away for long stretches. Fingerprints, of course. You'd think a man who was going to smash a jewelry store window, knowing he couldn't be interfered with, would have the sense to wear gloves. We've got the men who robbed Blakes', and Houton's, and a couple of others. Their fingerprints were on glass fragments inside the windows. They'd cut their fingers on them and flung them out of the way as they groped for the stuff on the trays."

"But no trace of Preston?"

"None. Oh, we've done what we could. We've third-degreed and sweated every man we've picked up. We've had the station houses full, too. And we've worked. We've caught a bunch of the little ones, and recovered a good bit of property, and we have the goods on half a dozen fences we've been trying to get for a long time; but Lefty Dunn and his mob got away clean, and Preston with them—and they got three-quarters of a million from the Merchants' National. In currency."

There was silence as the car sped on down the nearly deserted street, passing no vehicles except occasional brilliantly lighted taxicabs. It passed Columbus Circle, and a little later it passed Times Square, and still went on down town.

"I—I feel almost ashamed of myself," said Kathryn

soberly. "I tried to help all I could, when you were working to forestall Preston, but secretly I was almost hoping
you'd fail. It would let me scoop the town. And it did. My
salary was raised because I had all the story and Professor
Schaaf's explanation of what the darkness was. But—it was
terrible. And people are still afraid it will happen again."

"Why not?" asked Hines tiredly. "It can. We haven't a
thing to go on. Schaaf's had the American Electric laboratories put at his disposal, and he's buzzing about there
blissfully, talking about the possibility of heterodyning 'die
verdammte short Hertzian wafes that cause der trouble.'
But he's got to duplicate Preston's results before he can
try to neutralize them. And so far there's been no reason
why Preston shouldn't turn on his darkness anywhere in
the whole city and make another clean-up at any minute."

"BUT THERE'VE BEEN precautions—"

"Oh, yes. Sternutatory gases—sneezing gas bombs—in
show windows, ready to be set off. Half-million-candle-
power flares that will burn five minutes in every bank.
That much light probably won't be absorbed by those ions
Schaaf talks about. And guns. Most of all, there's the fact
that people know what they're up against, and will fight
back even in the dark. But I'm putting a lot of hope in
to-night's work."

Twenty-Third Street slipped by, and the humming
motor of the little car went on steadily, headed down town.
Union Square spread out abruptly to the right, with its
lights glowing upon emptiness save for rare and straggling
pedestrians.

"What's happening to-night?" asked Kathryn, as tall
buildings shot upward on either side again.

"The banks have been working by non-negotiable paper more than ever," said Hines uninterestedly, "Wall Street went into spasms for awhile, but took to issuing certificates for its negotiable securities. Short of getting currency out of the Reserve Bank down there, it would be pretty difficult for Preston to make much of a killing where most of the money is. But money has to be shifted now and then.

"There's four millions in money and securities that has to be shifted to-night. It was intended to do it secretly, but we found the news had leaked. We think it leaked, anyway. And if it did, it leaked to Lefty Dunn, and he'll make a try for it with Preston's help. We're going to try to step on it. I've helped with the preparations, Schaaf's helped more. He saw Preston's outfit up-State, you know, and he made a suggestion or two that looks promising. I'm going to park you with him, if you don't mind."

The car was far down town indeed now. Kathryn saw "Broome Street" brightly illuminated on a corner signpost. But the runabout went on and on, and the buildings grew taller and taller until the thin thread of sky overhead was almost lost between the desolate lean flanks of the structures on either hand.

Hines turned off to the right, stopped the car, and switched off the lights.

"We'll walk from here." He looked at his watch. "Half past three. Two hours to daybreak. You'll lose a lot of rest."

"I got some sleep," she said.

They walked on toward the Battery. Their pace seemed a crawl, after the swift flight of the little car, and they seemed rather to be moving through a cavern than any inhabited city, and the desolation of dead buildings seemed to press down upon them and appall them.

It was a long, long walk through a desert of brick and steel. Suddenly Hines turned in to a deserted doorway, and a voice spoke softly, and they followed a hall to where a shaded electric bulb burned dimly, and Kathryn saw figures sitting in readiness for something. She could not know what.

There were one or two uniformed men among them, but the others looked strange indeed, and Kathryn could not distinguish the cause of their oddity. She was hustled into a tiny elevator that promptly began to rise to the steady humming of a hidden motor, through dark and unoccupied floors with the smell of emptiness.

The elevator stopped. A walk along a dark hallway to an open door. Into an unlighted room in which a pipe glowed and in which there was the sound of movement.

"Hines?"

"Right," said Hines briefly. "I've brought Miss Bush. She gave enough information before that affair of two weeks ago to have given us a chance to stop it. She's entitled to a front seat."

A VOICE GROWLED. Kathryn smiled wickedly in the darkness. That was the commissioner, sitting up here in a darkened room.

"Ah, Miss Bush," Schaaf spoke amiably from the darkness. "You did not giff me der chance to thank you for making me famous. Come and share my window. Hines is going down into der street again."

She moved hesitantly through the darkness until he took

her hand and pressed it. He led her to the square of grayish light that was the window.

"We are ten stories up," he told her. "If you do not mind der height, look down."

She saw the street far below her, empty and gray and desolate, but peculiarly clear by reason of the shaded street lights.

"Der bank is opposite us," said Schaaf softly, as if afraid of betraying the presence of an ambush by normal speech. "You see der little lights inside. They haff four millions of dollars ready to be mofed in an armored car, when it comes. They feel, Miss Bush, about that four millions of dollars as I felt about my notes on der proof of der multiatomic nature of der sodium chloride molecule. That four millions is fery precious to them, Miss Bush, though they will nefer spend a cent of it. Just as my notes were fery precious, though I could not spend them."

He craned his neck. Far away, down the deep and narrow chasm below the window, a brightly lighted taxicab came in a peculiar silence. It seemed to roll noiselessly down the deserted street, and red and green and yellow lights glittered upon it, and the white paint of its hood glowed brightly as it passed close by a street lamp. It came on, and maudlin song arose faintly from it. It sounded like a drunken group of revelers, moved by some whim to invade the financial district at night.

It passed below and went on.

There was a muted whirring. The commissioner's guarded "Hello!" Then gruntings. He hung up the receiver.

"Their lookouts, most likely, in that taxi. They don't know we know about the leak, but they're scouting, anyway."

There was the movement of other bodies in the room. Kathryn suddenly realized that there were probably four or five other men in there, silent and waiting. One of them snapped a lighter and shielded the flame with his hand while he puffed a cigar into a glow.

Kathryn caught a sudden glimpse of a curious collar about his neck. It was a telephone transmitter hung in place, and there were headphones over his ears. This was an office already fitted with several phones, evidently, which had been taken over for use as a temporary headquarters for the night.

"Er—hadn't we better—" began the commissioner uneasily.

"Shush," said Schaaf placidly. "Lieutenant Hines told me how it should be done. Shush for awhile now."

Kathryn wanted to giggle. She felt very nervous and very much thrilled, and more than a little apprehensive; and her muscles were uncomfortably tense.

A man came out of the bank, far below. He looked up the street and then went back inside again. The bank became black and blank and dark again.

"They expect der armored car," observed Schaaf. "Now we can haff a little smoke. You might tell them."

He was talking toward the back of the room. A man spoke quietly into a transmitter.

Kathryn gazed about and saw nothing. Schaaf felt the movement.

"Wait. Der performance will be intricate," he said, and chuckled.

A MINUTE. TWO. Then there was a brittle little tinkling of glass somewhere. The scraping, musical sound of glass falling down the stone side of a building. Kathryn started.

"That—that's a fire over there! It must be!"

Smoke was welling hazily out of a broken window in a building on the opposite side of the street and a half block away. A wavering reddish glow began to be visible behind it.

"To be sure," said Schaaf tranquilly. "It is an excellent effect."

He glanced once at it and stared down, looking far uptown and ignoring the gradual accumulation of a vast mass of whitish vapor curling up the sides of the buildings across the way. A second window broke with a second brittle tinkling. A fresh billowing of smoke came out.

"Here is der armored car coming," said Schaaf.

A man spoke quietly into a transmitter. Kathryn looked down.

Far away, coming sturdily down the deserted street, one of the squat gray armored cars which carry valuables from place to place in New York was speeding noiselessly. Four motorcycle policemen ringed it about.

It swept up to the bank and stopped. One of the motorcycle policemen suddenly pointed upward. There was an intensification of the red glow back of the thick smoke. The motorcycle cop had stopped his machine. He now ran swiftly to the nearest corner and worked busily at a little signal box.

"Eferything according to schedule," said Schaaf. "He is turning in der alarm."

A muted whirring. It was a telephone bell, muted. A man answered, and said quietly:

"Two cars are coming down Church Street at forty miles an hour."

Kathryn felt a little electric thrill running over her. The commissioner stood up and came over to one of the windows, gazing down nervously.

Schaaf said meditatively: "I do not hear der engines. Tell der bank not to hurry. And tell them of der two cars."

A man murmured at the back of the room. Kathryn was staring at the fire. The smoke coming out halfway up the building across the way was thick and dense, and the red glow behind it was fiercer. Then she heard a faint clatter and clanging.

"Hines," said Schaaf in her ear, "he is a smart man. He thinks that somewhere in der buildings all about there are men watching who can report by der telephones, and can signal that der beans are spilled. That is der reason for der verisimilitude."

The clanging and hooting grew louder. Making a monstrous tumult, building up a tremendous uproar, fire engines came racing down the street. A steamer clanged to a stop and coupled swiftly to a hydrant. A hook-and-ladder came racing. A hose-tower after it.

The bank doors opened, and men made ready to come out.

AROUND THE CORNER of the nearest street two heavy cars came hurtling. A machine gun began to spit, and filled the cañonlike space between the tall buildings with a snarling uproar. Water geysered upward for an instant and swung sharply toward earth.

Kathryn, staring down, saw the four-inch stream from a hose strike the foremost car and crash in its windows like so much wet paper. Then, abruptly, the street and the lights and the armored car and all the puffing fire engines ceased to exist. And at the same instant something flared intolerably overhead and the buildings on either side of the street for many blocks to north and south began to gleam brightly.

"Breston," said Schaaf, very calmly indeed, "he has turned on der dark. I guessed right about der probable height of der phenomenon. Now, we shoot der works!"

A river of darkness seemed to have filled the street below. A dull black substance seemed to have welled up instantly and to flow silently and without disturbance between the tall rows of buildings, as the Styx itself must flow between its banks. Flares, the huge magnesium torches that are used by aircraft for landing at night, were burning atop buildings for blocks on either hand.

From the motionless surface of the darkness the smoke and steam of the fire-engines coiled upward into the glare above. The fire which had been the excuse for calling the fire-engines had abruptly gone out, and the welling smoke from the windows had ceased. The watchers in the tenth-floor office looked down upon a surface of blackness imprisoned between the walls of office-buildings. And submerged in that abysmal dark there were men.

Dull, thudding concussions sounded from below. Windows quivered.

"Bombs," said Schaaf calmly "They were ready to smash

open der armored car if they were too late to nab der ship-
ment before it got in. Now they use der bombs because
they are scared. I will bet anybody that Breston is shaking
in his shoes."

The horrible shrill scream of a man in agony came echo-
ing cavernously from the impenetrable blackness below.

7

FIGHTING THE INVISIBLE

A MAN SPOKE quietly at the back of the office.

"The bank doors are closed and the money's safe. They want to know if they can turn the juice into the doors."

"*Himmel!* No!" snapped Schaaf, as the commissioner rumbled an assent. "Firemen are sweeping der hoses all about. Do they want to electrocute them if a stream of water hits der doors?"

The commissioner hastily made his assent into a negative, and returned to his study of the incredible scene. The buildings rose out of nothingness, and their sides were apparently incandescent from the flames burning above.

Down there under the surface of the blackness, the fire-engines swept their streams of water to right and left and up and down. They were working blindly, of course, but whatever those streams of water struck would go down. Plate-glass, cars, men.

"*Verdamm!*" said Schaaf presently, though without dismay. "Hines is a smart man. He don't take chances. We were hoping, Miss Bush, that a stream of water would smash into der car where Breston had his apparatus working. If it got into der coils it would short-circuit them and der apparatus would work no longer. We could take a look at *die Schweine* then. But der engines are still working, judging by der steam that comes up, and still der darkness holds. Hm— Ah, here comes der first flare down."

A ball of fire, incredibly white and unbelievably fierce, descended before Kathryn's eyes. It was swinging down swiftly by a dangling steel cable. It went down in swift swoops of fifteen and twenty feet at a time.

"A magnesium flare," said Schaaf softly. "It has half a million candlepower. We try him on der dog. Ha!"

The flare reached the definite surface of the blackness. It seemed incredible that no glitter came from that surface. It dived into the flood of darkness. Its white light turned to red. Down and down— Fifteen feet in the black flood and it could be seen as a dully glowing red ball, no more.

"No more flares," said Schaaf quietly over his shoulder. "They don't work. Der darkness absorbs all der light. But keep der other flares going on der roofs. Now we try."

A voice spoke quietly from the row of telephone instruments.

"Lieutenant Hines reports that the street is full of gas. Sneeze-gas."

"No. 3 expedient gone to hell," said Schaaf calmly. "We hoped from der water, and we hoped from der flares. And we had sneeze-gas and tear gas bombs ready to smash in der street. But they intended to use it themselfs to disable der armored-car crew and der bank people, I suppose, and they must haff masks. It is der deffil that Breston got so much money two weeks ago. He has capital to supply his friends with all modern improfements. Hm. All right. Tell that fire-eater Hines to get ready to go out with his mopping-up party and raise hell. Set der gongs going."

A man spoke quietly at the back of the room, and to the chatter and chuffing of engines in the street there now was added the heavy, measured clanging of monster gongs. The engines shut off abruptly.

"Der gongs are signals," said Schaaf quietly. "It is Hines's idea. They signal to der firemen to cut off der water, and he and his gang go out hand and hand to sweep der street and grab anybody that has not a rubber suit on and smash him behind der ear. He and all his men are ex-soldiers, and they pretend it is a patrol between trenches. Also, der gongs keep them oriented so they know which way is which. Those motor cycle cops had orders to duck in der armored car if der darkness fell. I hope they remembered, or somebody is likely to sock them in der jaw."

THE COMMISSIONER GROWLED from the next window. There had been a sudden silence. The firemen had fumbled their way to their engines and climbed up on them. The street below should be empty of all living creatures except Lefty Dunn and his gangsters, desperate and at bay, and the sinister figure of the man who, allied with the under-world, seemed to have had the city at his mercy. Shots sounded suddenly from below.

"Somebody is going to get scared, now," said Schaaf. "Herr Commissioner, our Lieutenant Hines is out and fighting like der deffil. Der gentlemen for whom we are gifing this party will try to run away now. If you will giff orders—"

"I've got a cordon all about the darkness," growled the commissioner.

"Der idea is," said Schaaf patiently, "that Breston has not a full-power darkness-producing outfit with him, or else maybe der water got to some of his batteries and cut down his power. He can't drife a car in der darkness. He will try to walk, carrying that suitcase apparatus with him. Tip off der cordon of reserfs to leafe one man at efery corner, especially der corners where there are police telephones. Maybe they can tip us exactly where he arrifes."

The commissioner coughed, and swore privately to himself for not having issued the orders on his own initiative. He gave them.

"That, also, was Hines's idea," said Schaaf placidly.

He looked at his watch in the glare that came in the window. Another shot below. Three more. A shriek.

"It should be sunrise in half an hour more, maybe less," he observed. "I hope der *verdammt* fool is caught before der people try to come down this way to work. Otherwise we will haff to stop der subways."

He looked sharply at the girl beside him. She was shaking peculiarly. Her lips were caught between her teeth and her eyes glistened suspiciously.

"Shush!" said Schaaf in her ear. "I know. I am scared to der bottom of my marrow, too, but that fighting fool Hines is all right. He has to be! And if you cry now, I will tell him about it afterward! That is a threat! Shush!"

She caught her breath, struggling to fight down sobs of nervousness.

A man said briskly from the row of telephones:

"The cordon, sir, reports that the blackness is moving. It's moving on down town. It is three blocks long and three wide, and it has moved half a block south."

Schaaf grimaced, and then grinned.

"Haff somebody yell that out in der street to Hines. He

will know what to do. Are members of der cordon posting themselfs in der high buildings and smashing in doors to get at telephones so they can watch der darkness and tell us? I suspect Breston will switch it off for an instant to try and see where he is, after he mofes a block or two."

A man spoke briskly into a telephone. And Schaaf said pleasantly:

"Hines efen thought of that, in case all der other things did not work. I told him he was a pessimist, but I admit now that he is smart."

Silence. There were no more shots. The lights flared brilliantly outside. One dimmed, and another took its place. The unwavering, opaque blackness below—it was almost impossible to look at it without believing that it was a solid substance—seemed to flow noiselessly like a river of death between the starkly illuminated buildings on either side. But Schaaf said suddenly:

"It is going down! He has mofed a block or more with his apparatus!"

KATHRYN STARED. THE upper limit of the blackness had receded. It was hardly more than three stories above the street, now. As she watched, very, very slowly it went down still more.

"He is going south. On foot," said Schaaf, "as Hines predicted."

Five minutes later the street itself was dimly visible. The street-lights appeared as dull red glows, which grew brighter and turned white. The squat gray armored car appeared. There were two figures moving spasmodically on the pavement beside it. The darkness drew on toward the south. Two more figures, crumpled up and still. A car, slued around with its windows smashed and the hood torn off its engine by the force of a stream of water. Minutes later another car appeared dimly as the darkness became merely murkiness. It, too, was washed clear of windows.

"I bet," said Schaaf intently, "Breston almost got caught by a stream of water, and hid behind his car for protection from der hoses until they were turned off."

"Is—is *he* safe?" asked Kathryn in a strained voice. She was not, one gathered, asking about Preston.

One of the men at the telephones said quietly:

"Lieutenant Hines asked just now for the position of the center of the darkness. I gave it to him from the reports of the cordon around its outer edge."

Kathryn gasped in relief.

One of the other men at the telephones said swiftly:

"Report. The darkness was turned off for about two seconds. Preston was seen, carrying two heavy suitcases and staring about him. There were two other men with him. Lieutenant Hines fired on them and saw one of them fall."

Silence. Looking down from the windows now, the street was clear. But to the south the darkness rose from the pavement and filled the space between the buildings.

"It seems cruel," said Schaaf gently, "for all der whole police force to be hunting down three men as if they were mad dogs. But they are mad dogs. Der newspapers did not print all der crimes that happened on Fifth Afenue the other day. They could not. And Breston permitted those crimes deliberately. He arranged to turn der underworld loose for a share in der profits. He got that share. And he will do it again if we do not catch him."

The commissioner coughed, and said suddenly:

"See if the gas has cleared down in the street enough for us to go down."

A quiet inquiry.

"It is reasonably safe, sir."

The commissioner strode to the door. Kathryn looked appealingly at Schaaf.

"Surely," he said comfortably. "It is working like a well-oiled clock. We go down and follow der darkness, and maybe we see Hines, eh?"

The elevator was brightly lighted, now, and descended with a cheery hum. And the street was bright, though it was a ghastly brightness. They emerged to the sidewalk. An ambulance clanged up and stopped. Men had come out of the armored car and were bending over the writhing figures beside it.

"Sneeze-gas," said Schaaf quietly, "it is terrible. It produces a horrible exhaustion. But it is not fatal."

The still figures a little distance off were gangsters, with gas-masks adjusted in marked incongruity to their loudly checked and now soaked and draggled clothing. Uniformed figures were moving about, investigating. The firemen were cheerfully coiling up their hose and preparing a return trip to their engine-houses. Two more bodies of gangsters. A man in a rubber suit—one of Hines's men. Twenty yards on, another gangster.

THERE WERE SEVEN gangsters and two police in the space of a block. Beyond that the pavement was blessedly bare. Schaaf looked to the east at the first side-street.

"Der sky is lightening. Day will soon be here," he said quietly. "I think we get Breston."

They walked quietly after the slowly moving mass of

darkness. On the ground-level, here, it looked vastly different. It rose in an irregular, clumsy curve. Seen from behind it looked oddly like some monstrous, prehistoric monster edging itself painfully down a canon whose walls closed tightly upon its sides.

Four blocks down they found two policemen carrying off a figure on a litter.

"Lefty Dunn, sir," said one of them, satisfiedly. "Lieutenant Hines shot him, sir. He's dead."

Two blocks further a policeman was beaming as he inserted his key into the police telephone box.

"Just taking up cordon work here, sir," he reported happily. "The darkness is dwindling fast. It's hardly more than two blocks long and wide, sir."

"His batteries are running low," observed Schaaf. "Soon he is in der soup."

They hurried a little, now. It seemed as if the two fleeing men were, guiding themselves by the trolley-tracks and could make better time in the horrible darkness all about them. A little farther on there was a clatter and clanging, and a chemical engine appeared where a policeman was playing a hand fire-extinguisher on the awning of a corner cigar store.

"Ah," said Schaaf pleasantly. "They are getting desperate. They tried to make a diversion by starting a fire. That is foolishness. It only adds arson to der charges of robbery and murder."

The cigar store was at the corner of Wall Street, and Trinity churchyard showed a certain duskiness at its southern edge, but that was all.

And five minutes later they were able to view the darkness as a whole. It had moved out into the clear space which is Battery Park. The flagpole of the Aquarium rose above it. It was a circular, flattened mass of black with ragged, hazy edges. It stood like some monstrosity in the mass of green things. It was hardly more than two hundred feet in diameter, and it was certainly not thirty feet high. And it seemed to be still dwindling slowly.

Hines came up, with sweat-streaks on his face and powder-marks on his hands. He was wrapping his handkerchief around one wrist, which was bleeding.

"Cut it," he said quietly, "breaking in a door to get at a telephone booth. I called up Governor's Island, sir," he added to the commissioner of police. "They have some army planes there."

The sky was getting lighter and lighter. The harbor spread out as a lucent gray, and ships at anchor began to take definite shapes through the morning air. The Statue of Liberty rose gray and misty from its base.

The ominous mass of blackness was the only incongruous thing in the whole spectacle of the sunrise. That pancake of malevolent darkness was still, clinging to the outer edge of the park, with nearly half its diameter spreading out over the waves of the harbor. A sudden chug-chugging arose. The blackness began to move. It swept out over the water, moving steadily and doggedly.

"*Himmel!*" snapped Schaaf, his mouth dropped open. "They found a launch! Breston will make for der Jersey shore and land, and der Jersey police cannot make a cordon in time to stop him from landing and hiding himself."

"Don't worry," said Hines grimly. "Look there!"

A LITTLE DARK speck detached itself from the earth of

Governor's Island. It rose and rose, and a dull muttering drew nearer and nearer. The noise rose to a roar, and an army biplane swept above the moving monstrosity of blackness. It circled and swooped.

Something dropped. There was a heavy concussion, a vast and crackling detonation.

And then there was abruptly nothing upon the water, anywhere, except a spouting mass of spray and smoke, and a few remnants of a boat that swirled about and sank as the plume of spray subsided. The blackness had gone out like a blown-out candle.

"Good shooting," said Schaaf comfortably. "That must haff been a big bomb. Now we will haff difers hunt for der fragments of Breston's apparatus, and we will find that we can't do a damned thing with them. Which, from der scientific standpoint, is a fery great pity."

Hines unconsciously brushed his hands together.

"It's finished," he said, suddenly very tired.

The commissioner of police coughed. He was a civilian, and he had been a political appointee, and he had been learning of late that the force is much more important than politics. It was not altogether a pleasant dose he had swallowed. But he turned abruptly to Hines.

"Inspector Hines," he said, and coughed again, "I—er—I may not have coöperated with you as fully as I should when you first reported this matter; but—er—in the future you will find no cause for complaint. Come in to see me to-morrow."

He moved abruptly away. Hines stared after him.

"Inspector?" Kathryn gasped.

"Yes," said Schaaf placidly. "Inspector Hines. The

commissioner is like Napoleon in his promotions. Yes. All of us haff our Napoleonic moments, and he did this fery nicely. You are Police Inspector Hines hereafter, and I congratulate you. And I think, Miss Bush, that as a fery good friend of his, if I were you I would take der moment of congratulation as an opportunity to kiss him. It would be appropriate, and it might not be unpleasant."

Kathryn swallowed something.

Hines flushed a little. "You've got your scoop," Hines said awkwardly, ignoring Schaaf, "and this time there is nothing to regret about it."

"I—I don't care!" said Kathryn firmly. "About the scoop, that is. It doesn't matter. But I am going to kiss you."

And she did.

THE CITY OF THE BLIND

*Science Arms The Underworld With
An Astounding Weapon That Plunges
New York Into Black Horror*

1

DEATH TRAP

WHEN HINES DISMISSED the police chauffeur and started up to his apartment he was tired. Moreover, it was raining; one of those irritating, persistent, drizzling rains against which a top and windshield is no protection whatever. The street lamps and the entrance lights of the apartment building were reflected by the wetted pavements. The street lights, in particular, seemed to have little puddles of melted gold about their bases.

Hines started wearily across the pavement. Something stirred in the shadows. He faced it, instinctively alert. One does not rise in the detective bureau of the City of New York without acquiring ill-wishers; and one does not survive their ill-will without a little luck and more alertness.

But the moving figure was a slickered patrolman, who saluted.

"Evening, inspector."

Hines nodded, relaxing. He saw another slickered officer beyond the first. Others. His eyes sharpened by sudden curiosity, Hines saw four men within a hundred yards, waiting in the rain as if for something expected.

"What is it?" he asked. "How is it you men are posted here?"

"Guard, sir," said the patrolman. He smiled. "For you, sir. The commissioner's orders."

Hines stared. "But what—" He stopped.

"Mr. Schaaf, sir," said the patrol man, "is waiting up in your rooms. We were ordered to stand guard outside and look out for suspicious persons. It's believed, sir, that some one may try to assassinate you."

Hines grunted. "News to me," he growled. "Nonsense, anyhow. I'll call headquarters and have you relieved. No use your standing in the rain."

He went into the foyer of the building. An impeccably dressed man with the air of one waiting in boredom for a taxi was lounging inside.

The telephone bust with annihilating force.

Hines grunted again. "Hello, Davidson," he growled. "You, too?"

"Yes, sir," said the lounger. "The commissioner has been worried about you, sir."

Hines frowned. When one has been a lieutenant of police for a few years, seeing very slight hope of promotion, and then after a violent disagreement with the commissioner one enables the said commissioner to cope with something brand-new and extremely dangerous coming out of the underworld, it is natural for the commissioner to realize his debt. It is even natural— though unusual— to receive an arbitrary promotion to an inspectorship. But such solicitude over one's health—

The descending elevator clicked its stop. The door swept

open silently. Hines stepped in. Four patrolmen on guard outside his apartment house. A plain-clothes man inside the foyer. Perhaps other men posted about.

He got out on his own floor. Another man from the detective bureau looked up alertly, stood up, and Hines scowled at him.

"Hully!" he growled. "This is too much! How many of you have been taken off useful duty and stuck around guarding me?"

"There's a man on every floor, sir," said the detective.

"It's a hell of a note," said Hines angrily. "I'll phone and have you relieved at once. I don't need guards!"

He put the key in his door and went in. He entered pitch-darkness.

A voice said placidly.

"Now, der fluorescence of atmospheric ions under der influence of short Hertzian wafes—"

Hines snorted.

"Schaaf! What the devil is all this foolishness?"

Lights flashed on, and Hines stared blankly at the sight before him. He knew Schaaf, certainly. That tall German scientist had made all the difference between success and failure in his efforts to cope with the malevolent scientific genius Preston in his alliance with the underworld a month or so before.

Schaaf was six feet and something, with a luxuriant blond beard and an expression of complete placidity under all circumstances. Hines had been told Schaaf was waiting for him. But—

Schaaf was present in six separate incarnations. There were six men in the room, and each one of them was something over six feet tall and each one wore an expression of complete placidity and a luxuriant blond beard. It was practically impossible to tell them apart. After an instant's bewildered survey, however, Hines growled and nodded to the man whose whiskers were indubitably his own.

"Hell's bells!" he snapped. "What's the matter? Have you gone crazy and made the police department crazy with you?"

Schaaf beamed.

"These gentlemen," he observed placidly, "are a disguise. When you are encountering a fery intelligent man, Hines, der best way to confuse him is to do der most foolish thing you can think of. Then he cannot anticipate your actions, because if you are fairly defer you can think of a lot of foolishness."

HINES GROWLED AGAIN.

"You've done it, all right. What's it all about?"

Schaaf waved his hand.

"We go into executife session," he observed. "My disguise will now excuse us, and we think wise, deep, andt profound thoughts, and maybe do something sensible for a change. Where the deffil were you to-day? Eferybody on der police force was looking for you."

"Leg-work, practically," said Hines, frowning. "That Helman murder case. It looked bad. The idiot had insured his life and couldn't wait a year to commit suicide. Tried to fake his suicide as a murder, so his wife would get his insurance; and he didn't have sense enough to arrange an alibi for her."

"Which you broceded to do. You are always altruistic," said Schaaf. "Now sit down and don't smoke der cigars in your own humidor. Take one of mine. It is safer. My disguise is going out and we can talk."

The five men with blond false whiskers were going out of the room. Schaaf beamed upon Hines, who had halted with his hand on the humidor cover.

"Why—"

"Don't smoke it," said Schaaf with sudden grimness, "because Breston or some friendt of his has been in here today."

Hines jumped.

"Preston! But he's dead!"

"Like hell he's dead," said Schaaf placidly. "He is der most actif and most irritating corpse I efer ran across."

He passed over one of his own cigars. Hines took it, staring.

"But that bomb blew him—"

"Nowhere at all," Schaaf assured him. "He took der apparatus that makes darkness along with him down to der Battery, with us chasing after him gayly, shooting sneeze-bombs at him, trying to pour water on him, doing all that der combined resources of me, and you, and der Bolice Department could think of. And he got into a launch, we considered, and was blown to bits out in der harbor. Der army airplane dropped a bomb into his pancake of dark-ness andt we saw a boat that was sinking when der dark-ness vanished. And der police launches fished up farious fragments which they pieced together abbroximately into one corpse for burial. But that was all."

Hines sank into a chair and bit off the end of his cigar.

"But," said Schaaf placidly, "we knew he had two men with him when he started toward der Battery. You shot one of them when he lifted der darkness to see where he was. There was one more left with him. We assumed that both of them got in der launch that was smashed up."

Hines growled.

"He wasn't fool enough to stay behind, was he?"

"He wasn't a fool if he did," observed Schaaf. "My dear Hines, suppose he slipped oferboard from der piling while der launch went on out with his companion to be blown into little pieces? It was der sensible thing for him to do. If Breston fanished, der gunman with him would go like der deffil, carrying der darkness, and we would go like der deffil after him. Which we did."

HINES'S EYES NARROWED.

"We were a pack of fools!" he said grimly. "We should have looked under the wharf. But why are you sure he got away?"

"A man told me," said Schaaf. He puffed comfortably. "I haff a good job with der Research Department of der American Electric Company. I got it because Miss Bush made me famous when she wrote up Breston's party. To-day I was working fery hard and my brain went dead on me. And there is a quick lunch near by where they haff abominable coffee which is a great stimulant. I went there to get a cup of it.

"A gentleman came in and sat down beside me. He placed a large bowl of soup on der arm of der chair next to mine. He entered into conversation. He asked if I was Professor Schaaf, der great scientist. I admitted it with becoming modesty. And I saw a car waiting at der door with a number of fery efficient-looking gentlemen in it. I looked back and saw my friend getting out an automatic pistol to shoot me with. I beaned him, as you call it, with his own plate of soup. Then I carried him out to der kitchen and stuffed his head in a tub of mashed potatoes while police whistles were being blown and der deffil raised generally. Der others ran away."

He shook his head reflectively.

"A fery angry person, that gentleman. At der police station he said that Breston had offered him fife grand to bump me off, but that when he got out of prison he would do it for nothing, just for his own prifate pleasure. Der police want him fery badly, and but for der comestibles I beaned him with, he would haff shot me and got away."

Hines chewed savagely on the end of his cigar.

"Preston's alive, then," he said grimly.

"I went to der Commissioner. He began to throw fits at once, fery entertainingly. He knows it was by luck that we licked that *verdammt* Breston last time. He said to find you at once, before you were killed, for Breston will want to kill both of us because we know too much about him. So I borrowed der fife men to wear whiskers and follow me around for my protection. If a gunman wants to kill me, he will haff to kill all of us to be sure he gets der right one, and it will be confusing and possibly tedious. And then I ditched der research work and set people to work looking for you."

Hines chewed his cigar again, remembered and lighted it, and scowled.

"I'll be assigned to the job of finding him," he observed grimly. "And if he tried to have you killed, he'll try for me too. But why do you think he had some one in here to-day?"

Schaaf grimaced.

"When I came in to wait for you, I made myself at home as always. I sat down, and I reached in der humidor for a cigar. And like I always do, I cracked der cigar and smelled it. You smoke fery bad cigars, Hines. Fery bad. But der cigars in der humidor were good ones. So I got suspicious. I cut one open and there are some small crystals inserted in der tobacco which I suspect would not be healthy for you to smoke when der heat reached them. Yes?"

Hines's eyes glowed suddenly.

"I see," he said shortly.

"Breston is making ready to turn on der darkness of his, and he wants to get us out of der way. He is starting a new campaign—"

SUDDEN, DENSE, ABOMINABLE blackness filled the room. The glow of the lighted lamps went out utterly. The windows did not even show as grayish rectangles from the streetlights outside. Hines felt his heart pumping suddenly. He looked at his cigar. The glow of its tip was totally invisible. He touched his finger to it and was scorched. It was still burning, but the air no longer transmitted its light. The blackness seemed even tangible. Hines reached up to the electric bulb over his head and felt it. It was hot, but it did not glow.

Schaaf's voice came through the horrible darkness. It was placid as before.

"Yes. He is starting a new campaign. And this is der opening gun."

"Just a minute," said Hines.

He jerked off the shade of the lamp by his chair. The hot bulb scorched his fingers. He brought it close to his eyes. At eight inches he could see the filament as a dully glowing red line. At six it was bright. At four inches from his eyes he could see his fingers on the other side of the bulb.

"It's Preston's darkness, all right," said Hines coolly. "Nothing else on earth absorbs light like that. And at a guess he's aiming for us, somehow."

"I haff a hunch," said Schaaf in the absolute darkness. "It is a splendid hunch and fery comforting. If you will gift me your wordt of honor not to touch der telephone—"

"I ought to call headquarters," said Hines, every sense alert, "and report this right away."

"So you should. But for der luff of Gott don't do it! Wait!"

Silence fell. A woman screamed affrightedly somewhere, floors below. There was a hammering on the door of the apartment.

"Keep out!" barked Hines. "All right in here! The darkness will lift presently."

Silence, and blackness. Horrible, absolute blackness. The utter blackness in which the blind live always.

Sounds became magnified by the utter lack of light. Hines could hear his heart beating. He heard Schaaf breathing, five feet away. He heard the rustling of cloth as Schaaf seemed to lift his cigar to his lips. The ticking of his watch became suddenly deafeningly loud. There were sounds, a long way off, as if people were exclaiming alarmedly at something. A man began to bellow, "Get a doctor! I've gone blind! Somebody get a doctor!"

And then, with the barest possible flickering, the room leaped back into light. The bulbs glowed dazzlingly after the incredible darkness of a moment before. The torn-off lampshade looked astoundingly untidy, flung on the floor.

Hines's face was grim and hard and a trifle pale. Schaaf was much paler.

"It was a strain on der hunch, to wait," Schaaf said quietly. "But it worked out. I think der telephone is phony, Hines. Der apartment cannot be rung from der switchboard below. Come and stand in der doorway with me. If I did not stop you, you would have called headquarters at once, wouldn't you?"

"I'd have called while the darkness held," said Hines grimly.

"And that," said Schaaf soberly, "was maybe what der darkness was for. Now I ruin a book. Dodge behind here, Hines."

He motioned Hines back behind a wall and held a book ready. "If der instrument is phony," he observed, "it will spring its little surprise when der receiver goes off der hook."

He flung the book with a quick motion of his hand and darted back beside Hines. The book sailed across the empty room. The telephone was struck obliquely and knocked to the very edge of its stand. It tottered there a moment, wavered, and started to fall to the floor.

A terrific explosion rocked the building! It was so sharp a detonation that it was over before the ear had time to register its impact. It was stunning in its brittleness. It was incredibly loud and incredibly fierce and incredibly venomous. Plaster from the ceiling fell upon Hines and Schaaf, in the next room.

There was a huge, gaping hole torn in the floor. The walls were shattered, the furniture smashed. The telephone, the

stand—everything within five feet of the telephone instrument had been blown to powder.

If Hines had lifted the receiver to call Police Headquarters, every fragment of his body would have been annihi-
lated.

2

THE BLACK THREAT

IT WAS IMPOSSIBLE to keep the thing out of the newspapers. Too many people had been in the three-block circle which had gone dark for the sole purpose of making Hines pick up the telephone and so be blown to bits. But the bomb-explosion itself disturbed very few people. Hines could have been spattered against the walls of his apartment without causing any great commotion, had it not been for the accompanying darkness. It was the darkness which frightened New York.

Some six weeks before, a beam of darkness had been laid upon Fifth Avenue for precisely fifteen minutes. In that quarter of an hour a forewarned underworld had reaped a harvest. Jewelers had been robbed. Pedestrians had been stripped of their possessions. Every possible source of valuables that could be cleaned out in fifteen minutes had been looted. In addition, there had been many deaths in the panics caused by the darkness, and there had been some crimes too horrible for the newspapers to record.

For two weeks, New York was in panic. Hines knew, and Schaaf knew, and Kathryn Bush of the New York *Star* knew who had caused the darkness, and partly how it had been done.

A certain man, Preston, had made use of Schaaf's researches and had discovered that the ionized particles of the air absorbed all light that struck upon them, and re-radiated it as heat, when under the influence of certain short Hertzian waves. Preston had made a deal with the underworld for a share of the profits they could win in a street with all men blind. His profits had been enormous.

Two weeks after the Fifth Avenue episode, Preston had tried to use the same flood of blackness to make possible the theft of four million dollars in currency and securities in transit between two banks in the financial district. With Hines and Schaaf forewarned, the entire resources of the police and fire departments had enabled them to foil the attempt, and it seemed that Preston had been killed. New York breathed more easily. But in less than a full day from the bomb explosion in Hines's apartment, New York was a bundle of nerves again. Everybody knew that at any instant any part of the city might be plunged into abysmal blackness in which lights served no purpose at all; a blackness in which the forewarned hordes of the underworld would be quickly at work to loot and kill with complete impunity. And New York's nerves went bad.

First, of course, the Stock Exchange began at its opening to show symptoms of panic at least as great as that of the public in general. And the public in general was on the edge of hysteria and sometimes slipped over that edge.

A fuse blew out in a Lexington Avenue subway train. The lights went out, leaving it in darkness. A woman shrieked "The Darkness!" and there was a wild surge of fear-crazed passengers. Four people were dead when it was over.

At the Yankee Stadium, a dark thundercloud formed

quickly overhead and a deep shadow fell upon the grand-stand. The crowd went mad with terror, and fifteen people died.

For the rest, the Broadway theaters were nearly deserted, but there was instance after instance of mob insanity in neighborhood moving picture houses until the police rather desperately considered closing all public gather-ing-places until the tendency to panic subsided.

HINES WORKED. THE average man considers detective work as mostly the art of sitting still and thinking inten-sively about certain conveniently distributed clews. It is much more complicated and much less comfortable than that.

Hines was directing practically the whole detective force of the city in a frantic quest for Preston. First, of course, there was the attempt to locate the spot from which the short waves that produced the darkness had been trans-mitted. The area of the darkness was found by painstaking inquiry.

It was a circle some three blocks in every direction. Plot-ted on the map, the center of that circle turned out to be a tiny triangular park with a seedy patch of grass and a seed-ier statue of an obscure patriot.

"He was in a car," said Hines drearily. "He had his outfit in a car, probably parked there, as he watched for me to pass going home or maybe just for lights to go on in my windows. Then he turned on the dark knowing I'd identify it for what it was and start to telephone headquarters at once. He probably heard his damned bomb go off."

But no car had been noticed as parked where the center of the darkness had been. That was a blind lead.

The investigation of the bomb was similarly fruitless. The fake telephone instrument had been blown to fragments too small to offer any clews. It seemed to have been loaded with mercuric fulminate, an explosive so powerful that it is commonly used as a detonator for the ordinary "high explosive."

All that could be learned about the bomb was that an elderly telegraph messenger had been deposited on Hines's floor with a box apparently of flowers. But no telegraph messenger had been sent to the building by any messenger service.

It seemed most probable that the messenger had been a lock worker and had opened Hines's door, changed telephone instruments and the cigars, and gone peacefully out again. He had left no finger-prints in the apartment. And the elevator-boy, though he gave a voluble description of the elderly messenger, was unable to identify any photograph in the Rogues' Gallery until a picture of a messenger's uniform was cut out to be held over the standard photographs to assist his memory. Then he identified nine separate photographs as those of the messenger in question, and ultimately gave up in despair.

That also was a blind lead, so Hines set grimly to work to check up on every person in New York who had bought certain essentials of all shortwave radio sending outfits within the past four weeks. It was a task of titanic proportions.

The cigars were examined minutely, and offered no suggestions whatever. They were a standard brand, sold by thousands of stores and counters. The cyanide crystals had been inserted with a needle from the trimmed end. They were untraceable.

The gangster who had tried to assassinate Schaaf was obstinately silent, but it soon became evident that he knew nothing to tell, even had he been willing to talk. The others who had waited in the car outside had vanished utterly.

The last possibility came to Hines as he was racking his brains desperately for some other possibility, however unpromising. He was chewing at a cigar he had allowed to go out, and talked to himself in default of a more inspiring audience.

"He covers his tracks, always. We stepped on his last scheme by jumping ahead of him. What will he try now? What was the weakness of his last scheme? Hm. Lack of power. He could only blanket a certain area. He'll want to make the whole city dark, for safety, next time."

Inspiration came. He jumped for the telephone and had Schaaf on the wire in minutes.

"LOOK HERE!" HINES snapped. "If Preston wanted to design a bigger outfit, would he have to look anything up? Consult authorities, charts, figures, or anything of the sort?"

Schaaf's placid voice came over the wire.

"It is fery probable. Yes. A good technical library would safe him fery much trouble. I haff an idea, Hines, all my own. Der ionization—"

"Hold it!" said Hines. "Get a stenographer and dictate as many titles of the books Preston will need, as you can think of. I'm sending down some of my men. Give each one a copy. They'll go to all the technical libraries in the city and try to check up who's used those books lately. See?"

"Smart!" said Schaaf approvingly, over the wire. "Der more especially as Breston will surely want certain titles, like Strutt on der Differential Ionization of Isotopes, which not forty men in der United States can make head or tail of, and then they can't see der difference. Yes, you haff an idea, Hines. Send them down. And I haff a little idea of my own. When you get a chance to see me, I will tell you."

Hines rang off, satisfied. It wasn't a bad idea. The chances were against finding anything useful, but every man makes some slip, somewhere, and most detective work depends exclusively on finding that slip.

The door of his office opened and Kathryn Bush came in. She looked at once excited and apprehensive; thrilled and filled with an uneasy dread. Hines jerked to his feet and took her hand.

"My friend," said Kathryn with a queer smile, "why have you set two detectives to guard me?"

Hines turned brick-red and scowled. "Confounded, clumsy—" he began.

She shook her head.

"They were awfully careful, and very good," she protested. "It was fully half a day before I noticed them. And—I need them, I think. Preston knows we're friends, you and I."

Hines's muscles grew taut.

"He telephoned me to-day, at the *Star*," said Kathryn quietly. "He used your name to clinch my interest, and made threats. Then he told me, very unpleasantly, to look for—this."

She dropped an envelope on Hines's desk.

"It was in the morning mail, not yet opened. There's a

leg-man waiting to take it back to the *Star,* when you've read it."

Hines picked up the envelope, felt it over, went to the window and carefully tore it open. He sniffed at it cautiously before he came back to his desk and shook it out on the blotter.

"He's got me nervous," he admitted with a wry smile. "Gas, for instance. He might have anticipated your bringing it to me."

He opened the sheet with the ends of two rulers.

"I've been wanting a good set of his finger-prints," he observed, in a certain amount of apology for his caution. "The ones we got last time weren't perfectly clear."

And then he read:

To the Editor of the *Star:*

To-day, at twelve fifteen o'clock, daylight saving time, I shall blanket the entire metropolitan area in darkness for five minutes.

To-morrow, at three o'clock, I shall blanket the city in darkness for one-half hour.

Thereafter, each day, I shall blanket the city in darkness for such times as please me, at such hours as I shall select, until my terms have been met.

I will agree to leave the City of New York unmolested for one year for the sum of ten millions of dollars, to be remitted to me as I may later direct, and when Police Inspector Hines and Professor Albert Schaaf are no longer living. The news of the acceptance of my terms may be broadcast by all radio stations.

I am not concerned with the source of the ten millions of dollars. I do not care who shall kill Inspector Hines or Professor Schaaf. But I will pay, personally, twenty-five thousand dollars to any person who will kill either one of them, or fifty thousand dollars for them both.

Other newspapers in the city are receiving copies of this letter.

THOMAS PRESTON.

HINES LOOKED UP and smiled pleasantly.

"I'll give your leg-man a photographic copy in ten minutes," he observed. He pushed a button. "Now I begin to have hopes!"

Kathryn was deadly white.

"Sit down," said Hines. "It's ten five now, and I'm going to get busy. You'll have a story for your paper, and if you want to phone it in, there's a telephone."

Kathryn moistened her lips.

"You're going to—let the letter be printed?" she asked unevenly. "Offering money to kill you?"

Hines laughed and went out. In five minutes or less he was back. He took up the phone and began to give crisp orders. As an inspector of police, he had vastly more authority than as a mere lieutenant, and moreover the commissioner was in nearly as bad a nervous state as the city at large. Hines had been given nearly unlimited authority in the matter of Preston, and he began to use it.

Kathryn heard him give a blanket order to all traffic stations and all traffic officers. Another to go to all patrolmen on duty. A third to be transmitted to all business houses. A statement to be broadcast by radio. An order to the subway and elevated operating departments. To the surface car lines. Then a series of directions as to the redistribution of police reserves.

He swung about in his chair.

"There's your story," he observed, "on the answer to Preston's threat. Why don't you phone it in? The *Star* will be getting out an extra, won't it?"

Kathryn tried to smile.

"When I left, for here, they were clearing the way for one, holding a blank front page and all the rewrite men champing at their typewriters."

A voice came up from the street below. "Wuxtry! Wuxtry!"

"We're beaten to the street!" wailed Kathryn. "Because I brought the letter to you instead of having it opened."

Hines smiled.

"You've better stuff to go in the extra of the *Star*. Here, use this telephone."

He got the connection for her. A leg-man was streaking it for the *Star* offices with the photographed letter. And Kathryn began to dictate feverishly over the wire to a swearing city room which was collectively tearing its hair over having carried an honorable cooperation with the police to the extent of being beaten to the street with an extra on Preston's announced intentions.

But as Kathryn began to talk, that swearing died down. Typewriters began to hum and rattle. The crashing roar of linotypes began on the lower floors. The *Star* was ready for its story. The story was written, set up, matted, cast, trimmed, and inserted into the waiting presses in time which beat all records for the *Star* or any other paper.

It was, as a matter of fact, little more than thirty minutes from the time Kathryn hung up the receiver before trucks began to spread over the city with huge bundles of papers being tom apart and hurled wildly at news-stands by bulk distributors already racing at full speed toward other stands.

It was a little after eleven when Hines spread out the paper on his own desk. Kathryn had once absurdly visualized Hines's name in hundred-and-twenty-point type in a *Star* headline. She saw it now in hundred-and-sixty-eight point. The headlines screamed.

HINES FIGHTS PRESTON!
Traffic Ordered Stopped Before Darkness Falls—
Pedestrians to Get Under Shelter at Noon—All Buildings
Closed During Darkness—Subways to Stop—All Travel
Suspended

As news-matter in a city already terrified by the threat of universal blindness, the moves taken against that darkness were vastly more important than anything else. Preston's letter and its photostatic copy were on the front page, to be sure, but "Ten Millions Ransom Demanded," with its appropriate write-up, was crowded away down to the bottom of the sheet.

AT A QUARTER to twelve the streets of New York seemed almost deserted. There were vehicles parked by thousands. Parking rules were not only suspended, but parking was ordered by the police. The sidewalks were empty. At twelve o'clock the sun shone down brightly upon a city that seemed to have been deserted by all its inhabitants. Stores were closed and barred. Banks had drawn huge grilles across their entrances. Surface cars stopped short at any spot their motormen chose and remained still.

The city was motionless without movement of any sort.

Even the boats in the harbor were docked or anchored wherever they happened to be. Railroad trains puffed and hissed, quite stationary, upon their tracks. Only the windows of the city were alive. Every window of every building was packed with faces, staring out for the beginning of the darkness.

But it came on with an utter absence of the spectacular.

An aviator was flying twelve thousand feet up, by Hines's order, to take an air-photo of the phenomenon. A slow-motion motion-picture camera clicked inaudibly beside him, its noise drowned by the roaring of the motors. He leaned over the side of the fuselage, his companion waiting with a ray-filter camera and its plates. Gazing down upon the city, the aviator saw no sign or symptom of anything wrong. The city lay bright and glittering below him. Extraordinarily still, of course.

Only the ever-present tiny plumes of steam from the tops of tall buildings moved. No ships steamed about the harbor. No crawling traffic stirred in the streets. The city was extraordinarily still, but bright and brave and glittering in the sunlight.

And then—it *was not*. The city was there no longer. Instead of the city, there was a vast expanse of blackness. It extended to the outskirts of Newark in a dense black flood. It reached up toward Yonkers, and it overwhelmed all Brooklyn, and it blotted out even the Narrows. From aloft it did not seem to possess a substance. It looked rather as if a bottomless gulf, the abyss itself, had opened a gaping mouth nearly twenty miles wide and swallowed the city into oblivion.

3

BLACK HORROR BROODS

A LITTLE MORE than twenty-four hours later the streets were similarly and singularly dead when the big police car drew to a stop before the American Electric Building. It was half past two in the afternoon, and New York had been warned that all its inhabitants would be blinded for half an hour, at three.

Coming down Broadway, all through the wholesale district there had been the same spectacle. Empty store-windows, with grilles in place where grilles could be provided. Doors locked. Few cars, or none. No pedestrians at all. Worried policemen looking more and more suspiciously at the few scurrying vehicles darting uptown.

The city already seemed like a city of the dead. The five minutes of blackness, the day before, had made New York a city trembling on the verge of blind panic. There were nervous persons already having chills from terror of the darkness which would come on at three. The hospitals already began to experience an influx of hysterical patients, in advance of the event which called forth their hysteria.

Always, of course, there are a certain number of people with unstable mentalities in a city the size of New York. Always there are a certain number who will be pushed over the edge of complete sanity by any exciting event. A doctor at Bellevue can estimate with a near approach to accuracy just how many citizens of New York will go insane over almost any given event, from a transatlantic flight to a national election.

In the case of the darkness Preston turned on at will, the estimate ran below the probable figure for, say, a comet visible to the naked eye, like Halley's comet, but it was considered that more mental patients would be produced than even by a financial panic in Wall Street. The event justified the prediction. Bellevue's observation wards were nearly filled by bright-eyed feverish people who could think of nothing but The Darkness.

There were a dozen people lingering before the American Electric Building when Hines got out. Policemen on duty there thrust them back. But they eyed Hines nervously, or hopefully, or bale fully, as their natures dictated. One man began to shout hysterically, and was promptly collared by a burly patrolman.

"It's Bellevue for you, me lad," said the cop philosophically, "an' don't be bringin' the Lord into it, because 'tis your own nuttiness that makes ye think the Inspector is at the bottom av all the trouble."

Hines's expression was grim, and he was beginning to look very, very tired, when he turned to Kathryn inside the building.

"That man's typical," he said, smiling without any mirth. "Since the publication of Preston's letter sixty or seventy crank letters have come in, explaining why I should permit myself to be assassinated for the good of the city. One woman wrote that I would be dying heroically if I permitted her to do the job, because I would be dying for the benefit of millions, and letting her bump me off would give her twenty-five thousand dollars she needed very badly."

"You—you are in danger," said Kathryn, unevenly, "with people getting hysterical like this."

"After to-day," said Hines, smiling wearily, "I'm to be given a bodyguard. But we're progressing. We've got a picture of Preston now, thanks to you, and we're printing posters by the hundred thousand."

The elevator began to carry them swiftly upward. Hines looked at his watch.

"Twenty minutes more," he said tiredly. "I hope Schaaf's little tricks work. I'm still hoping for something from some of mine."

KATHRYN WATCHED HIS face anxiously. He did look tired. He had been working night and day for four days, now. Ever since the bomb explosion in his own apartment. His eyes were beginning to be sunken in.

"That picture," he said suddenly. "We got a clear set of Preston's finger-prints from that letter he sent you yesterday. We sent them to Washington by telephone transmission. They were all ready to work on them, and had twenty clerks looking them up."

At Kathryn's expression of mute interrogation, he explained wearily.

"Preston is thirty-five or so. He should have been in the army in the last war. And the finger-prints of every man who was in the army are on file in Washington. They found him. Private, Chemical Warfare Battalion. Found his home town, Clinton, Delaware. The police there jumped to work, hunting up his relatives. All dead. They finally found a girl who'd been engaged to him. She had a picture. They sent it on to us by airplane. Schaaf and I watched a photographer retouch it—age it, to look just as he does now, beard and all. The posters are being run off now."

The elevator stopped. Armed guards watched them come out of the elevator. Hines smiled.

"Schaaf doesn't like to be shot at. Quite sensible, really. I hate to be trailed around, though."

He followed a guide through a wide-open door marked, "No Admittance Without A Pass." A man with yellow whiskers started to his feet, then sank down again. A second man, identical with the first in whiskers, height, and clothing, even to a tiny flower in his button-hole, pointed silently to another door.

Then four yellow-whiskered men—the exact doubles of the first two—were seen. Three of them were tugging some heavy piece of apparatus into place under the direction of the fourth. It was the fourth who waved his hand abstractedly to them.

"Just in time, Hines. Ah, Miss Bush! Sit down! We haff fifteen full minutes, because that *verdammt* Breston is always on time to der second. Just a minute."

He went on, busily superintending the dragging into place of a huge screen that seemed to be made of wire netting. His three doubles worked willingly, but unskillfully.

"It looks," said Kathryn under her breath, "like something he does with mirrors—all those doubles of his."

Hines managed to smile. Schaaf seemed to be satisfied, looked at his watch, and emitted an anguished howl. Instantly, it seemed, men were running and seating themselves at various predetermined positions and taking up pieces of apparently complicated apparatus in their hands.

"I did der placing of der instruments with members of der Whisker Sextette as my assistants," explained Schaaf placidly, "because I can shout at them, and they do not giff a damn. But der people in der laboratory here mostly understand German profanity and they find themselfs insulted. Do you want to sit there in der dark, or ofer here where we may possibly throw a little light on Breston?"

Hines and Kathryn moved forward.

"A screen," said Schaaf amiably, "which intercepts all der known lengths of Hertzian wafes. Here is an apparatus with a bit of radium emanation in it. Radium emanation ionizes der air about it. We compare der intensity of der darkness when a known ionization is present, and der intensity of der darkness in normal air. Here we see if der *verdammt* darkness prefents der transmission of light in a closed metal container. We haff an hour in which to work. Here are farious apparatuses trying to measure der wafelength Breston uses. Here is a spectroscope with a thermocouple and a relay instead of an eye. It is to measure how much of der spectrum is absorbed by der atmospheric ions and re-radiated as heat. Here is a soft X-ray, and here der spinthariscope screen. We see if X-rays penetrate der darkness. Here is a mercury fapor lamp, which is rich in ultra-fiolet rays, and here a rhodamine plate with a filter. We see if der ultra-fiolet end of der spectum is affected. That is my pet idea, Hines, that I told you on der telephone. We haff a hell of a lot of apparatus all around. When we finish, we ought to know efery thing about Breston except der size of his collar and does he like blondes or brunettes. Sit down here. We haff three minutes more. We rehearse."

FOR TWO MINUTES more he conducted himself like a general. The men at the separate instruments closed their eyes. At his order they made their tests. And little bells rang, or buzzers buzzed, and curt reports were snapped in the silent laboratory.

"Good. Fery good," said Schaaf. "We work this, Hines, like an astronomical obserfation of an eclipse of der sun. Now, *Gott strafe* Breston! It's time!"

There was half a minute, three-quarters of a minute of dead silence. And then, with utter soundlessness, the world went dark. Hines felt Kathryn shrink, beside him. He groped for her hand and held it fast. They were in the horrible blackness for which there is no simile.

The darkness was so deep, so terrible, that it clutched at one's throat. There was an hysterical impulse to make a light—any sort of light. To strike a match. To flee from this horrible blindness. It felt as if there were massive walls all about, shutting off the light, as if one were buried alive, as if the boards of a veritable coffin were about one, and solid earth atop.

A man said in a staccato fashion:

"Selenium cells do not respond."

"The wave-length is not above five meters," said another curtly.

"Not above two meters," said a third voice shortly.

"Not above one-half meter," said a fourth voice.

Schaaf swore audibly in German.

"Light is transmitted in the closed tube," snapped a voice. "I shall open one end and try to get a bearing."

Schaaf stopped swearing, then began again.

"X-rays penetrate the darkness, sir, quite normally," said a tranquil voice at one side.

"Sir! The rhodamine dye is fluorescent at a distance of six feet!" said another.

Schaaf began to swear again, but this time with satisfaction.

And then a voice, shaking with excitement, said:

"Herr Schaaf, I have the honor to report that the screen absorbs the short waves Preston is using. I am in light, sir, and can see the screen from six feet by the light of an electric bulb."

SCHAAF EMITTED AN explosive whoop.

"Hines! Miss Bush! Walk here and shake hands with me where we can see each other! Der rhodamine dye means that we practice all der faforite forms of *Schrecklichkeit* on that deffil!"

Hines felt Kathryn's hand close convulsively on his. He stood up and fumbled his way with a peculiar feeling of helplessness, through the absolute opacity. And suddenly an arm caught at his outstretched, fumbling hand and pulled at him, and Hines felt absolutely the most peculiar sensation of his life.

His head came out into brightness. He was in a triangular space where sight was visible. At the base of the triangle there was a square of ordinary wire screening, some four feet square. It rested on a table, as Hines remembered. An electric bulb burned brightly before it. At its edges the darkness began again, and the area of lightness narrowed to a point.

His head seemed disembodied. Kathryn's face was

pale and bloodless, and seemed dismembered from her body. Schaaf sputtered and gesticulated—judging by the motions of the head—but Hines had a singularly ghastly feeling that the three of them were decapitated heads, talking together in some noisome vault into which they had been thrown.

And then through the wall of darkness all about them a voice said harshly:

"Inspector Hines! Herr Schaaf! Police Headquarters speaking on the telephone. Fires are breaking out. Panic-stricken people, in a frenzy for light, are setting fire to their houses in hopes of being able to see. Headquarters wants to know, in God's name, if there is any way to get the fire engines to the flames?"

The three bodiless heads stared at each other, there in their little tomb of light.

"Tell them," said Hines steadily, "there's only one way. Broadcast by radio that Schaaf and I are to be executed summarily and that all of Preston's terms will be met. If they want to do that, Preston will turn off the darkness. Not otherwise."

Kathryn's eyes turned to him in horror. And Schaaf said angrily:

"And tell them that now we know how to lick der *Schzveinhund,* and that they are *verdammte* fools if they do it!"

And the darkness held... and held... and held. Somewhere off in that darkness buildings were burning, wholly without light, and human beings were dying in the flames they could not see.

It was very still in the research laboratory of the American Electric Company. But suddenly a new sound arose. It was wind. It began as a humming noise. It arose to a whine, and then to a shriek. A gale of unparalleled intensity blew through the darkness which enveloped New York. When it had reached its height there began a torrential down- pour of rain. Storm and flame and flood had their will for a space, of the city which was a city of the blind.

4

DEFIANCE

THE HEADLINES WERE in the largest obtainable type, and a good part of the reading matter below was in leaded twelve-point, double column, instead of the more customary seven. All the papers had nearly identical stories, but that of the *Star*, as having been written by Kathryn, was perhaps the most complete.

HINES DEFIES PRESTON!
Declares Darkness Can Be Neutralized

To the public these stories offered hope, because they told of a way by which the darkness could be locally defeated. Since it was produced by the action of short Hertzian waves on ionized bodies in the atmosphere, anything that would absorb Hertzian waves would "absorb" the darkness.

Metallic screens, placed vertically and grounded, had been proved to allow a space of transparent air to remain on the side away from the transmitter of the darkness-producing waves. The public was informed that ordinary bed-springs, placed upright and connected to a water-pipe, would cut off the darkness on one side. Four such springs, all grounded, would make a room in which lights could be used. It was advised that such areas should be formed in houses and apartments, and that on the falling of darkness the occupants of the houses should place themselves within them.

The interiors of bank vaults, likewise, would not be affected by Preston's darkness, and it was believed that if metal-sheathed buildings had their sheathing grounded that lights could be used in the interiors. The essentials were a screen of metal and a connection to the earth.

Less important than that information, but horrible enough, was the account of the damage that had been done by the storm. Thirty fires had broken out in the darkness, too, and had raged uncontrolled for half an hour. And people had been in those houses, and unable to see the flames which licked at them.

Newspapers are commonly considered callous, but the horrors of those fires could not be described—not in words which any man could bear to read. And panic was widespread enough without added horrors. The observation wards of all the hospitals were wholly inadequate to take care of the hysterical and mental breakdown cases that poured in.

The darkness was nerve-racking to any one. It was terrible to a strong man, deliberately exercising self-control. To the ignorant, to the excitable, to the inherently unstable among New York's population, it was literally intolerable. Cases turned up which in all their symptoms were exactly like those cases of shell-shock of which the public had learned in the last war.

When the darkness lifted, mobs surged crazily back

and forth in the streets. Stark terror filled all the city. The underworld, this time, took little advantage of the blackness, because the underworld was terrified too.

The storm was described as a totally unheralded cyclone of which New York City was the center. It had reached a velocity of more than a hundred miles an hour toward its peak, and the list of damage done was heartrending. Many shacks and flimsy frame buildings in Jersey City had collapsed from the sheer impact of the wind. The summer cottages of the Rockaways formed a tangled heap of débris. Nearly half the death list of the darkness was caused by the collapse of buildings insufficiently strong.

And then, too, the later editions of the newspapers carried additional news of further disasters to shipping, and of mobs fighting for places on outgoing trains, and of mad panics on bridges and ferries among people fleeing from the city.

THE COMMISSIONER OF police spread out a newspaper on his desk and pointed to the headline. Hines and Schaaf and—it seemed quite natural by now—Kathryn had been summoned to him by a peremptory message. The commissioner looked drawn and haggard.

"I want this retracted," he said in nervous doggedness. "We've got to deal with Preston. We'll try to save your lives, of course, but we've got to buy him off. We can't stand another day like this one. The whole financial district is going to pieces, the stock market's closing, and there were four hundred people killed. We can't stand another day like this!"

He pointed to the headline again.

" 'Hines Defies Preston!' " he quoted bitterly. "That's

daring him to do his worst. And four hundred dead in half an hour! Of course the storm was an accident, but—"

Schaaf snorted.

"Accident, der deffil!" he said disgustedly. "Of course, Breston may not haff anticipated it. He is no meteorologist. But do you realize that when der atmospheric ions fluoresce under der influence of his short wafes, der light-energy they receife is turned into heat? Der air gets hotter. When it gets hotter, it rises. More air underneath is heated. That also rises. Der result is like a gigantic chimney der size of der City of New York, or of der blob of blackness, full of hot air and rising like der deffil. It draws in der air from round about, starting a wind. Der wind becomes a storm. Der storm becomes a cyclone. Der cyclone—well, Breston had to turn off der darkness fife minutes before he intended."

The commissioner ran his hands through his hair.

"That makes it worse! We can't stand such storms! We've got to buy him off!"

Schaaf snorted again.

"Buy off my grandfather Schmidt!" he said wrathfully. "My dear sir, you do not realize that now we haff Breston up a tree! He was in a car before, a truck, most brobably, and der wind nearly scared him into fits. We had bearings on der source of der darkness, and it mofed. Der fact that we gafe instructions for neutralizing der darkness profes to him that we had bearings on him. Now he knows that der darkness produces a storm in which it is not safe to be out in a truck. He knows that we can take bearings on him and find out where he is, so it is not safe for him to be under shelter. He will not dare to leafe on der darkness more than fifteen minutes at a time! Buy him off? It is foolishness."

"But we can't fight him!" snapped the commissioner. "He did more than ten millions' damage to-day, and Wall Street—"

Schaaf sputtered. Hines said steadily:

"Do you realize that he gives only his promise to leave the city alone for one year? How much will he ask next year, if he keeps his promise? And how much the year after?"

"Not mentioning," said Schaaf scornfully, "that Hines and I now haff der scheme that will smash him, and that it will be necessary to bump us off before Breston will permit you to grofel in der mud before him."

Kathryn added quietly:

"And the *Star*, of course, will print the fact that a way to beat him is known and that you won't permit it to be used."

The commissioner paced back and forth, nervously.

"WE'VE GOT TO do something to reassure the public," he said harshly. "There are mobs forming and dissolving. Mobs the police can't handle! The people won't stand this darkness! They've got to be reassured!"

"Der next edition of der papers," said Schaff scornfully, "point out that Breston don't dare leafe der darkness on for more than fifteen minutes, and eferybody knows how to be comfortable for that long."

"But he can get under shelter," insisted the commissioner.

"And we can blow him out of it," snapped Schaff. *"Himmel,* man, haff you no brains?"

"But you can't see him!"

"Der hell we can't," said Schaaf. He snorted "In fifteen

minutes after der last darkness went off, der staff of der research laboratory designed a fision apparatus to take advantage of der fact that ultra-fiolet rays are not affected by Breston's short waves. There are twenty optical shops smashing up kitchen ofenware and grinding lenses. All der rhodamine dye in der city is cornered for our use. And der American Electric Company is equipping automobiles and motorcycles with mercury-fapor lamps. Of course we can see!

"Herr Commissioner, it may not be polite, but you forget that Hines is a smart man, and there is *ein Herr* named Schaaf that is no dumbbell either. Pfah! I am going out to take a smoke!"

He got up and marched disgustedly out of the room.

"I've given orders," said Hines quietly, "on my own authority. Preston is not going to be bought off. He's going to be licked. If you choose to countermand my orders, you may try it. But I wouldn't advise it. My orders will stand."

The commissioner flushed.

"You're relieved of all duty," he said shortly. "Preston's terms have to be met. The business interests of the city demand it. And you will be under arrest in two minutes, for mutiny."

Hines laughed softly.

"Mutiny is a hard word," he observed. "But treason is a harder one! The national government is interested in this, now. It's more important than any one city, even New York. Washington has been talking to me on long-distance. Also to the Governor of the State.

"I've told what I know and what I intend to do. I'm ordered, from Washington, to go ahead. Try to stop me and

I'll have soldiers and marines take over the job of the police, and the Governor will call out the militia to cooperate with them. You can try surrendering Schaaf and myself to mobs to be torn apart so you can grovel in the dust before Preston. You can try it. But I'm afraid it won't work."

The commissioner swallowed.

"The next long darkness," said Hines grimly, "is going to be the worst. Just before nightfall every newspaper in the city will be on the streets with an extra, challenging Preston to do his worst. He will, and his worst will be pretty bad. He's not a meteorologist, it's clear, so he's going to get under cover to stand a storm. He's going to turn on his darkness and keep it on. For hours. For days. "Until New York starves or goes mad in the blackness."

The commissioner gnawed at his nails.

"And what are you going to do?" he demanded at last.

"Find him in the darkness," said Hines, "and kill him, and turn the darkness off."

He went deliberately out of the room, and Kathryn followed him. And almost as if his movement had been a signal, the darkness fell. Utter, deadly, terrible darkness. KATHRYN GASPED. HINES reached out his hand.

"Steady!" he said quietly. "This won't last long. He said he'd turn on the darkness whenever he chose and for as long as he pleased. He'll probably try a bunch of short doses, to wreck the nerves of everybody in the city."

"But—why?" demanded Kathryn.

Her eyes stared helplessly at the nothingness about her. And she began to realize the deadly danger that Hines was in. His death and Schaaf's were necessary before Preston's persecution could be stopped by a huge money payment.

And the darkness was so horrible, unbearable that there were thousands of people in the city who would have killed him in hopes of an escape from it.

"Why—must you—"

She sobbed, clinging to him in mingled terror for herself and for him. And Schaaf's dry voice came to them.

"Hines," he was saying placidly, "you are der damnedest fool I ever saw. If Miss Bush were clinging close to me, as she is to you—well, personally, I would kiss her. I haff heard that it is an excellent remedy for fears, terrors, tremors, and agitation in young ladies."

Hines whirled.

"The glasses work?" he demanded eagerly. "They work?"

"Of course they work," said Schaaf placidly. "They were designed on scientific principles, and der sun is sending plenty of ultra-fiolet rays down through der darkness; I obserfe that Miss Bush has turned away from you and is staring about as if she should see also."

Kathryn gasped. A hand touched her shoulder.

"I haff only one of der fision outfits with me," said Schaaf. "I came to demonstrate to der commissioner, but he gafe me a pain in der neck. Hold to Hines's hand and come on."

Hines took hold of her arm, and Schaaf went on before. It was an incredible sort of situation. Utter blackness all about and Schaaf walking with a possibly exaggerated confidence, leading them through what might have been a sea of ink. And, as always, the darkness was so complete that it seemed to possess a substance. It was too black to be intangible.

Without warning, the darkness vanished. It had lasted

five minutes or less. Schaaf was just leading them out of the entrance to headquarters.

Kathryn gasped in relief.

"Here," said Schaaf, "here is der car. Ha! Der light has come on?"

He took down an elaborate contrivance, much like a blindfold with two huge goggling lenses at the front. He blinked.

"Oh, well," he said placidly, "I was getting too proud of my smartness in seeing what other people could not. Get in der car, Hines, and drife like der deffil. Breston will keep this up awhile. Now a minute or two. Now half an hour. He will make it dark nearly all night, I bet you, because he can do that without making a storm. There is no sunlight to heat der upper layer of darkened air. So we will haff to get busy. Home to der American Electric Company, James."

He lolled back, waving his blindfold contrivance negligently, as Hines meshed the gears and shot away along the empty streets. The city was queerly quiet, but there were people everywhere. They saw heads staring out at the blessed night, after the recent darkness. Once they heard a woman screaming in a fit of pure nerves. And once they heard a whole roomful of people laughing horribly in unquestionable, indubitable hysteria.

The darkness came on twice more before they reached their destination. Once for less than half a minute. The other time it stayed on for a full quarter of an hour, and a steady, rising wind began to blow. Then the light came on again and the wind died down fitfully.

"This," said Schaaf meditatively, "will giff der Weather Bureau fits. It will mess up der weather maps terribly."

But then they reached the American Electric Building. The street in front of it was blocked with vehicles. There were half a dozen huge trucks. Twenty or thirty touring cars. Quite as many motorcycles. Mercury-vapor lamps burned bluely in the bright sunlight, and workmen were busy with all the cars at once.

It was just at sunset that newspaper trucks went racing about the city again, scattering papers for all the world to read. The headlines of all of them were nearly identical.

"TURN ON THE DARKNESS, PRESTON, I DARE
YOU!" SAYS HINES.

Half an hour later the darkness came on, and remained.

5

IN A RED WORLD

KATHRYN FELT HANDS touching her. She shivered and stood still. She might have been buried under ten feet of earth, for all the vision she possessed.

"Now, Miss Bush," said Schaaf placidly in her ear, "if you will stop shifering, I will bestow upon you der gift of eyesight. Take off der hat."

Fumbling, with her hands shaking uncontrollably, she tried to obey. She could not. She heard movements all about her—confident, purposeful movements. The starter of a car whirred and a motor caught with a roar. It was throttled down and began to purr comfortably. And Kathryn had all the sensations of the blind, even the horrible depression which is enhanced by hearing the movements of those who can see.

Schaaf helped her clumsily.

"Der theory," he observed cheerfully, "is fery simple. To-day at three o'clock we obserfed that ultra-fiolet rays were not absorbed by der darkness. They penetrate Breston's dark just as well as daylight. But they are infisible to our eyes. Yet, just as Breston makes der light we can see turn into heat we cannot see, there are substances which turn rays we can't see into the light we abbreciate fery much, just now. Hold der head still."

Kathryn felt a rather clumsy headdress fitted over her hair. Something hard and uncomfortable covered her nose.

"A football head protector is not designed for ladies," said Schaaf placidly, "but you can stand it for der story for your paper. Rhodamine dye, as I haff told you, has der faculty of absorbing ultra-fiolet light and emitting bright red. So, we took opera-glasses to look through. We would make der front lens form an infisible image on a plate coated with rhodamine dye. Der image would become fisible, and so close to der eye that der darkness would haff no time to absorb it. You—"

Kathryn uttered a little exclamation of relief.

"I see light!" she panted. "Red light!"

"Precisely," said Schaaf placidly, "but I brag a little anyway. It is like a camera, making an image on a sheet of film, but in this instance it is defeloped at once by der fluorescence of der rhodamine dye. Der only trouble was that ordinary glass is no good for der infisible ultra-fiolet rays. It is as opaque to them as a brick. Only quartz glass is good for them. So we bought a quantity of ofen-glass, which is glass that ladies cook cakes and bake pies in, and broke it in small pieces, and had all der optical shops in der city busy grinding them into lenses. Ofen-glass is made of quartz only. Therefore, we haff put a football headdress on your head to hold a nose protector, and a nose protector to hold der remade opera-glasses; and if you will turn around—"

Kathryn turned about. She gasped.

IT WAS ALMOST impossible to believe that she was not looking directly at the world about her. But what a world!

There were monstrous, flaming, crimson flares overhead. Only after minutes did she associate them with the blue mercury-vapor lamps she had seen in the street before the American Electric Building, and before that only in the windows of photographers.

They were lurid, unearthly glares of scarlet, licking all about the tubes which were their sources. That same unearthly glow, was cast upon the street and upon the buildings. She seemed, in fact, to be in a filmy scarlet fog, at once formed and driven back by the monstrous flames above her.

The people who moved below those lights wore curious, unhuman heads. The long, hard-rubber nose-guards of the football headgear had the protruding lenses of binoculars above them. The human beings looked rather like gigantic insects. She saw a glowing crimson machine move forward and stop. She saw other machines tested. More unearthly lights flared.

And curiosity overcame Kathryn. She lifted the nose-piece and the glasses from before her face. Instantly she gasped. The horrible, tangible blackness closed upon her the more terribly because she could still hear the sounds of movement all about.

Hines came out, monstrous to look at with the expressionless, insect-like seeing apparatus covering his face.

"Hello, Hines," said Schaaf placidly. "Haff you got der bearings from der other observation stations?"

Hines nodded.

"But we don't need them," he said curtly. "I found Preston's slip. One of my men found his name and address in his own handwriting. A slip, all right!"

Schaaf's jaw dropped.

"Der deffil!"

"You gave my men a list of book titles he'd need," said Hines. "They went to every technical library. And they found his trail. He'd used a dozen of those books, several times each. He was copying, I understand, a list of—er— dielectric values—"

"Fariations," said Schaaf. "Fariations of der dielectric constant with Hertzian wafes of different lengths. He wanted it to extrapolate for his own wafe-length, I bet a nickel. Oh, dammit, why can't I figure out der wafe-length he uses? I would play der deffil with him!"

"We'll do it anyway," said Hines grimly. "When he asked for books in the reading-room, he had to give his name and address on the requisition-slip. My men found those slips. On most of them he'd used a fake name and address. Just once, he'd been absorbed or absent-minded. He signed his real name to one slip—and an address!"

"Where," said Schaaf, "we go and pay him a fisit. Good work, Hines! Where is der address?"

"The same place the observation-stations have bearings on," said Hines. "When will we be ready?"

"In two minutes more. They are fixing der last flare now."

But a crimson workman dropped a crimson tool and nodded to some one in a chauffeur's seat. A starter whirred. A motor roared. Two more glaring crimson flames came into being.

"We are set," said Schaaf. "Now we climb in and start."

"Stay with Schaaf, Kathryn," said Hines curtly. "I'm going to be with the dirty work."

Shouts, orders, a scurrying of men, and the street was

empty of all but machines. Those machines moved on in a purring, compact mass.

STARING ABOUT IN the extraordinary crimson world, Kathryn saw the vehicles as flaming, unearthly monsters in a crimson mist, with expressionless heads as of insects staring out of them. They moved in a glow of fiery light that died away before and behind them. It was weird. It was incredible. It was like some peculiar nightmare, or perhaps a cavalcade upon another planet. It seemed wholly unlike any scene that could be upon earth.

But when she lifted the extraordinary vision apparatus from her eyes, it seemed more strange still. Darkness pressed upon her like a solid substance. She had an almost hysterical impression that something pressed physically upon her, that if she moved her hand it would be found to be held fast, held firmly. She felt the unreasoning terror of nightmare, the unthinkable horror of those who are buried alive.

There were sounds in that darkness all about her. The purring of motors. The clankings of metal. And once she heard a far-away hysterical screaming. The motors went grimly on.

She fought off her own panic to try to imagine the feelings of people in those buildings on either side. If there were people! Somewhere in the city there were children crying heart-brokenly, and folk stumbling with wide and straining eyes to answer their cries.

There were curious, rather dreadful little cubbyholes whose four walls were made of bed-springs, through which the flood of darkness could be seen. Bright, unshaded electric bulbs were burning in those cubbyholes, and people would be crowded in them, sweating and staring at the devouring darkness without, and waiting—waiting without hope.

There were other places, other scenes, on which she dared not dwell. Men gone hysterical in the singularly complete emotional breakdown of the manual laborer when he does break down. Men turned into raving beasts by pure panic, gone into maniacal, destructive rages because they could not hope to escape the darkness which broke down all thought of self-control.

In the filmy crimson mist she saw a man upon the sidewalk. A policeman. He was upon his hands and knees, crawling the length of the curbing. She saw his head lift up and saw him staring blindly at the machines. They were invisible to him, but he could hear them passing.

"Hines gafe orders," said Schaaf in her ear, "that all der cops should go to der beat-telephone and wait. They could crawl along der gutters for guidance. Some of them will go nutty, but some of them are brafe men. That one, for example."

They left him behind. They moved on uptown. Things began to appear parked in serried rows, which it took thought to identify as cars. Buildings seemed all a vivid scarlet, all the same shade, varying only in brightness.

Hines's car dropped back, and the monstrous head of Hines—machinelike and inhuman with its goggles—peered out at them.

"Have you got cross-bearings, Schaaf?" he called above the thunder of their progress.

"To be sure," said Schaaf placidly. "Of course. Def darkness is coming from der same place as before. It worries me, Hines. Maybe der deffil expects us!"

"It's not unlikely," said Hines grimly.

CARS SPREAD OUT to right and left, vanishing down side streets as moving specks of vividly crimson light.

"Hines is surrounding der place," said Schaaf. "Der bearings remain der same. I am badly worried, Miss Bush. Breston is too clefer to let us take him easily. But he has der darkness on, I wonder if he has remote control. If he has, he would be using either batteries or der city current for power. And it would need a hell of a lot of power to make all der city dark. I haff an idea!"

He began to think busily.

The procession clanked on. Suddenly, the cars stopped. Hines came back. At an order, all the motors were silent.

"Listen!" said Hines curtly.

Stillness. The queer, unavoidable sounds of bodies moving in their seats. Muted, nerve-racked noises from the houses about, the houses in which men and women crouched in tiny cubbyholes of screening, watching electric bulbs in desperate terror that those lights also would go out and leave them in utter blackness!

Motor horns began to blare, a long way off. Hines grunted in satisfaction.

"Bearings the same," he said shortly. "We'll go from here on foot."

"Hines," said Schaaf nervously, "I don't like it! I tell you, I don't like it! Do you think Breston didn't hear our motors coming? Do you think he did not hear der horns? There is something defilishly wrong. He has a great predilection for bombs and gas and poison and such. Haff you gas-masks?"

"We have," said Hines grimly.

"We'll go on."

Kathryn lifted the vision apparatus from her eyes. She was blind, but this abysmal blackness seemed somehow a cover for the terror she knew was showing on her face.

"One minute more," protested Schaaf. "Hines, I haff a hunch. It is a silly hunch, but I belief it. Go to der nearest police telephone and say to der headquarters to haff der electric current cut off from this part of der city."

Hines's goggled face turned to him.

"But the poor devils in those houses, in those screen-coops you told them how to make—"

"They'll go crazy," said Schaaf irritably. "I know it. They will lose what little hope they haff left. But it is a hunch, Hines! Do it!"

It was very queer to Kathryn, to be sitting there in utter blackness, filled as she was with an unnamable terror for Hines and with tears rolling down her cheeks through sheer anguish—to hear footsteps go confidently to one side of the street, and to hear the metallic clanking of a police street-telephone being opened, and to hear the crisp little ring of the instrument.

"Tell them," said Schaaf nervously, "to try it. Cut off der current for three seconds. If der darkness lifts, leafe it off. If it does not, put it back on again."

He moved uncertainly in the seat beside Kathryn.

"It's not natural," he protested miserably. "I know that we should haff der deffil licked, and because it seems so complete I haff fears."

The man at the street-telephone was talking curtly.

"If my suspicions are right," Schaaf said, more miserably

still, "Breston has let us come here to be destroyed. He has used der city current for power so that he can haff remote control of der darkness. And—"

Kathryn started and cried out. Her eyes were dazed by the glare of mercury-vapor lamps above her, by the radiance of automobile headlights ahead.

"It's off!" she cried sharply. "The darkness is off!"

SCHAAF TORE AWAY his vision apparatus. He thrust it into his pocket with a shaking hand.

"We are licked," he said miserably. "Hines, I know it. We haff beaten him in one way, because we haff fixed it so he cannot do this same thing again. But I know that he has beaten us in some other way. I am afraid, Hines! I am afraid!"

Hines stared about grimly, his clumsy headgear in his hands.

"I suppose," he said curtly, "he's got his outfit mined, so we can't examine it; or has it filled with gas. We'll wear gas-masks and go cautiously."

He gave orders. Men got out of the cars and began to group themselves on foot.

"Skirmish order!" snapped Hines impatiently. "Masks adjusted, too! You know what the man looks like. If you see him, shoot to kill!"

He started forward. Kathryn made a futile gesture after him. She heard a chattering noise beside her. It was Schaaf's teeth. He swore to himself in German and climbed clumsily over to the deserted chauffeur's seat.

"I am a *verdammter Esel!*" he said bitterly, "and I am scaredt to der marrow of my bones. But I haff to do it."

He pressed on the starter of the car. The motor whirred

and caught. In a moment more the car was crawling along the street after the men on foot.

"It is a garage," said Schaaf, through chattering teeth. "A big garage according to der bearings we haff taken. And der apparatus is inside it. *Ach, mein Gott,* how scaredt I am!"

Slowly the men on foot moved down the street. A dilapidated sign appeared in the headlight glow. A dirty, unpainted, seemingly deserted building with the monstrous doors of a storage garage.

No lights showed within. No sound of movement. Emptiness. Silence. Desertion.

Other figures on foot appeared far ahead. They hastened to join Hines.

"In there," said Schaaf in a quavering voice, "is der apparatus that would make der scientific reputation of der man that first described it. And I am scaredt!"

With masks adjusted, Hines's men reached the face of the building. A man tried the door. Hines barked at him and took his place. He tried it with his shoulder.

Schaaf fairly screamed.

"Hines! Hines! Look! *Die Katze!*"

An alley-cat had crept shivering to the feet of the uniformed men, in the instinct of all domestic animals to turn to man in the face of the inexplicable. The surrounding darkness had been too deep for even her eyes to penetrate. She was rubbing her side against Hines's legs, mutely begging to be comforted.

And suddenly she staggered and kicked crazily, and fell!

"Gas!" gasped Schaaf. "From der crack at der bottom of der door! Hines, der place is full of gas! You haff to get der people out of der buildings around and about. You know what gas can be!"

Hines snarled. He had drawn himself back to fling his whole weight on the door, to break it in. But he gave the orders.

With a dozen men he waited before the building while policemen went shouting through adjoining buildings, flashing their flashlights and ordering all occupants out. The street, illuminated only by the stars, became flooded with humanity, almost hysterical with joy at the sight of the stars again, until fold that the source of all the darkness was within the building near by. Then they fled in senseless panic. The street became empty again.

"NOW," GROWLED HINES, "I suppose it'll be all right."

"Please!" begged Schaaf. "I ask you, Hines, to leafe der gas escape. And when we enter, let us tunnel in through der walls. He will haff expected doors to be broken down, and he could leafe bombs."

Hines growled again.

"I'll put a cordon around four blocks," he grunted. "The government at Washington wants to know how the thing was done, for a weapon if we ever have war again. I ought not to risk ruining it."

The buildings all about were emptied of people now, and those people were racing toward lighted streets in the distance.

The city is divided into many districts by the electric companies, and any one of them may be isolated, in case of damage to the wiring. The street was utterly empty. Hines reached a police telephone. Within minutes there were wild clangings. Load after load of reserves rolled up and climbed down to the street. There were a thousand men available for duty in twenty minutes after the cutting off of the darkness. And Hines made a cordon about four square blocks that not even a cat could have broken through.

"We're going to wait," he announced curtly, reluctantly, "for the gas to dissipate. Meanwhile Washington will be telephoned to, and Army gas-experts will come by plane. The apparatus is wanted by the national government."

Schaaf was heart-broken. But then Kathryn said timidly:

"Do you—do you suppose Preston is in the building? That he may have killed himself when he found he was defeated?"

"We haff no such luck," said Schaaf morbidly. "I am worrying, Miss Bush, because I haff a hunch that: my brain has been dead. There is something that I haff not thought of, which I should haff thought of."

He sat with his head in his hands, muttering impatiently at intervals, Kathryn most deplorably forgot even the *Star*, waiting to see Hines, for whom she had felt such horrible terror. He was back in the isolated district, combing the deserted buildings for possibly overlooked human beings.

And then, very suddenly, there was a terrific explosion. A sheet of flame shot upward to the skies. The streets shook. Buildings rocked. Glass fell in tinkling showers from buildings all over the city. And then there were crashes— horrible crashes—as shaken and undermined buildings collapsed.

Kathryn went deathly pale. Her body was rigid. After minutes she whispered.

"He—he is in there!"

And Schaaf cursed frantically in German because he

believed the same. But a group of men came running, in advance of a thinning, wavering cloud of smoke. Hines broke out in front of them. He came on, calling anxiously:

"Kathryn! Kathryn!"

She stood up, sobbing in relief.

"Here I am! I thought you were killed!"

They seemed to melt into each other's arms.

SUDDENLY SCHAAF GROANED, and swore more deeply than ever before, and said bitterly:

"Of course, Hines, der deffil has destroyed his apparatus. But more important, and much as I hate to interrupt der party, I beg to inform you that you are one terrible boob, and a guy named Schaaf is another."

Hines flushed deeply and said:

"Why? What's the matter?"

"We did not kill Breston, as you know," said Schaaf disgustedly. But der worst of it is that we nefer efen guessed what he was drifing at all der time! He had no hope of getting ten millions' ransom from der city of New York. But he has got rich, all der same. Before he started any of der works he had sold stocks in der stock market, going short of all der stocks in creation. And when he began to pull his stuff, der stock market went to hell and gone, and he cofered, and began to buy. When der world knows, in der morning, that we haff licked der scoundtrel, and haff fixed it so he cannot do der same thing again, all der stocks will go up again. Instead of ten millions, der son-of-a-gun may haff made twenty or thirty of them by der way der stock market behafed—which he was der only man to know in advance!"

Hines growled:

"Any police force in the world can beat him now, though!"

"If he tries der same stunt again," agreed Schaaf. He eyed the two of them wrathfully. "Oh, you aren't interested! Go on and hold hands! Make lofe! Go on! I giff you up!"

And they followed his advice to the letter.

THE STORM THAT HAD
TO BE STOPPED

*Preston, Evil Genius Of Science,
Defies America's War Weapons As
He Hurls Nature's Malignant Forces
Against His Blinded Attackers*

1

WITHOUT WARNING

ON THE MORNING that saw the beginning of the Storm That Had to be Stopped, Police Inspector Hines had his life saved by an amateur driver who drove a second-hand flivver into his roadster. It was pure accident, of course. Hines's left mudguard, his left front wheel, and his front bumper were all wreckage when the amateur driver stared wildly about, assured himself that he was still alive, and then burst into tears.

The amateur driver passed forthwith from history. He had nothing more to do with the affair. He merely kept Hines from driving up into the Catskills in the very early morning of August 5, when, as all the world knows, the Storm began.

You will remember that morning. There had been a heat wave over all the Atlantic States for two weeks or more. The cities sweltered. The beaches were crowded. In New York, Central Park was opened to any one who chose to sleep in the open air instead of the stifling tenements.

Those who could leave the city did so. The Catskill and Adirondack hotels were packed. The seashore resorts swarmed with people.

Kathryn Bush was up in the Catskills, and Hines had

She crouched against the fragment of wall that still remained standing.

started up to be with her until Monday. The fact that his car was wrecked in Yonkers almost certainly saved his life, and quite positively determined the events that followed. If he had been up in the storm-center, he would have been utterly helpless.

IT WAS CURIOUS that the storm seemed to start so gently. Kathryn Bush wrote an account of the beginning, for the New York *Star*. It was her vacation-time and she was staying in the house of Heracles Tribble, at Rosedale Farm, North Weddensdale, Greene County, New York. She expected Hines to come up, and had risen early. A room was reserved for him at the farmhouse, where there were four other boarders. She may have been sentimental, or she

may have been restless. In any event she was looking out of her window when the sun rose.

While birds began to sing abstractedly in the mountain-shadows, long-streaks of golden light became visible on the flanks of monster hills. The invisible sun was gilding their sides. Later, a long time later, the red disk of the sun appeared.

The sunlight was gratefully warm after the dawn-chill, though even in the first rays she thought regretfully of the blistering, terrific heat that would come at midday when this same sun would be a ball of intolerable fire, hanging overhead in a brazen sky. Irrelevantly, she remembered the weather forecast—fair and warmer.

And then, quite suddenly, the warmth seemed to go out of the sun's rays.

It was as sudden, as abrupt, as the turning off of a light, as the closing of a furnace door from which a fierce glare had poured forth. The sun was no darker, however. It seemed to shine as brightly as before. It did not give off heat.

Kathryn stared about her. She looked back at the sun. It glowed vividly, but it seemed obscurely to have changed color. She held out her hand to it to catch the warmth of its rays. There was none.

A cloud over its face? No. The sky was wholly clear. There was simply no more heat coming from the sun.

Puzzled, but quite unalarmed, it seemed to Kathryn that the sun's ruddy tint had vanished very suddenly. It even seemed as if instead of a normal gold, the great disk had taken on a faint bluish or greenish tint. The change—if it was a change—was so slight that she could not be sure.

The seeming lack of heat was so extraordinary that, instead of turning away, she gazed and gazed, and presently took a tiny reading-glass and focused it on a bit of paper. The paper should have turned brown and burned luridly. Nothing happened.

More curious still, now, she focused the light upon her hand; then upon the sensitive skin of her forearm. A vivid spot of light formed at the focus of the lens. The speck of flesh seemed white-hot. But there was not the faintest, not the tiniest sensation of heat.

It was at just this time she noticed that a wind was blowing far away. Where she stood at her window, looking eastward, the air was utterly calm. Her window, as a matter of fact, was open wide. But she suddenly saw trees, a long distance off, bending and tossing furiously as if in a gale of wind. There was a long straight stretch of white road reaching far away toward infinity. A cloud of dust was racing along it.

"It's wind!" said Kathryn vaguely.

Still she stared. Then she saw something rolling crazily across a distant pasture. It was a smother of dust and débris. But there was one gigantic, darker object that rolled and rolled. She saw suddenly that it was the top of a tree, sheared off from its trunk in some freak of wind-pressure, and rolling like a monster ball.

The wind struck a farmhouse three miles down the valley. Kathryn saw a cowshed open and vanish. She saw a fence-line disappear. The dwelling leaned and leaned.

It sank quite gently to a sloping mass of wreckage, save that its roof went ballooning off insanely and mowed down a lane of trees through a planted orchard before it crashed against an upward-jutting outcrop of granite and was torn to bits about it.

WHEN THE WIND struck the house from which Kathryn had watched it, the windows were all down. She had shouted of a storm approaching. Clouds, too, began suddenly to appear in writhing, ominous masses. The house had been closed tightly by the agitated Mr. Heracles Tribble, who hastened out to his hen-houses to see to their security before the storm came, and did not come back.

Kathryn watched from the window. The rolling cloud of dust that was the forefront of the wind drew nearer with incredible speed. As it drew close, the monstrous size of the disturbance became apparent. It was hundreds of feet high, and it was rolling over and over upon itself like a monstrous comber.

There seemed even to be striations, in it like those the stranding of a rope will make. But there were objects carried in the smoke-colored rolling cloud. Dark objects, of all shapes and sizes. Kathryn, staring and almost paralyzed by sheer astonishment, saw the tree-limbs and it seemed even whole trees caught up in the monstrous turmoil.

Somehow her eyes swept to the hen-houses at the rear of the house. Mr. Heracles Tribble was standing in the open, peculiarly puny and ineffective, staring incredulously at the thing that bore down upon him. He was small, and rotund, and bald. He wore silver-rimmed spectacles, and he stared at a rolling wave of smoke and dust and utter destruction, hundreds of feet high, that swept toward him irresistibly.

Mr. Heracles Tribble turned suddenly, and fled toward the house. Kathryn saw his mouth dropped open in horror. His fat little legs twinkled. He ran with incredible speed. But the rolling cloud of dust and débris had reached the pasture-lot. It touched the hen-houses and they vanished as if blown to atoms.

Unpausing, the monstrous thing came rolling up. Its bellying edge was over the house while its base had still not yet touched the running little fat man. But then Kathryn saw smoke-like dust envelop him. She saw—or thought she saw—that he rose crazily from the ground. And then the wave of wind struck the house.

It was absurd, but Kathryn was not frightened even the instant after she knew the wind had struck. Her first conscious thought was that the house had been lifted away from around her, leaving her untouched.

Then she realized that the house still stood. There was no roof over her head, to be sure, but the walls remained intact. The feeling of being in the open air came from the fact that without warning or a sound that could be heard above the deafening uproar of the wind, the windows had ceased to be. The glass panes broke out of them with no more disturbance than so many breaking bubble-films would have made.

Kathryn had been at one moment safely housed, behind glass panes. The next instant she was merely sheltered behind a thick brick wall while a dense fog of dust blotted out even the farther side of the room.

Something crashed into that farther wall and kicked feebly. It was a pig, picked up no one could guess where and carried no one can guess how far. Then a tree-trunk thrust itself through the brick wall, horribly splintered, and heaved upward, tearing the wall apart, and then somehow went reeling off into the thick dust-cloud.

KATHRYN PUT HER hand to her throat. Sheer professional training alone saved her from panic. The newspaper woman's acquired instinct said:

"What a story! I've got to get to safety. It will be a big story when the wind stops—and I saw it!"

She dropped to the floor and began to crawl past the window toward the stairway. Once she ventured a little distance away from the wall, and a solid stream of air— as solid as a board—that came through a window, rolled her over and over until she struck with a crash against the leeward wall.

It held her there, then she battled her way on hands and knees down the stairs. The wind beat at her terribly, trying to fling her up again. It came in through the smashed lower windows.

She saw the dining room table flat against the wall. Its top covered a window and it was held in place by the wind-pressure. It was very probably that measure of protection which enabled her to pass so close to the leeward wall without being picked up and hurled off into nothingness.

She heard a terrific crash upstairs, in the room she had just left. Fragments of brick came down the steps. She reached the cellar stairs, tumbled down them, and heard more terrific crashes still.

Then there was darkness, while the wind roared by overhead. The noise the wind made was not a hum, not a whistle, not a shriek. It was a steady, a terrible, deep-toned roar. That roaring of the wind was characteristic, throughout, of the Storm That Had to be Stopped.

2

IN AN OPEN CAR

HINES HAD STARTED out at five o'clock in the morning, in hopes of getting away from the city before the heavy traffic began. But, of course, he turned out to be only one of many thousands who had the same idea. The heat wave in New York had been terrific. It is recorded that the traffic had piled up as early as 3 A.M., and when Hines started at five he was promptly swallowed up in a long lane of cars going up-State at a bare crawl.

His accident happened just out of Yonkers at a little after six, but it was nine before his wheel was replaced and a new mudguard in position. By that time the Storm had begun.

Down there, quite sixty miles from the storm-center, its development was less spectacular. Up among the mountains it is fairly certain that the wind began at a very few minutes after six. Watches found on victims of the first terrific rush of wind were almost invariably stopped at that hour, and clocks in houses, overturned and crushed, corroborate the figures. But it was nearly half past six when a strong wind began to blow from Yonkers toward the mountains.

The sun was just up. Hines was seething over the delay.

He was engaged to Kathryn, and he resented anything that kept him away from her. The Catskills had been his suggestion in the first place. Kathryn, as a feature writer on the *Star*, didn't want to get too far from New York anyhow.

Other matters aside, there was a man named Preston who was rather definitely dangerous and who was still at large. Not less than twice, with his artificial darkness, he had set the whole city of New York by the ears, to his own enormous profit.

Hines, and Schaaf—now up in the Catskills, too, making some abstruse experiments with very short Hertzian waves for the research department of the American Electric Company—Hines and Schaaf had managed to checkmate him each time.

Each time Kathryn had been in at the death, and each time the *Star* had scored a newspaper triumph. With Preston still at large, and both Hines and Schaaf convinced that sooner or later he would try to strike again, Kathryn had not wanted to get too far away even on her vacation. She wanted to handle the next battle with Preston for the *Star* as she had the first two.

Hines moved restlessly about the garage, or scowled at the never-ending but often pausing line of cars that went crawling, crawling, creeping away from the heat of the city.

Those cars were leaving a sweltering city behind them, to steam upon sweltering roads in an atmosphere of exhaust-fumes, but at least they had hopes of reaching the hills and coolness. Instead, only too many of them reached the hills and disaster.

Hines noticed a breeze at twenty after six. At half past it was a wind. At seven, it was half a gale, blowing under a clear sky with a brazen sun already sending down a blistering heat.

Hines swore under his breath, but it was no use trying to hurry the mechanics. He was an inspector of police in the city of New York, but at a roadside garage he was merely a customer, and the traffic outside promised plenty of customers before the day was over.

It was shortly after eight that Hines saw the top of an ancient touring car torn to ribbons by the wind. Before nine o'clock came, he had seen dozens of them.

THE TRAFFIC BEGAN to thin, abruptly. Cars headed for the mountains turned aside. They began to fight their way into storage garages, battling a terrific, solid mass of air.

Some of them stopped where trees on a side-road promised some measure of protection from the wind. Others were wiser and parked themselves in swarming masses wherever deep cuts or valleys ran across the prevailing direction of the wind.

The galvanized garage roof was a drumming tumult, now, rattling and booming from the wind that went sweeping across it. The mechanics finished Hines's car and very reluctantly opened the doors—closed a half hour before— to let him out.

He came out into a rather incredible world. Trees were leaning toward the mountains. The roads were nearly clear. The traffic had lessened almost to nothing. The noise of the wind was a distinct deep booming sound, to which the tortured trees added shrill whistles and shriller screams, and now and then sharp cracking sounds as limbs or trunks gave way under the intolerable pressure.

Hines turned toward the mountains and shifted gears.

They clashed, horribly. It was seconds before he realized that the wind had pushed his car ahead of the motor-speed. He had to race the engine to get into second, and race it again to get into third.

The car seemed to be possessed of unlimited power. It sped toward the mountains like a mad thing. Every man comes to know his motor, but Hines found his own car acting like a thing possessed. With his foot off the accelerator it made forty-five miles an hour. The barest touch on the gas-pedal sent it leaping to sixty, seventy miles.

He saw an ancient flivver turned over, at the side of the road. There were no people near it. He braked, instinctively, and found his brakes nearly useless. His car flashed past, and he heard the brakes squealing, but felt hardly any diminution of his speed.

There was a ripping sound behind him. His back curtain had blown in. The split upper half of the windshield opened out, and wind poured from behind him out over the front. Another wreck. Two more.

He saw a car coming toward him and passed it with the speed of light, but in the instant of his passing saw the man at the wheel of that other vehicle working frantically at gas-lever and throttle, and it seemed to him that for the fraction of a second he heard the roaring of a motor laboring horribly in low gear, battling against the wind alone.

The road shot into a deep cut, and the abnormal acceleration of the car diminished. Hines jammed on the brakes and stopped with difficulty. The ripped fragments of his back curtain were flapping about him and he got out his knife to cut them away.

Now he felt the wind as a savage, gusty pressure. It was

terrifically strong, even down here in a cut some thirty feet deep. Something was stirring in Hines's breast, just then, which he was grimly refusing to recognize. After all, there have been storms and storms. Kathryn, up in the mountains, would be safe enough.

The thin tooting of a horn came to him. A car had drawn aside from the road, some fifty or sixty feet ahead. A man in it was waving to him to come on ahead. Hines merely released his brakes and his car moved sluggishly for twenty feet and stopped. He put it in gear for the rest of the distance.

Here, remarkably, the air was calm. The man in the other car was smoking placidly. Overhead the wind rushed past with its deep, ominous roaring sound. At just this point between the sides of the cut there was a perfect lee, where no wind-currents of any sort were noticeable.

"I THOUGHT I'D tip yuh," said the man in the other car. "This is the best place I've hit yet. Pull over off the road an' you'll be all right. Better get off the road, though. A car come through here like a bat out o' hell. Turned over at the end of the cut, yonder. The wind's near crosswise there."

Instinct made Hines ask: "Anybody hurt?"

The man spat.

"Hell! They fell out an' the wind picked 'em up an' carried 'em off somewhere. Ain't it a wind, though? What y' call a hurricane, I guess."

Hines was staring, oblivious. Far, far away, a cloud was forming, but unlike any cloud Hines had ever seen before. Something, the sheer distance of the formation perhaps, told him that it was higher than any cloud he had known.

It rose as a vast, incredible column, and then it spread out as a mushroom might spread above its stalk.

"Yeah," said the man in the other car. "It's been like that for half an hour, now. Looks like a volcano cloud, but it ain't. No earth shocks. Just wind. I reckon that's the storm center. It's a peach, this storm. That cloud 'll be over the Catskills, somewheres."

Hines started, and then he turned grimly to his car-top. He slashed at it, wrenching away the cloth and flinging it away.

"I'm going on," he said, rather absurdly.

The man in the other car shrugged.

"I ain't stopping you," he observed. "But you better stay here. That wind is a hell-cat. If you want your car to stay on the road an' you're bound to go, load 'er down with rocks. Plenty of 'em. I mean that wind 'll blow you clean to hell and gone if you don't."

Hines's brain was busy with a real, an acknowledged terror now, but something in the suggestion jerked at his mind.

"Right," he said suddenly, "Thanks. I'll do it. I believe it's needed."

The other man unfastened his car-door and stepped out.

"I'll help," he said amiably.

In silence they worked. The empty seat beside the driver was filled with bowlders and smaller rocks. All the floor-space filled up. Hines flung up the back of the rumble seat and they filled it with stones of smaller size.

"One more tip," said the other man thoughtfully. "Some flat rocks alongside your hood 'll help."

They found two huge stones, loosened by the dynamite

that had made the cut. They wedged them in between the mudguards and the hood. Hines held out his hand. There was a bill in it.

"Go to hell," said the other man cheerfully. "Me, I'm a socialist and a proletarian, an' judging by your car you're a damn' capitalist—a bourgeois anyways. But one guy can help out another one, can't he?"

Hines put away the bill and shook hands instead.

"My girl's up there in the mountains," he said briefly. "I'm going up to see if she's all right."

"Good luck!"

HINES'S CAR, WITH its top gone and its windshield laid flat before it, went into low gear with a vast groaning. It was burdened with over half a ton of stone. It went into second with a little difficulty. Then the wind began to make itself felt. Despite its added weight, the car went into high gear quite normally. It was rolling along at twenty miles an hour when it came out of the cut into the full blast of the wind again.

Hines was flung against the side door. The car shuddered horribly. Gasping for breath, with his head bent over, his hat gone instantly, Hines fought to keep it on the road. There was a curve here, and for two hundred yards he went squarely across the wind. Without the rocks, no vehicle ever built would have stayed on the road in such a blast.

Then the road turned again and the wind was behind him once more. Instantly the car picked up speed. Thirty, thirty-five, forty miles an hour. Forty-five miles—fifty—

The landscape flashed past, a mass of wrecked trees and débris. Hines saw the body of a motor truck a full hundred yards from the road, smashed against a rocky hillside. He saw two, three, a dozen cars overturned—always on the side of the road to which the wind would have flung them. He came to a town which was nearly obliterated. Wreckage littered the streets. He jammed on the brakes, raced his motor, got it into second, and slowed by the braking action of the engine. He raced it again and got into first and turned off his switch.

He was going no more than fifteen miles an hour when the car careened over a heap of rubbish which once had been part of a building, swung about insanely and crashed where splintered planks had piled up against a massive stone wall.

It was part of a road tunnel underneath a railroad track.

Then Hines saw a man crawling on the pavement before him. The man had a rope about his waist, which was evidently tied to something. A paint-pot slopped white paint about as he pushed it ahead of him. He was painting huge letters on the concrete roadway.

> HINES STOP!
> HINES STOP!
> HINES STO

That was as far as he had gone. He was painfully working on the last letter of the third "Stop" when Hines opened the side door of his car. Hines slid out, gasping for breath, and dropped flat on his belly on the road. He went crawling about the splintered planks to windward until the man saw him. Then he shouted, uselessly, while the man stared. **IT WAS NOT** until Hines had pointed repeatedly to his name and then to himself that comprehension slowly

THE STORM THAT HAD TO BE STOPPED

dawned on the crawling man's face. The fellow waved and shouted an order across the ten feet of intervening space, then hauled himself along the rope in the very teeth of the wind to a doorway in the side of the road-tunnel. Seconds later he was out again with another rope. He flung it into the air, and the wind stretched it taut.

Hines crawled, knotted it about his body, and felt himself hauled across the road.

For the second time he was in a blessed calm. He stood up, panting. The man who had been painting on the road made a peculiarly absurd salute.

"You're Police Inspector Hines, sir?" he asked woodenly.

Hines nodded, still unable to speak.

"Corporal Woodford of the State Police, sir," said the man who had pulled Hines across the road by a rope. "All wires are down, sir, but every broadcasting station that hasn't been wrecked has been broadcasting orders to every possible agency to stop you from going into the storm.

"Professor Schaaf managed to get a message out by radio, sir, from a spot very near the storm-center. He says that the storm is caused by Preston's darkness-apparatus, and that you are the only man able to stop it. And the storm, sir, simply has to be stopped. Will you step inside and give your instructions?"

Hines blinked, and then the meaning of the message came to him. Rage filled him, consumingly. And then he went sick with helplessness. Because, of course, he could have no instructions to give for the stopping of a storm.

3

DECLARING WAR

UNDER ORDINARY CIRCUMSTANCES, it is probable that
the little room in which Hines found himself would have
seemed extraordinarily cramped and crowded.

It was perhaps eight feet by ten, certainly no more, and
it was inset in a railroad fill which here was pierced for a
vehicular roadway. A door opened upon the curbstone, and
from the narrow doorstep it was no more than ten feet to
the painted white line which normally marked the center
of the road.

On the farther side of the railroad embankment there
was another concrete highway, which explained the presence of the room. Here was a dangerous crossroad, and
this little cubbyhole was a shelter for the State policemen.

There was a tiny stove, and a bench along one side of
the wall, and a cupboard and a table. There were nails,
from which a slicker, a belt with a holster attached, and a
patched motorcycle inner tube depended. On the table a
tiny radio blared forth intermittent sounds from an even
tinier loudspeaker.

"To all authorities in New York State," said a voice
crisply. "All traffic must be stopped where the wind has
now reached a velocity of forty miles an hour. The storm

is expected to increase in intensity until four o'clock this afternoon. Wherever possible the population must be warned of this fact. The storm will lessen markedly at about sunset and may have ceased entirely by morning.

"It is imperative also that Inspector of Police Hines be reached and warned not to enter the storm area. Where practicable, signs should be painted on stone walls or the pavement. 'Hines Stop!' will be enough to cause Inspector Hines to stop and make inquiry. He will probably travel on one of the following roads—"

Hines turned to his companion, who was busily raking together a heap of wires from the drawer of the table and twisting them together into a single long strand.

"I'm getting a buzzer signal ready," said the State trooper woodenly, "to use the railroad rails overhead. The radio said half an hour ago that all State troopers were to use buzzer signals and railroad tracks where they couldn't report otherwise. Not many of us left, sir, and very few of us can report, anyhow. I didn't bother with that until I'd put up signs to stop you, sir."

The radio had finished a long list of highways. It began again, repeating the previous message word for word, while wind roared overhead in a deep-toned bellow which did not seem to vary by the fraction of a semitone. It was rising slowly in pitch, as a matter of fact, but so slowly that Hines's ears could not follow the change.

"THIS IS AN emergency means of communication, sir," said the trooper, joining wires together with painstaking care. "It's the old buzzer line that used to be used in the Army. I take an induction coil, the one from my motorcycle, sir, and put the secondary into the rail up overhead. The rail's iron, sir, and it isn't insulated, and it's not very efficient, but they can pick it up with amplifiers at the other end."

He bent two wires and fastened them to the storage-battery which ran his radio. He was busy for a minute or more, improvising a make-and-break contact.

The trooper put it down, satisfied, and tied a rope about himself.

"We have ropes here, sir, for towing," he observed. "I'm going out with the wire, sir, and try to fasten this to the railroad rail. If I'm blown away, sir, will you try to haul me back?"

"Wait a bit," said Hines shortly. "I'm going to do that. I don't know Morse code; and you're needed for signaling. I'll make the connection... It's my order," he added sharply as the trooper shook his head.

Reluctantly, the trooper gave him the rope-end.

Hines knotted the rope tightly about his body and stepped out of the door. Wind struck him, and took his breath away. But that was the wind that blew through the relatively sheltered traffic-way. He was crawling on his belly when he came out on the lee side of the railroad fill, and a monstrous eddy of wind lifted him six inches off the ground and flung him crashing ten feet away. He gasped, and began to crawl desperately up the incline toward the rails.

The wind, here, had formed a monstrous whirl over the slight obstruction. The dried cinders, dust, and small stones which once had covered the side of the embankment had long since been sucked up and flung madly away. It was naked damp clay that smeared him as he crawled toward the tracks.

He seemed to be weightless, as the wind-whirl tried to lift him upward. Hines had been in the European war, and he thought that he had learned to hug the ground, but never before in his life had he clung so desperately to the earth as he did now. He was blinded, strangled.

There was a vast, malevolent force pulling and tugging at his body. And then quite suddenly his fingers scraped concrete, and he fought the wind that strove to push his exploring hand aside and found a steel signal-post that must be beside the track.

It was that post that really made it possible for him to reach the rails. The blast that came over the top of the embankment was as fierce, as savage, as nearly irresistible as a flood of swiftly-flowing water. Nobody knows what velocity the wind ultimately attained in the Storm, but it had reached a hundred and forty miles an hour when the self-registering anemometer in the Burton observatory was wrecked.

Hines faced that wind, and fought his way inch by inch by means of the steel bands connecting the signal-post to the rails. An outstretched arm caught the wind. The sleeve ballooned out and burst. A flapping end was seized by the wind and the rest of the garment was literally peeled from him.

Here, of course, the wind was at its worst as far as Hines was concerned. He was protected by no more than the four-inch steel rail from its full force, and constantly there poured over him dust, smaller fragments of débris, and above all and over all the overpoweringly dense and solid wind itself.

When the connection was made, Hines was sobbing

with sheer exhaustion. He slid back down the incline, an inch at a time. And then suddenly the wind caught him, and he felt himself lifted up. The rope about his body tightened and hurt intolerably, and then he felt a crash and lost consciousness.

WHEN HE CAME back to himself he was lying on the floor in the little eight-by-ten room again, and the State trooper was working the buzzer signal steadily. He stopped, and came over to Hines.

Hines stirred, and the trooper nodded to himself. He went back to the buzzer and worked it again.

The radio broke off in the midst of its tediously repeated message.

"Corporal Woodford!" said the loud-speaker crisply. "Since Inspector Hines has recovered consciousness, we will give him the message from Professor Schaaf. He is in communication with the American Electric Company by means of a short-wave set, and we will rebroadcast it to you."

There were clickings. One or two curious crashing noises. Then a reenforcement of the roaring of the storm, only this extra roaring came from the speaker. It was evident that wherever Schaaf was speaking into a microphone, the storm was there too.

"Hello, Hines," said the placid voice of Schaaf. "This is a fery pleasant situation, I dondt think. Now I giff you der works, and you use your head. Here is what I haff found out.

"At six this morning der sun changed color. From where I am, I obserfe with a spectroscope that der infra-red part of der sun spectrum is completely gone cuckoo. I haff examined electric lights in der same manner, and der infrared spectrum is missing there, also.

"Der air where I am no longer transmits radiant heat. Der air, in other words, is opaque to heat-wafes, as our friendt Breston has been able to make it opaque to light. I think he is up to some more of his deffilment. As you remember, he was able to make der air absorb and neutralize light, producing his infernal darkness.

"I conclude that he has contrifed to make der air absorb heat instead of permitting it to come on down to der ground, and in consequence der air within range of his sending-apparatus is getting hot as der deffil because it is absorbing all der heat that should pass through it to warm the earth. Getting hot, it expands and rises. More cool air is rushing in underneath. That, in turn, is getting excited and rushing to der upper stratosphere.

"Der result is der Storm, that is raising hell. From der communications I haff received from der American Electric Company, der storm-center is fifty miles across, which makes it a hell of a storm. Der aferage for a typhoon is ten to fifteen miles.

"Der information I haff for you is that it is definitely Breston who is making this storm. He has a sending-apparatus with a range of twenty to thirty miles in efery direction. Where his *verdammt* short wafes reach, der air is no longer transparent to heat-wafes and all der heat of der sun is being used to heat der atmosphere, instead of der earth. There is bractically a chimney fifty miles across, full of hot air which is rising toward heafen and raising hell.

"You can locate der sending-station with apparatus like we used to line up der source of der darkness, before. I will be in communication with der Electric Company for some time to come. You can reach me, of course. But be careful as der deffil how you talk. Breston is no doubt listening in.

"I don't know what you are going to do, or how you are going to do it, but you haff got to do something. Der chimney of hot air will stop working, of course, at sunset. But it will probably begin again at sunrise, and in der meantime there will be der deffil of a storm all night long because of der hell that was raised all day. Good luck, Hines. I sign off now."

THERE WERE MORE clickings and the storm-roar from the loudspeaker stopped. Then the crisp voice of the announcer came once more.

"Mr. Hines! I hope you received Professor Schaaf's message. Woodford's communications are coming through quite clearly. It is not yet known just where you are. If you will send word, every effort will be made to reach you. In the meantime, will you give what orders you can about preparations for stopping this storm?"

The trooper, with his improvised key poised, looked expectantly at Hines.

"My messages are getting through, sir," he said woodenly. "And I imagine that they can't be read by anybody except at the other end of the rails. Before you recovered consciousness, the commissioner of police in New York City broadcast a message giving you full authority. The State authorities have done the same. What shall I tell them you want done?"

Hines's hands were clenched tightly. Kathryn was up in the mountains somewhere, somewhere near the center of the storm which was Preston's work. Preston's work!

She was probably dead by this time. Few buildings could stand the blast that blew outside. There was nothing to do, now, but get Preston.

Preston was the one man on earth that Hines unfeignedly hated. He had seen the man once. He had fought him twice, with the scientist Schaaf's aid. Preston should have been one of the greatest scientific geniuses on earth, but instead had now made himself the most cold-blooded murderer in history.

Preston found that certain short Hertzian waves produced a state of fluorescence in the air* so that the visible waves of light were absorbed by the ions of the atmosphere, and an utter darkness was produced.

Once, some months before, he had sent a beam of those waves down Fifth Avenue, in New York. In fifteen minutes of utter blackness the forewarned underworld of the city reaped a harvest of which Preston received his share.

With every resource of science and courage, Hines and Schaaf had fought him then, and had won. His apparatus for producing darkness was destroyed, and he seemed to have been killed. It was that success that had won Hines promotion to an inspectorship of police.

PRESTON, HOWEVER, WAS not dead. Three months since, he had reappeared with a new and larger apparatus for the broadcasting of his short waves. He filled the whole city with the unbelievably high-frequency broadcast, and

---

* The fluorescence of atmospheric air under the influence of certain wave-lengths of radiation was described as long ago as 1911 in a lecture before the Royal Institution of Great Britain by Professor R.W. Wood of Johns Hopkins University. The very short rays discovered by Schumann were demonstrated to produce fluorescence in air. The experiments and a photograph of the phenomenon may be found reprinted in the Report of the Smithsonian Institution for 1911, which is available in many public libraries. See page 165 *et seq.*

the air above the whole metropolitan district absorbed all visible rays and transformed them into invisible heat. The whole city was immersed in an ocean of oblivion.

Again Hines had fought him, with Schaaf's assistance. That bulky blond German scientist had invented instruments for locating the source of this radiation which had an almost catalytic effect in producing darkness. The effect of the waves was out of all proportion to the power used in producing them.

By Schaaf's instruments and Hines's courage, again the menace to the city had been nullified; but Preston had gone scot-free, and had become a millionaire through the panic in the stockmarket his horrible weapon had caused.

He remained undiscovered and at large, and his captured apparatus had been destroyed by the explosion of an evidently prepared bomb before it could be examined.

Now he was again at work. He had prepared apparatus which could send over a circle from fifty to sixty miles across. Wherever that station maintained a field of force of the extremely short radio waves, there the effects of the unholy radiation were evident.

He seemed to be using now a slightly different wavelength than had caused all light radiation to be absorbed by the air. Now it was that all heat was arrested by the atmosphere. The warmth of the sun did not reach the earth. The air itself became heated instead. Heated, it rose, and created a cyclonic storm beyond all parallel.

Preston, in the midst of that storm, was as safe from any danger save that of the storm as if he were protected by armies. No man could reach him, alive. He was invulnerable, protected by the sheer destruction he had invoked.

HINES CLENCHED HIS hands in the cubby-hole dug in the railroad embankment. His eyes narrowed. Kathryn was very probably dead, and Preston still lived. Preston would have to be killed for the sake of humanity alone; yet Hines would kill him to avenge her only.

"First," said Hines in a cold and utterly bitter tone, "I want everybody who's sold stocks short for a week past to be checked up. Preston will be operating in terms of millions. I suggest that the stock-market be closed, because when it's closed he can have no motive to continue the storm. And then—"

He paused to marshal his thoughts, while rage pumped in every artery and an almost insane hatred maddened him.

"Then," he said harshly, "I want the biggest tanks in the United States Army to be sent up here as soon as the wind dies down a little. They'll have to travel under their own power, because the roads and railroads alike are useless. I want the big forty-ton ones. I want at least two gun-carrier tanks with six-inch guns and a supply of gas and high explosive shell. And I want some bombs."

He went on to list cables, more bombs, and airplane photo maps of all the Catskills.

Meanwhile the Storm increased in force. It had been unbelievable before. Now the wind reached an intensity hitherto unknown upon the earth.

4

INTO THE DESOLATION

WHEN SUNSET CAME and the Storm died down temporarily, it had left its marks all over a circle of territory a full thousand miles in diameter. The damage done ranged from a mere blowing-down of signs at the edge of that circle, to the absolutely unparalleled devastation of the territory immediately about the storm-center.

In the center, of course, the damage was terrific. Forests, houses, hamlets, towns, all were leveled to the ground. Yet, there were survivors. Cellars protected some, as did valleys and hollows. Probably four or five thousand people lived through it.

The fifty-mile circle of the storm-center was devastated, but it was not destroyed. And beyond the storm-center, where the wind had not reached its ultimate velocity, the amount of damage was neatly proportioned to the distance from the focus of the storm.

But about the edge of that central area—the space Schaaf had spoken of as the chimney—there was a ring-like strip of utter desolation, five to fifteen miles wide.

Every particle of vegetation had been swept away by the sheer force of the wind. The fields were bare even of grass. In spots apparently even the topsoil had dried to dust and gone sweeping away into oblivion in the storm-wind. The forests were shattered areas of splintered stumps. The houses had left as traces only small mounds of masonry, or else no signs at all.

The storm died down at sunset and for half an hour there was almost peace. But the vast chimney of sun-heated air which shot upward for miles had acted as a vacuum, drawing to itself air from every direction with terrific speed. When the vacuum abruptly ceased to be, the winds continued to blow for a time from sheer momentum, and piled up a colossal high-pressure system which was as intolerable as the previous storm-center had been.

Over all the North Atlantic States, then, there was atmospheric chaos. Dense clouds formed at nightfall. Rain in unexampled volume fell, while electric storms wrought havoc. In the Catskill section mountain streams, choked with the débris of the wind's creation, became flooded with falling water and abruptly turned to inundations.

In that terrible strip of desolation about the storm-center itself, the bare, stripped earth turned to a vast morass of mud. And that morass claimed victims when survivors in the central area tried to cross it during the darkness and the rain.

AT NINE O'CLOCK, rain was falling in sheets, in columns, almost in solid masses. Lurid, unbelievable bolts of lightning leaped from one horizon to the other.

There were no electric lights, of course, in two thousand square miles of New York State that night. Beneath monstrous clouds which poured floods upon the earth, there was only blackness, save at one spot. There, pencil-beams of light stabbed futilely at the falling rain, where twelve huge tanks rocked and lurched and slid on up toward the mountains.

They had stopped in their advance and picked up Hines. He sat up in the control-room of the largest of all of them, and asked dreary questions and dully gave instructions which organized the attack.

The tanks would go on up toward the site of the storm-center. They would gather, presently, and Hines would give instructions which would be final. Then they would scatter to their several strategic points.

With dawn, when the Storm That Had to be Stopped began again, they would use the instruments Schaaf had originally designed for determining the point of origin of certain other short waves. They would find Preston's station. It would probably be a dugout, underground, for safety from the storm he could create at will. The tanks would bomb that station mercilessly. Or if he had intrenched himself upon a mountain peak, the gun-carrying caterpillars would come into action. Six-inch guns would assail a solitary man who essayed to devastate the earth.

Only colossal things such as they were weighing forty tons each—could hope to exist and move in the atmospheric turmoil that would begin with sunrise.

The tanks rumbled and lurched as they made their way in a sedate long line toward the hills. Rain poured in rivulets from their steel sides. Sheets and masses of falling water scattered the beams from the searchlights mounted upon them. From the control-room it was possible to see perhaps twenty feet with some clarity, and dimly for thirty feet more. But after that even the searchlight glare was dissipated by the rain.

Hines looked weary and worn and haggard. All day long he had been in communication with New York, giving orders which men leaped to obey.

The State had given him full authority. He had shown his ability. Besides, the scale, the scope of this disaster was one to induce panic. The leadership of Hines, who had twice defeated Preston, would restore some confidence in a public otherwise more than inclined to be panic-stricken.

THESE WERE ARMY tanks, shipped on flat-cars as far as the rails were undamaged, drawn by a locomotive that had crept on and on, as far as it dared, while the Storm still blew in the daytime. They had come at full speed immediately darkness fell.

Now they went lurching and pounding up toward the hills. The clanking of their mighty treads was thunderous in their reverberating interiors. The roaring of their motors was deafening.

They were full of the smell of hot oil and exhaust-gases and fuel, but up in the control-room the lightning and thunder blotted out all sights and sounds, and the sheer desert of mud over which they traveled toward the hills made it impossible for any man who saw it to think of anything else.

Hines, alone, thought of Kathryn. The awful desolation over which the tanks traveled had been covered with farms and houses and forests only twelve hours before. People had lived here—people who now were torn and draggled corpses flung haphazard amid the other débris of the Storm.

Hines had been cooped up for twelve hours knowing his helplessness, knowing that Kathryn was either dead or desperately in need of help. Now, he was sure she was dead. The desert of mud over which the tanks passed was enough to convince him of her death.

The radio had told them that over most of the United States the wind had reached gale intensity.

The weather bureau in Washington was working like mad to predict the unpredictable, but from the one day's storm alone weeks of chaotic weather could be foreseen.

Already meteorologists were speculating upon the effect of the Storm upon the climate of Europe. California, it was certain, would be visited by subsidiary hurricanes, and from Texas on north there would be cyclonic whirls of terrible intensity as the air of the earth moved to fill up the vacuum Preston could create at will.

What news there was of the loss of life was so monstrous as to have lost all meaning. The record of towns destroyed, of villages wiped out, became monotonous. From the standpoint of property destroyed the Storm was one of the major catastrophes of history; and if the death toll was lighter than certain plagues and earthquakes, it was only because the larger cities were fortunately far from the circles of highest wind-velocity.

THE FEEL OF slippery mud beneath the tanks' great treads changed subtly. The earth became curiously more solid. A great bowlder appeared not far from the leading tank's track, glistening and running with rain. The tank changed course to avoid it. Hines looked back. Despite the falling water, he could detect a long lane of white glows, which were the searchlights of the following tanks.

The tanks still went on. They were in what seemed to be a semi-solid mass of water, intermittently made into a greenish universe of light by lightning-flashes which were blurred by the rain to mere indefinite illumination. In the periods of darkness between those flashes, the searchlights gleamed brightly ahead. And water poured from the tanks in floods.

Débris appeared, water-soaked and shredded. The stumps of wind-whipped, obliterated Indian corn began suddenly to the left. The treads of the tanks clanked suddenly on concrete. There was a road beneath the leading tank.

A speaking-tube whistled in the leading tank.

"Headquarters," came up thinly to the control-room, "orders you to try to locate yourself by road signs or any other evidences of position."

The officer in command of the tank snorted and made no answer.

The tank went on. There was concrete under the left tread only. The tank wallowed around and climbed back on the road. It went rumbling blindly on in the rain. Presently bare concrete was visible. Mud had not washed across it here.

"There!" said Hines sharply. "A road-sign bent over by the wind! It's in place!"

An unearthly hooting set up. The tank stopped with a grinding noise. Hines peered out of the little vision-slits and saw a dripping man with a flash light bent over something by the side of the road. It was one of the cast-iron road signs one finds in the Catskills. They are set up on wrought-iron posts, which are fixed in concrete.

Originally the sturdiness of construction was made necessary by the vandal habits of a motoring populace, but it served a useful purpose now. Set facing the wind, the cast-iron plate had caught the full blast. And the wrought-iron shaft had bent slowly but definitely until the sign lay nearly flat, facing upward.

The dripping soldier came sprinting back into the tank. The speaking-tube whistled again.

"The sign says 'North Weddensdale Corporate Limits,' sir."

Hines clenched his hands. This was the village where Kathryn had been staying! He strained his eyes desperately through the rain.

A rectangular hole to the left of the concrete caught his eye. It was a cellar. The house had been taken cleanly away from above it. Nothing was left. Nothing.

"Go on," he said hoarsely.

The tank ground into motion again. Rain poured from its sides. Its searchlight ray stabbed into the darkness and was dissipated by falling water.

Then the searchlight ray went out.

ALMOST INSTANTLY THEREAFTER the speaking-tube whistled.

"All the tanks, sir, report their searchlights have gone out."

The officer commanding the leading tank swore to himself. "All right. Everybody stop and repair them."

Hines heard his voice speaking hoarsely:

"It's the Darkness. The metal walls of the tank act as shields, so we can see inside, but it's the Darkness—the same darkness Preston turned on in New York. If you send a man outside to make sure, keep up a noise so he can find his way back."

Hines went, himself, to the exit door of the tank. He heard two men moving about outside. The interior of the tank was brightly lighted, and the door was opened wide, but the light from inside did not strike upon the earth beneath the tank. It seemed to be absorbed by some solid black substance which surrounded the metal monster and stretched solidly almost with an inward bulge, across the open door.

Thunder shook the earth. There was a crashing and crackling of electricity. From the violence of the report, the lightning-flash must have struck somewhere near by. But there was no faintest flickering of light.

Then, in a peculiarly ghastly fashion, a groping hand came out of the solid wall of blackness across the tank's exit door. It seemed disembodied, detached from any body. It caught at the edge of the door. A man came, wild-eyed and staring, out of the apparently solid opacity. His teeth chattered as he swung into the illuminated tank.

"The—the flash light don't work," he gasped. "I held it up to my eyes and it just glowed, but it don't give any light. See?"

He pressed the button. A brilliant gleam shot from the flash light. His jaw dropped open. But Hines nodded his head very bitterly.

The Storm had been made by the broadcasting of very short Hertzian waves which caused the atmosphere to be opaque to heat; a mere variation of a device that Preston had used before. Now he had gone back to the use of his first device again.

Now, from somewhere within a thirty-mile radius, he was broadcasting short waves differing perhaps by the fraction of a millimeter in length from those that had produced the Storm. And these tiny ripples in the ether caused the absorption of all that band of frequencies which made visible light.

There was darkness outside the tanks so dense as to be tangible, so complete as to constitute utter blindness, so thick that it caused the perfect absorption of even the ten thousand candle-power searchlight beams within a distance of three feet.

HINES THOUGHT GRIMLY, staring at the apparently solid wall of darkness without the door. The metal walls of the tanks, of course, absorbed and grounded the waves that impinged upon them. The darkness could not invade the tanks themselves. But it blinded the drivers beyond the possibility of a remedy.

The engines of the tank stopped suddenly. The officer in command swung down from the control-room, his lips twisted wryly.

"I reported to headquarters," he said briefly, "and received orders to stop my motors and wait for dawn. It is believed that the darkness will be lifted when the Storm is started up again."

Hines did not hear him. He was listening with his ears strained to their utmost. In the near-silence that came with the engine's stopping, the sound of the rain and thunder outside seemed to redouble. The rain was invisible, the lightning unseen, but there was a tumult without the tank that was terrifying. Yet in the midst of that tumult Hines thought he heard a faint cry.

It was repeated. Again, and again. And cold sweat came out upon Hines. He could not believe his ears, yet he dared not disbelieve them. Out there in a storm such as would have been called a tornado if the Storm itself had not given a new meaning to the word, he heard a voice which he could swear was that of Kathryn!

The storm itself was violent enough to make venturing into it madness—and he would have to go into it as a blind man.

The cry came once more. It was fainter, this time.

5

TRICKED

TWO MEMBERS OF the crew of the tank volunteered to go with him. They went out as Alpine climbers travel, tied together with a long strand of wire that paid out behind them. It would insure that they returned to the tank, or would lead them to any of their number who was injured.

Hines went first, groping over unfamiliar ground, unable to guess where his next step would bring him. He had broken out the glass of a pocket compass proffered by one of the tank's company and steered by the feel of its needle, with the tank hooting dismally behind him at regular intervals for his better orientation.

He went on into the blackness which seemed almost familiar. His flash light bulb glowed dimly when three inches from his eyes. Farther away, its light was absorbed by the opaque air, and he seemed to swim through it as a diver might swum through a sea of ink.

A fall into a ditch crammed with débris corrected the sensation of swimming, however, and he blundered on and gashed his leg against the splintered stump of a tree whose knife-edged fragments were in nowise softened by the rain.

Rain pelted downward through the darkness. It poured from him in streams. He had to bend almost double to protect his open compass from the falling water while he felt of the needle.

The tank hooted behind him. He went on. The wire attached to his waist dragged. It jerked, and he halted to allow the following man to move forward and give him slack. He shouted, and the beginning of his shout was loud, and the end of it was drowned out by thunder. He listened, and heard only the terrible drumming of miles of rain.

Then a cry in answer. He shouted again, and plunged forward and stumbled ten feet on and gashed his forehead horribly, and went on again with warm blood mingling with the rain that beat down on his face. Suddenly he was sprawling on hands and knees on a monstrous heap of broken bricks and field-stone.

A cry came up almost below him. He cursed the darkness then, and called once more; and Kathryn sobbed.

"I—I'm all right, only some brickwork fell on me and I can't get up," she said unsteadily a moment later.

"I'm coming down to you," said Hines hoarsely.

"Be careful! There's an open space just above me, where the floor broke in, but there's loose rock there. You may fall."

Hines gritted his teeth and fumbled here and there with infinite caution. Loose rock above a hole over Kathryn's head meant not so much danger to him as to her.

He tore his hands on splintered planks. A figure came blundering near by. He heard it gasping, but he saw nothing, anywhere.

"Easy!" snapped Hines. "We're here! Standstill!"

Kathryn said steadily from below: "You're nearly above me. I think you're at the edge of the hole in the flooring."

He found it, and called quietly to the other man.

"Our belts," he said briefly. "We'll put 'em together and you lower me. Then you can haul her up, and after her, me."

He went down, dangling in the blackness with no more knowledge of his whereabouts than a blind man would have had. He landed in a foot and a half of water.

"Here," said Kathryn unsteadily. "B-but be careful of the m-masonry."

HE STUMBLED AGAINST her shoulder before he realized that she was trapped near the floor. The cellar was filling with the drainage of the rain. Hines was two men then, for an instant. One felt coolly until he had located the mass of brick and mortar that pinned her down, and had envisioned its position and its size. The other man was sick with horror at the thought of the death that had awaited her as the cellar slowly filled with water.

He had more than two men's strength as he wrenched at the mass of stone, though. It fell with a turgid splashing that was louder than the drumming of the rain and the constant splashing of water that came down into the stone-lined depression.

He lifted her and held her close, there in the unbelievable blackness. He sent her up, by the linked belts. And he carried her himself, the long, stumbling, rather terrible way back to the hooting tank, which slowly hauled in the wire as he advanced. The other men blundered on ahead of him to take any falls there might be while he carried Kathryn.

Her arm was broken, and she was badly bruised, but that was all. Hines set the arm himself, while she smiled at him gamely in the smelly, machinery-crowded war-engine.

Then Hines turned to the commander of the tank with

a new and more savage grimness. He had gained a new motive from Kathryn's injury. Oddly enough, he had felt defeated in advance while he believed her dead; but a new and throbbing rage swept over him because of her injury, a fiercer passion than the hopeless hatred her death would have caused.

"Look here," he said savagely. "You've had orders to take directions from me. Preston's turned on the dark, outside. He thinks we're helpless. You radio headquarters and tell them I order you to go on. I take all responsibility."

The officer grinned.

The ordnance department maps of the Catskills leave some things to be desired, to be sure. There are errors, in spots, and they are not wholly up to date. But every road and bridlepath and every grade and hollow is shown upon them.

With a concrete road under their treads and the North Weddensdale corporate limits sign for a position-sign, the tanks could very nearly go to any spot in all the mountains, blinded though they were.

Men had walked about each of the tanks, with flash lights held close to their eyes. They discovered that for a short distance beyond the tank, in the direction away from the sending-station of the waves of darkness, there was a lee, a "shadow"—a relatively small and cone-shaped shielded area, in which the air was protected from the Hertzian waves that made it opaque to light. In those shielded areas lights could be seen. And those small spaces of transparent air gave a bearing—rough, to be sure, but still a bearing—on the station that was sending the short waves.

THE DARKNESS WAS being transmitted from a spot nearly north-northeast of the steel monsters. A man swung up in top of each one with a flash light and a hammer. He worked himself around the central turret until he had the turret between himself and Preston's transmitter of darkness. His flash light gave him proof of his direction. He rapped on the turret-plates. One rap for each division of the compass to the east of north, and two for each division to the left, was the agreed signal. He would transmit the bearing of the source of darkness whenever the turret was pounded on from within.

"One more thing," said Hines crisply. "Arrange with the other tanks to navigate by whistle-signals instead of radio. Preston will be listening in, you can be sure."

Then through the sound of thunder and of rain, there came the multitudinous hoots of many whistles. There was a whirring and the roaring of engines. Then with a monstrous grinding, the tank set off.

Hines and the tank officer bent over the map of this locality. Kathryn looked on, though her eyes rested most, often upon the haggard, draggled figure that was Hines.

"The road curves here," said Hines quietly. "That will place us definitely."

The officer laid his finger on a certain spot.

"A bridge," he observed, all of sixty feet high in the middle. We'll be crossing it—blind. And it may be blown out."

Hines shrugged. The tank rumbled on, and on…. Its whistle hooted, and was answered from behind. Then a long line of blind monsters hooted one after the other as they swam through obscurity as black as the blackest ink.

Concrete under the treads. They were steering the monster by compass, now, and the sound of the treads.

Quite suddenly, the tank wallowed off the concrete. It lurched, Careened, swung about and then found the way again.

"That's the curve," said the officer. "We're located all right."

From this time on the navigation of the monster vehicle was confident and crisp. A modern tank records its course and distance so accurately that even in the densest fog it can retrace its way for miles without a landmark.

From the map a forecast of the course to be followed was being made and the tank lumbered on through oblivion. Utter darkness filled the world without its steel walls, save where one man sat in a terrific downpour in a triangular small space of transparent air, and watched a dripping compass by the light of a flash light.

From time to time he pounded savagely on the steel deck with a hammer, signaling to those within. From time to time, too, there were vast hooting noises, feet only from his head, and there were other dismal hootings behind him in the utter blackness.

THE FEEL OF the concrete underneath changed subtly. The forty-ton weight of the tank was making the huge bridge sway slightly. The tank's whistle howled, in a succession of long and short blasts.

"They'll wait until we're across the bridge," said the officer shortly. "One at a time is load enough."

The leading tank ground on. The bridge quivered and shook. Presently the earth was solid under it again. It halted and seemed to bellow into the surrounding bedlam of rain

and wind and thunder. An answering hoot came faintly.
There was stillness, and presently the earth-quivering that
told of the near approach of another monster. More hootings of whistles. Another great tank, and another.

The fifth tank was on its way across the narrow cause-
way which the map said spanned a ravine some sixty feet
above the mountain stream. Suddenly, there was a wild
screaming of its whistle, a terrific crash, and then a deafening detonation. The waiting tanks trembled from the
concussion that ensued.

"It fell off the bridge," said the officer of the tank in
which Hines rode. He spoke very calmly. "I suppose the
rest of us weakened the bridge in passing over it. Maybe
the Storm helped, too. It gave way and the bombs went off
when the tank crashed."

He looked at Hines.

"We'll go on with those that are here with us," said
Hines grimly. "Signal the rest to hunt for shelter from
to-morrow's wind."

The hooting, dismal cavalcade of four tanks began again
to fumble its way along the narrow ribbon of concrete that
wound among the mountains. Twice the treads crunched
shrieking metal beneath them. Cars, wrecked and, it was to
be hoped, abandoned. Half a dozen times, in one relatively
sheltered valley, the leading tank crushed a way through
splintered masses of limbs and foliage that were heaped
up in monster windrifts.

The half-drowned men out in the flood of rain pounded
regularly their signals of the source of the waves of darkness. The tanks had gone five miles in all in a little over an

hour, when the poundings on the outside became frantic. A new signal of direction came through. Hines said shortly:

"Stop the whole line. Check with all of them."

The tanks had been boring their way through the blackness by map. The darkness-producing ether waves demonstrably had been coming from the north-northeast. Now, abruptly, they were proved to be coming from a little south of west.

Hines studied the map and the line that had been drawn to indicate the tank's ultimate destination. The sending-station was no longer there. It had changed position.

"Either," said Hines harshly, "Preston's moved his sending apparatus, or he has two or more of them. He turns one off and another one on. We haven't a burglar's chance of locating them if they turn off as we draw near them."

They were playing a deadly game of blind-man's-buff with Preston. Now Preston showed an unexpected resource. He had more than one outfit for producing darkness. When the tanks drew near one, that ceased to operate and another took up its task.

It seemed as if Preston had Hines beaten.

6

SCIENTIST AT BAY

HEAVILY, LABORIOUSLY, CLUMSILY, the tanks crawled on through the darkness. They were blind and they were fumbling. They went clanking through a blackness as of the Abyss, with the peculiar confidence of things that have long been sightless, while rain beat upon them and thunder roared about them.

Hines and the tank officer were again bent over the map.

"Schaaf's experiment station was here," said Hines shortly, touching a spot on the engraved sheet. "It was more or less a secret, but he was trying to work out how to make these same darkness-producing waves. He was trying, in fact, to duplicate Preston's results in hopes of finding some way to neutralize them. That accounts for his short-wave set and the experimental license that enabled him to use it."

The tank officer received a crossbearing from the tanks they had left behind at the wrecked bridge, and drew a line on his map.

"This is the third darkness-transmitter Preston's brought into use," he said quietly.

"And he's using underground aerials," said Hines shortly, "because anything above ground would have been blown away by the Storm. We can't locate the transmitters closer than within a quarter of a mile, by crossbearings, and we can't count on destroying them even with explosives unless we locate them more closely than that. Poison-gas will be useless in the wind that will be blowing by dawn."

"We're licked, then," said the tank officer.

"Not yet," said Hines grimly. "We've got the bearings now. Let's go on. I've still got one hope. Schaaf's a smart man."

The tanks crawled on blindly, like gigantic eyeless slugs creeping along the bottom of the ocean's deepest deep, while within a vast irregular circle fifty miles across, the drenched, shivering, hysterical survivors of the Storm itself went closer to madness from the terror of the dark.

AT ONE O'CLOCK in the morning, while all over the United States people sat up by their radios and listened fascinatedly to the never-ceasing broadcasts of news and orders, reports and fragmentary pleas for help, there was the first direct word from the man who had caused the Storm That Had to be Stopped.

Radio broadcasting was, of course, the next most important factor, after Hines's activities in lessening the damage Preston did to the earth.

All the first night of the storm a warning was broadcast to the isolated folk who hastily turned to the radio as their sole link with the outside, that the wind was to be expected to begin again at daybreak. By broadcasting the location of the few hamlets protected by fortuitously placed mountains, much good was done.

Mostly, though, the radio served to make all the world realize the extent of the catastrophe. It is to the credit of the people of America that trains loaded down with supplies for the devastated area were already on their way while the Storm still raged on its second day.

The radio enabled all the continent to share in the horror of the Storm, and also the radio was the means of communication with Hines and the blinded tanks in the storm-center, so that a hundred million people shared in his adventure, in his attempt to stop the Storm.

Perhaps the most spectacular feat the radio performed that night was an accident. It was at one o'clock. The tank officer in charge of Hines's tank was communicating with headquarters. The Red Cross had arranged for half a dozen sentences from him, describing the devastation the tank had passed through on its way to the mountains. If rehabilitation was to take place, vast sums would be needed, and money could best be got while the catastrophe was fresh in peoples' minds.

The tank officer spoke curtly into the microphone to headquarters. His words were amplified and rebroadcast and sent over the nation-wide chains of radio stations. A hundred million people heard his voice and even the noise of the machinery of the tank, crawling through the darkness where the Storm was made.

But he had spoken no more than a dozen words when another voice cut in. This other voice was harsh, metallic; an abominally cocksure and arbitrary voice. It spoke with a studied insolence.

"THIS IS PRESTON speaking," said the voice arrogantly, and instantly folk all over the United States stiffened in their chairs as the unexpected tones came from their loudspeakers.

"I have been much amused by the accounts of the efforts

made to find and kill me. I have been listening in, of course, from my entirely secure retreat in the storm-center, and I am speaking on the same wave-length the tanks have been using. I hear my own voice in another speaker, being rebroadcast as the lieutenant's voice was supposed to be. I think it about time that the people of the United States should know with whom and what they deal."

Preston's voice stopped, and millions of people waited breathlessly. Static interrupted his words, and whole phrases were sometimes obliterated by the crashings made by the lightning, but on the whole his message was clear.

"I have made this storm for my own private purposes. I can continue it for days, for weeks, even for months. In one week, I am informed, I will have so deranged the normal atmospheric conditions in the United States that the crops of this fall will be practically ruined.

"In two weeks, by drawing down the colder air from the Arctic Circle, I will have brought on winter in Canada. In three weeks there will be four feet of snow in London, Germany will be frozen in, and all the north of France will have a semi-arctic climate, while the United States will face a famine. I invite the meteorological experts of the world to verify my statement.

"I shall continue the storm I have created until the governments I have mentioned make it worth my while to stop it. In the meantime, I assure you that the tanks that are trying to locate me have no chance of success. The Storm will continue until I wish it to stop. I will stop it only when I am sufficiently paid for my trouble."

The arrogant voice ceased. Announcers' voices, quivering with excitement, followed with a statement that radio compasses had picked up the message before its cessation and that it had actually come from the Catskills, from the storm-center.

The United States began to be afraid. The Boards of Governors of the Stock Exchanges of New York and Chicago began to arrange, quietly, for the closing of those exchanges. Cables began to carry long messages in diplomatic code across the ocean-beds.

Suddenly another broadcast, as widely distributed as the first, came from Schaaf, in his tiny laboratory set in a hillside. He had a national reputation, now, as an associate of Hines, and he was frantically called upon for a statement to nullify the panic that Preston's announcement would cause.

Schaaf's speech, repeated in the same ten million receiving sets, was entirely characteristic of him.

"I haff heard Breston's speech," he said dryly. "I remark that my friendt Hines is on the way to join me in a little Schrecklichkeit party, to be bractised on Breston. I consider that as imbortant as anything Breston has said. We will haff him in a matter of hours. As for his threats to mess up der weather of two continents, I say one thing: No matter how thin you slice it, it is still boloney."

SCHAAF'S SPEECH HAD just the tone necessary to restore confidence without lessening the public's sense of the real urgency of the situation. There were speculators in foodstuffs and other necessities, of course, who immediately grasped the opportunity Preston's threats created. They, by the way, suffered considerable losses by their enterprise as things turned out.

But on the whole the public reacted in highly favorable fashion to Schaaf's dry reassurance. Americans will always pay more for a good joke than a pathetic story, and Schaaf raised more money by the last line of his speech than all the tear-jerking efforts of radio spellbinders during the rest of the night.

Schaaf did not listen in and hear himself eulogized on the ether-waves, the details of his scientific career sandwiched in between casualty lists and weather predictions. He was placidly unaware of his sudden celebrity.

In fact, until the restored mail-services brought him sacks of admiring and begging letters, and an astounding number of proposals of marriage from female admirers, he was not aware that he had done anything out of the ordinary.

He was busy. He turned from the microphone with a grunt of disgusted relief. His experiment-station was a tiny stone-walled building half sunk in a mountainside. It consisted of four rooms.

The laboratory alone was of use to him now. Experimenting as he had been with short radio waves, he had needed a workshop in which the only etheric disturbances would be those he made himself. The walls of the workshop were lined with copper sheeting and the windows covered with heavy copper gauze, all of which was grounded. The interior was insulated from all Hertzian waves from without.

Now that laboratory glowed brightly with electric light, though he had only to open a door to see the apparently solid mass of no longer transparent air which resulted from Preston's devices.

He took down a screen from a window. Instantly the blackness seemed to pour, to stab, into the brightly lighted laboratory. Through the opening in the grounded shielding, Preston's short-waves penetrated, depriving the air of its ability to permit light to pass through it. A long cone of darkness, so definite as to seem a solid substance, projected into the room—more powerful than the shielding because of the nearness to Preston's headquarters.

Schaaf grumbled and measured it, carefully making his measurements from accurately marked points. He wrote down his figures and replaced the screen. The seemingly tangible cone vanished with much the effect of magic.

Schaaf sat down at a little table and began to calculate absorbedly. He scowled as he worked, and mumbled irritatedly as he took down a book of logarithms and ran his fingers down its columns.

THE TABLE TREMBLED, from time to time, with the violence of the thunder without. There was a very slow leak in the roof over in one corner, and now and again a drop fell glittering to an enlarging puddle on the floor. The wind howled outside. The rain drummed on the roof.

Schaaf finished his calculations, leaned back and absently combed out his luxuriant yellow whiskers with his fingers, then filled and lighted his pipe. Its poisonously strong odor filled the air.

The thunder was deafening and nearly continuous. The shrieking of the wind was daunting. The drumming sound of the rain was unspeakably depressing. Schaaf smoked comfortably for a space, and picked up the remnant of a half-eaten sandwich. He bit into it, stopped, and listened keenly.

There was a thin and dismal hooting above even the tumult from the skies. Schaaf beamed, and then growled impatiently. He swathed himself in oilskins, muttering something about "Der *verdammt* Breston!" and took a huge reel of cord from the wall. It looked like the extra-strong braided cord that is used for scientific kite-flying—or for getting a kite aloft that is to carry up a temporary aerial. He fastened the end inside the door, knotting and double-knotting it. He went out, unreeling the cord behind him, and fought the door shut again.

There was no longer any movement or any activity in the laboratory. A loudspeaker made nasal noises in one corner, which the booming of thunder and of wind and rain drowned out to inarticulateness. The lights burned steadily.

An open fire alternately leaped madly upward and died down to nothing beneath an improvised damper closing off most of the chimney-space above it. Rain made rattling noises on the windows, and wind screamed overhead, and always, always, always, the thunder boomed and crashed.

Then the door burst open and Schaaf came in again, fumbling his way back along the cord. He was soaked. Behind him, guiding themselves by the cord, came three other people. Hines was one of them, tattered and ragged and with a great gash on his forehead. He carried Kathryn lightly, in spite of the storm. She was wrapped in an oilskin, one arm in improvised splints.

Hines set her down carefully and blinked with the air of a man whose sight has suddenly been restored. The third person was the officer in command of the leading tank.

Schaaf put his whole weight against the door and closed it.

"It was not bad work," he observed comfortably. "You stopped on der concrete road where der big tree had blown down, as I told you by radio. I came down, blundered into you, and banged on der door. Here we are. Now, where is der map?"

The tank-officer produced a sheet he had carried under his slicker. Schaaf began to unroll it.

"I haff sworn—*Gott!* How I haff sworn!—because I didt not haff a map of der locality. Miss Bush, go ofer by der fire and get warm. Now, Hines, show me my bresent location and tell me der scale of der map."

The tank-officer, instead, obeyed both orders. Hines was settling Kathryn comfortably by the fire. And Schaaf took dividers and a pencil and calculated feverishly, grumbling in guttural German at the absurdity of calculating distances in feet and inches instead of meters. Eventually he measured with painstaking accuracy, drew six lines from the location of his laboratory to very precise and exact lengths, and put large dots at their ends.

"THERE," HE SAID decisively. "That is der best I can do. I have watched der *verdammt* darkness. Look!" He pulled out a window-screen and a black cone of opacity stabbed across the brightly lighted room. He replaced the screen and it vanished. "Der wafes that destroy der transparency of der air," he said briskly, "can come in der window-opening when I remofe part of der copper insulation inside. They interfere with each other, dissipate, and generally lose der original effectifness. Which gifes me my information. By der shape of der cone of blackness, I haff calculated der direction and distance of six different points from which Breston has transmitted darkness. At these six spots he has sending-stations."

The tank-officer said warmly:

"Splendid, sir! We took bearings as we came along—see my pencil-lines, sir?—and they intersect your lines at just the spots you indicate! It looks as if you are correct."

"Of course I'm correct! And if I had had der intelligence of an angleworm I would haff made der same measurements of der wafes that made der storm and we would know where Breston is. He is not at all of those places, certainly."

"No," said Hines. "But what I'm hoping for, Schaaf, is some way to see in spite of the darkness. Once—"

"*Gott in Himmel!*" cried Schaaf angrily. "Haff I not kicked myself forty-sefen times? Before, when we fought Breston in New York, his wafes made der air opaque to fisible light, but not to ultra-fiolet, and we did tricks with that to find our way about. But now, he has juggled his wafe-lengths to make der air absorb der ultra-fiolet rays also. I am as blind as a bat at der bottom of der sea, Hines, and I am mad! I am mad as der deffil, Hines!"

Hines frowned at the map.

"He'll keep the darkness on, even after daybreak," he said coldly. "He'll shoot the storm-producing waves out as an addition. And since he turns off his sending-stations when a tank draws near—"

"Maybe he has microphones in der ground," said Schaaf gloomily. "Der sound of a tank is unmistakable. Or maybe he switches them on and off for der mere purpose of being confusing. In any efent I haff done all I can. I tell you abbroximately where his sending-stations are. But you cannot find them without seeing them or tracing der wafes home, and he turns them off when a tank comes near. It is like trying to catch a mouse that is in six holes at once."

Hines smiled faintly.

"But we have lots of cats," he observed. "Lieutenant, I want these orders given."

Schaaf listened critically, then appreciatively, and then he beamed as Hines's voice went on.

"Hines," he said comfortably, "if your brains were dynamite and they went off, der report would be like Vesuvius. We got der son-of-a-gun!"

Even the tank-officer grinned confidently as he prepared to make his way back to the tank by the guiding cord.

7

THE HEART OF THE STORM

RAIN DRUMMED ON the roof and clattered on the windows. Wind shrieked outside the little stone building. A mountain-flank had protected it from the blast of air that had blown all the day before, and the storm that raged during the night was merely a gale such as uproots trees and sinks ships at sea. But it was uncomfortable to listen to, with thunder making the tumult of a bombardment.

The smoke of Schaaf's pipe floated about the room. The loud-speaker had been turned off, Hines turned it on with an air of impatience.

"The lieutenant's been gone a long time. Do you suppose he was blown away?"

Schaaf grunted.

"Of course not, Hines. He is a smart young man. He got to his tank, and he has been gifing orders by radio to der other tanks that were left behind when der bridge gafe way. Breston will see that there is a cat at efery mouse-hole, in a little while."

"Preston probably has more than the six you marked down," said Hines shortly, "but we have eleven tanks."

He was worried, though. Abominably worried. All but four of the tank-force had been left behind early in the night, when one tank was destroyed as a bridge gave way under it. Those land-warships had now been ordered, separately, to make wide detours and somehow get to the six spots Schaaf had indicated.

They would approach the stations from which Preston was transmitting his darkness-waves. If the station did not cease to transmit, the tank could ride it down and crush it, or bomb it with heavy bombs and destroy it utterly.

Preston had undoubtedly planned to alternate in the use of his transmitters for the precise purpose of preventing their location. But if every station he had ready to transmit had a tank waiting to pounce upon it— It was exactly like the posting of a cat at every mouse-hole. If the mouse showed his head—if a known station emitted the waves that produced the opacity of the air—the tank would pounce. But Hines was worried. Preston was clever.

"I am thinking, Hines," said Schaaf placidly, "that it should be near sunrise. I go and look."

For the third time he unfastened and opened a screen. For the third time a seemingly solid mass of blackness stabbed into the room. Schaaf disappeared into the tangible darkness. The noises of the outer air were suddenly magnified as he opened a window.

And the outer noises were changing markedly. Rain still fell and thunder still boomed. But the rain diminished. The drops became fewer and less regular. Then the thunder dwindled.

The listeners in the laboratory realized that a steady, even wind was blowing. It was a strong wind when they first noticed it. It gave forth a low hum whose pitch rose in minutes. It became a scream, and then a whistle that grew

more and more shrill until human ears could not detect it.
And then a steady, regular roaring noise took its place. It
was the wind of the Storm That Had to be Stopped. On
the second day of the Storm it rose much more rapidly
than on the first.

Hines and Kathryn looked at each other. Kathryn was
pale, but she smiled at Hines.

"We've got to get out to the tank," he said harshly.

Schaaf popped magically out of the blackness.

"Of all der double-barreled imbeciles!" he said bitterly.
"We haff to reach der tank, and it is impossible! Der
wind already is as strong as it was at its worst yesterday.
Nobody could liff in it a second! Der laboratory nearly
went yesterday! It will not stand another half hour if der
wind increases!"

THE WIND DID increase. Shielded though the laboratory
was by a mountain-flank, and thick stone as its walls were,
the beams that upheld the roof began to creak. The walls
quivered. Plaster fell from the ceiling. Windows burst
outward, suddenly, and all light and movable things leaped
toward them and vanished. Hines seized Kathryn and bore
her to the mountainward side of the laboratory.

"We haff," said Schaaf calmly, "maybe fife minutes.
Maybe less. I am sorry as der deffil, Hines, that we did not
get that *verdammt* Breston."

Then there was a vibration which seemed to shake the
very flooring. And suddenly a wall reeled and caved in,
and a section of roof tore out. Then, quite incredibly, the
monstrous beak of a tank thrust its way delicately into the
laboratory and stopped. A door slid aside and the tank-officer stood beckoning in the opening.

"I figured it was the only thing to do," he shouted above the wind-roar as they struggled inside the tank. "The wind's unbelievable outside, and if you were kept from blowing away, you'd strangle."

"As der poet says," observed Schaaf calmly, "you said a library-full. What do we do now?"

"I've been getting reports from the other tanks," said the officer cheerfully. "Three of them have reached position. They know they're within a quarter of a mile of a darkness transmitter, but each time it has turned off. The others are going on. We'll carry out the rest of the plan. All ready?"

The tank lurched backward. The laboratory collapsed, and instantly there was a savage bombardment by the wind. Beams, sections of roofs, stones, articles of furniture—everything the wind could wrench from the shattered building it flung with maniacal fury upon the tank.

The metal monster shuddered and clanged and reeled, and then turned about and slid on downhill with a ponderous clanking of its mighty treads. But the noise of the wind sounded even above the internal roaring of the tank's machinery.

There were hootings, unbelievably faint, and the tank-officer shook his head. He spoke curtly into a speaking-tube, and turned apologetically to Hines.

"Sound-signals are useless, sir. We are having to use radio again. We'll have quite a time of it anyhow. Better find seats of some sort. Or you can come up in the control-room."

The control-room was a tiny cubbyhole. There was room for the man who steered the cumbersome war-engine, and normally there was bare space for the commander of the tank. Now Hines squeezed in between them for the second time, and there was only the light of the dimly-lit instrument-board and a curious fuzzy appearance about the vision-slits where the darkness came a little way into the tank's metal interior.

"Six of the tanks are going to their posts. The other four are following us," said the officer in Hines's ear. "We're going to try to keep hundred-yard intervals, but we're all blind."

And the tank went crawling on.

THE INSTRUMENTS GAVE their varying indications. The wind roared without. In the dead blackness the air had assumed not only the appearance but the solidity of a substance. It pressed upon the forty-ton tank with such force that even the monstrous engine was edged steadily to one side.

The line of tanks, crawling through blackness, was following a concrete road by map and the feel of the treads.

There was no one in the tanks who did not think in shuddering horror of what the blinded monsters might be doing as they lurched and swayed across a place that had been inhabited. There might be people yet living who would be crushed beneath the tanks' broad treads.

But they went on. Their destination was a spot which Hines had chosen. The located transmitters of darkness formed an irregular circle, and Hines guessed that the form was not an accident. And if it were intentional, and if the transmitters were governed by remote control, then sheer efficiency would dictate that the controlling spot should be in the center of the circle. If anywhere, Preston would be at a spot nearly equidistant from all his transmitters.

Hines watched the vision-slits of the control-room. They were narrow slits in a bullet-proof steel wall. Wind came in them so fiercely that it stung exploring fingers. And the darkness crept in. The walls near the vision-slits looked fuzzy on the side nearest the darkness transmitter then in action. A man outside could have taken the station-bearing accurately, while this method was rough at best; and no man could live outside now.

Hines craned his neck suddenly to look behind. The blurry little bands of darkness had vanished before him. Now they reappeared at the back of the control-room.

Hines clutched at the tank-officer's arm.

"A transmitter, behind us!" he barked in the officer's ear. "Have that last tank turn back and try to smash it!"

A snapped order went down the speaking-tube. The trailing tank turned about. Its steersman had but little to do save keep a certain disgusting fuzzy appearance at vision-slits exactly before him. The tank went blundering into heaps of still-standing masonry where the town had been. It surmounted or destroyed them. It careened and teetered upon the edge of a cellar, plunged boldly into it, crashed blindly to the other side and reared upward clumsily to crawl out.

The officer in command of the trailing tank saw that the fuzziness had vanished from the control-slits ahead. It had reappeared behind. As near as this, even the roughest of observations would serve. He yelled an order down below. A monstrous, misshapen egg went rolling down from the back of the tank. The monster went blundering on.

Thirty seconds, forty. There was a concussion which

drowned out even the roar of the storm. Vast fragments of masonry struck the tank.

Suddenly there was a light outside the vision-slits. There had been a transmitter of darkness in the destroyed town. Deep in a sub-cellar, evidently, and sending out darkness from a buried aerial. Two hundred pounds of TNT had gone off above it. The transmitter might be destroyed, or it might be merely jammed. But for a space, there was light.

Those in the tank could see that there was a valley all about, and hillsides rearing up on either hand. Except for the inevitable motion of objects past the tank, and four slug-like monsters crawling up a ribbon of concrete road, the tank-officer's main impression was that of utter deadness and lack of motion.

Wind blew upon his own machine with an unbearable, terrible force, but there was no sign of movement outside. There was no dust, no flying débris; there were no clouds. The wind blew with an awful force which had already demolished all things that could be destroyed, and now it kept up a horrible steady pressure that held all things immovable.

The sun shone down from a brazen sky, giving forth no heat, and wind blew and blew and blew.

Utter blackness fell again. Another transmitter of darkness had taken up the work of the one destroyed. And the wandering tank swung about and went crawling after the others on the now-blotted out concrete road.

8

PRESTON'S FORTRESS

HINES GRINNED SAVAGELY, up in the control-room.

"We got one of them!" he said grimly. "We got it by accident, maybe, but we got one of them!"

The speaking-tube whistled. The tank officer answered, then turned to Hines.

"Tank Number Four thinks it has located another station. It is going ahead. The moment of light helped."

Grinding, pounding, roaring progress, with the wind a terrific pressure all about: One minute passed, two, three....

Light again. The leading tank was at the crest of the hill-road. Desolation was all about. Far away—miles and miles away, it seemed—there was a smother of white which would be a lake, with a dark spot upon it which would be a rocky islet.

Again the speaking-tube whistled.

"Number Four reports it set off two bombs. Light came on after the second."

Hines's jaws were clamped tightly.

"Every one destroyed," he said coolly, "helps to get the others. That's two of them, and we've got cats at the mouseholes now!"

Again utter blackness. Mountains, the long straight

stretch of white road descending, the frothing lake and the island at the end of the valley, all were blotted out. There was only the clanking of machinery and the bestial roar of the wind that thrust with a terrible force at the tanks.

Down the long road which no man could see. Despite the wall of wind without, the green mountainsides had seemed strangely inviting. And the sunlight had seemed brighter than ever the sun had seemed before. The deadly blackness was the more intolerable because weary eyes had looked upon the light again.

The machinery clanked and rumbled.

"Number Three tank reports—Number Seven also, that they have located transmitting stations—"

"One of them is wrong, maybe," said Hines coolly, "but let them both try."

The man at the steering-bar said quietly:

"We're nearly out of gas, Lieutenant. I just noticed it. Enough for two more miles, maybe."

The speaking-tube again.

"Number Three tank reports it exploded two bombs. Its station ceased to transmit, but the darkness still holds. Number Seven is letting go now.... Number Two has located a station.... Seven reports its station has ceased to transmit darkness. Number Two is bombing now.... Five has found its station."

"That completes the list," said Hines steadily, "if none of them made a mistake."

Again the voice from below.

"Two has put its station out of action.... Five fell into some sort of excavation. Can't get out at the moment. Asks for orders."

"If the ship can stand hand-grenades," said Hines savagely, "have them tossed out of all ports and see what happens."

Darkness. The pressure of the wind and its terrible steady roar. The noise of the machinery of the tank—

Light!

AGAIN SUNLIGHT. AGAIN the mountains. Again the smother of white which was the lake ahead. The leading tanks advanced heavily until the concrete road divided into two, and one went along each shoreline. This lake had been a summer resort once, but now the trees were splintered and blown away. The houses were utterly destroyed. There was only the uncannily blue sky and the still-green grass carpet of the shores, and a rocky small island half-smothered in foam.

The tank came to a cumbersome halt. Schaaf popped his whiskers through the companionway that led up to the control-room.

"Ha!" he said exuberantly. "We haff der son-of-a-gun! Hines, I haff to take some observations! I think and I suspect, but I haff to be sure where der last of der excitement takes place."

Hines stared about, and then pointed. A stony cliff reared upward some hundreds of yards to the right. It was forty or fifty feet high, and a heap of débris beneath it was proof that it created a lee. He indicated it in silence. The tank crawled heavily, smashing a way into the heaped-up trash.

Its engines coughed and stopped.

"Out of gas, sir," reported some one from below.

"It is no matter," said Schaaf blandly. "I haff a hunch. Der island ofer yonder is a charming place. One could establish a residence there and put in a power-house."

"Get a range-finder reading on it," said Hines curtly. "Have all the tanks range it."

Schaaf was cautiously opening the tank-door. He put one hand cautiously outside.

"Tie a rope around me," he said comfortably, "and I take a chance. There is a wind, but not such a hell of a wind. Der bank makes a lee."

He stepped outside with an electric-light extension and a square sheet of iron. It seemed peculiar, even futile, to be carrying an electric bulb in the overpoweringly bright sunshine. Schaaf balanced himself precariously.

Radiant heat could not be felt from the electric bulb; only in contact with the glass could its heat be detected. It was an exact parallel with the lightwaves that Preston could neutralize, but with a metal plate between the bulb and the source of the neutralizing short waves.

A gun went off not ten feet above his head. Schaaf swore and sat down violently. His necktie flopped about his face, blinding him for an instant. Then he heard the dull concussions of other guns. Every tank was firing madly with every gun it could bring to bear. And Schaaf swore bitterly as he saw what they were firing at.

THERE WAS A little rocky island out in the lake. The lake itself was a smother of white foam. But projecting upward above the water there was a mass of dark-brown rock some fifty or sixty feet high. There were traces of grass still upon it, but if there had been trees they were gone, and if there had been a summer residence that also had long since vanished in the Storm. But now, quite insolently, there was visible a signal of Preston's presence and of his defiance.

A globular mass of darkness had formed about the islet's peak. It looked as if Preston had turned on a transmitter of darkness and had deliberately begun to transmit the short waves with an absolute minimum of power. The fraction of a watt, perhaps, was being put into a hidden or a buried antenna. An irregular, amoeba-like globule of darkness hovered about the islet's tip.

Shells were bursting in and about it. A section of rock split outward from the island's side and fell into the foaming water. Instantly, it seemed, the globule of darkness expanded. From feet, its size could only be measured by hundreds of yards. The tanks were firing into a vast expanse of nothingness, and one by one they ceased to fire. There was nothing to aim at.

Then, very swiftly, the darkness increased in size. Preston was putting more power into his transmitter. And quite suddenly the world was dark again.

It had been a gesture of pure insolence. Tanks could not reach the island. He had seen the gray monsters gathered on the shore, and Preston had blanketed the world in darkness after showing the only men to reach his stronghold the utter futility of further effort to reach him.

He was protected by the deep waters of a mountain lake from attack by tanks, by hills and the Storm from all other means of attack, and by the unthinkable blackness of his own creation even from assault by projectiles.

Up in the control-room, the tank-officer swore bitterly and turned to Hines.

"I think we're done, sir," he said savagely. "We can't wade out through the lake to him, and of course the Storm—"

Hines's eyes were slits.

"Let's look at the map," he said shortly. "We might as well get the other tanks alongside us, by the way. In the lee of this cliff, we can go from one to the other."

He had taken figures from the map before Schaaf came back inside the tank, cursing mightily in German. Hines was asking curt questions and giving even curter orders, and when the other tanks came clanking into place men went out into the alleviated storm beneath the cliff and made demands of gasoline and wire cable and bombs.

Two tanks only had fuel for a run of another two miles. The rest supplied cable and bombs, and men gingerly unscrewed the fuses of the monster bombs and emptied four of the huge cases of all their contents. Then they labored terrifically to bind four still-loaded cases to the emptied ones, and fastened wire cable to the clumsy mass.

All this was done in darkness with the Storm roaring overhead, and while Schaaf was calculating feverishly at Hines's demand and the tank-officer was writing out his results in terms of formal orders, according to the customs and ordinances of the United States Army.

Then the ground quivered as two huge tanks moved away from their fellows. Now was the moment of greatest tension. The bombs had to be dragged over soft earth, and if they exploded with their loads of two hundred pounds each of T.N.T.—eight hundred pounds in the four loaded bombs—then the tank-force would be wiped out and Preston would win his single-handed war against the world. But the fuses had been changed, and they had hopes.

THERE WERE STILL three people up in the control-room
of the tank that had carried Hines. One was Hines, of
course, and one was the tank-commander, and Kathryn
was the third. Hines knew the chance he was taking. If the
tanks were wiped out, he wanted to be near Kathryn when
the end came. Schaaf was down by the wireless transmitter,
biting at his nails and growling guttural profanity at the
intervals between reports.

"Both tanks have reached their first position," came the
report up the speaking-tube. "They're reeling in the cable."

Hines held Kathryn protectively close. But it was rather
useless. They had combined four depth-bombs with four
empty depth-bomb cases to make a monster floating bomb.
They had fastened it in the center of a long, spliced-to-
gether steel cable, with a tank hauling at each end.

Those tanks were now posted where the shores of
the lake began to curve together. They were reeling in
their lines. When the lines tightened, the bomb would
be dragged away from the now fuelless remnant of the
tank-force and out into the water of the lake. With luck,
the bombs would not go off. But if luck were bad, and a
purposely insensitized fuse struck a rock or stone or bit of
débris—

Long minutes went by. The speaking-tube whistle was
a blessed sound.

"Reeling completed, sir. The cable is taut."

Two tanks now went crawling through the blackness
down the opposite shores of the little lake. Between them
stretched the cable with the monstrous floating bomb.

It is well known that fifty pounds of T.N.T. will shatter the walls of a submarine, and that a torpedo carries a

hundred and fifty, and that the effect of an explosion varies as the square of the amount of explosive present. Eight hundred pounds of T.N.T. in one blast would sink any ship or shatter any rock.

But against the massive walls of even a small island?—well, it would produce a concussion. It might shake down fifty tons or a hundred tons of rock. It might do impressive local damage, to be sure, but the damage would be strictly local. The rest of the island would feel nothing worse than a sharp concussion. And that was all Hines could hope for.

Schaaf had assigned arbitrary coördinates and positions for the tanks' reports. When their treads had covered so much ground in such-and-such directions, the cable should be out so much....

"Second position reached," said the speaking-tube briefly. "All figures are as anticipated."

Hines's hands clenched fiercely. The range-finders had given the distance 6f the island. The map had given the outline of the lake. Down the center of the turmoil of frothing water a bomb of colossal destructive power was moving with two straining tanks towing it from the shore, and all for an absurdly trivial physical effect which was all that could be looked for.

"Third position reached," said the speaking-tube. "All figures seem correct. The tanks await orders."

"Tell them to go ahead," said Hines. His voice was hoarse. On this everything depended.

There was no movement inside the tank. There was no sound except the deep, deep roaring of the Storm overhead. But then, quite suddenly, the tank quivered all over. It was as if the ground had slipped, had quivered suddenly; as if it had been struck an abrupt though far from dangerous blow. It was just enough to bring Hines's elbow sharply into contact with the steering-bar.

But suddenly the tank-commander was snapping orders. "Open fire! All guns!"

And the whole inside of the tank resounded with the sledge-hammer blows, the terrific impacts of guns firing at their highest rate.

FOR PERHAPS THE last time, it seemed to Hines, the island was again in view. It was already the center of a storm of bursting shells. There was a colossal wave of water yet subsiding from beside it, and a huge column of rock was topping soundlessly and very deliberately into the lake, and every tank on the lake-shore was pouring shell after shell after shell upon the mass of stone that remained.

Hines had made his last gamble. The destruction of the other darkness-sending stations by concussions seemed to him to show one possible weakness in Preston's preparations.

It was not likely that in every case the dropped time-bombs that had put the other darkness-transmitters out of action, had made direct hits upon the apparatus. It seemed most probable that Preston, like all other experimenters with radio waves, had used vacuum tubes for his oscillators. And vacuum tubes are made of glass, and they are thin, therefore concussion will break them.

Hines had not expected the shock of the explosion against the island's rocky shore to destroy Preston's apparatus. Not at all. He had only hoped for a single sharp shock, a single smart snapping effect.

As a matter of fact, on the island itself there had been

exactly the impression of a sudden and terrific earth-shock. And it was sudden enough to make the glass vacuum tubes of the short-wave transmitter shiver to atoms in their sockets. The transmitter was quite unharmed, but it was thoroughly useless after that!

Watching, with the flashes of high-explosive shells breaking about every portion of the island, Hines saw a sudden thick cloud of smoke arise. It was too dense, too thick, to be dissipated even by the wind which still blew madly. And great cracks appeared in the rocks of the island, and steam poured forth.

Schaaf went out of the tank with his hands over his ears. He held up his face to the sun and abruptly began to dance with a wholly elephantine lack of grace. Because the sun's rays were warm!

Gradually, slowly, the tanks ceased firing. They exhausted their ammunition upon their target, and the surface of the island was a mass of splintered rock and steam poured in dense clouds from its interior.

Then it was possible to hear Schaaf bellowing.

"Der storm-wafes are off! Der storm-wafes are off! We got der son-of-a-gun! We got him!"

And very abruptly, it seemed, clouds were forming overhead, and the wind of the Storm began to change from a monstrous steady blast to something no worse than a mere tornado, and in an hour it was hardly more than a terrific gale.

Before nightfall thunder was rolling over a circle two thousand miles across, and rain was falling in torrents only precedented by the night before. Two weeks or more of chaotic weather conditions were being predicted by the weather bureaus, but after that the air conditions would again become normal.

SCHAAF WAS THE first man on the island, and his gloomiest predictions were verified. Preston's apparatus had been destroyed by explosions from below. Not only had explosives been placed by Preston to ruin the apparatus and prevent it from being examined, but great masses of thermit had been placed here and there to complete the destruction. Apparently, Preston had intended to destroy his devices when their use was completed, and so had been prepared, by accident, for the disaster that came upon his plans. No notes, no diagrams, no single article of any value to Schaaf was ever found, on which account he swore bitterly. But a human skeleton was found charred and half-consumed in the ruins of the underground workshop. It was assumed to be Preston, but Schaaf regarded even this hopeful thought with disfavor.

He expressed his bitterness after a complete round of the six other transmitting-stations showed them all destroyed with thermit and explosive, apparently by some contrivance which would act automatically when they were no longer operable.

"Der *verdammt* scoundrel," he said bitterly to Hines. "He gifes me a pain in der duodenum. If I had der information he had, I would be der greatest benefactor of der world! I haff an idea, and if I can only find out how he did his tricks, I show you der Golden Age again! *Ach, Gott!* Why is it that fillains haff der best brains?"

He was smoking furiously in Hines's apartment when he made his plaint. The telephone rang. Hines spoke into it, smiling. When he had ended, Schaaf said suspiciously:

"That was Miss Bush. She is clefer, Hines. But—is she too clefer?"

"Did you see how she wrote up the whole business for the *Star?*"

Schaaf nodded, and puffed at his pipe.

"She made you a hero, and me a hero, and she threw enough flowers at der tank-men to make der worldt see how brafe and courageous and altogether der cat's-whiskers you are, Hines. Yes. She is clefer. But as your friend I ask it; is she too clefer?"

Hines was standing up, now, and absently looking at his hat on a nearby chair.

"Too clever?" he repeated abstractedly, but smiling nevertheless. "What is too clever?"

"A woman," said Schaaf shrewdly, "that makes eferybody see how clefer der man she lofes is, is clefer. But when she sees that she has brains also, and that when she marries she will haff to take der back seat, and she sees that she is a darned fool to do it—then she is too clefer."

"She's not," said Hines blithely. "She's going to marry me. In fact, we're going down town now to pick out some rings and such things." He added perfunctorily: "Want to come along?"

"Nix," said Schaaf cynically. "You don't want me now. But I come in, Hines, *ach,* I come in when it is time to buy der teething-rings and der baby-mugs. Then I won't be in der way!"

THE MAN WHO PUT OUT THE SUN

"As Surely As The Sun Will Rise To-Morrow"
Goes The Saying—But That Day The Sun Did
Not Rise, And The Blinded World Was At The
Mercy Of A Merciless Scientific Madman

1

THE MORNING THE
SUN DIDN'T RISE

MAY THE FIFTH was scheduled to be Police Inspector Hines's wedding day, but it happened that on that morning the sun did not rise, and so the wedding was postponed.

Otherwise it was just like every other morning. There were no storms, no earthquakes, no unusual phenomena of any kind. A great many people, as a matter of fact, simply disbelieved their clocks when they got up and therefore yawned and went back to bed again.

Others, checking up with the telephone company's time, reasoned sensibly that there was an eclipse or something of the sort, and searched the morning newspapers for details while they breakfasted by artificial light. But the morning newspapers, at least on the Atlantic Coast, bore only their usual quotas of divorces, embezzlements, ax murders and other diverting narratives. Having been printed during the night, they were entirely silent about the sun's eccentric absence. So it was quite a few hours before people became really alarmed.

Probably the first man in the United States to notice any oddity in the morning was a man wearing a green celluloid eyeshade, in the operating office of New York's gigantic

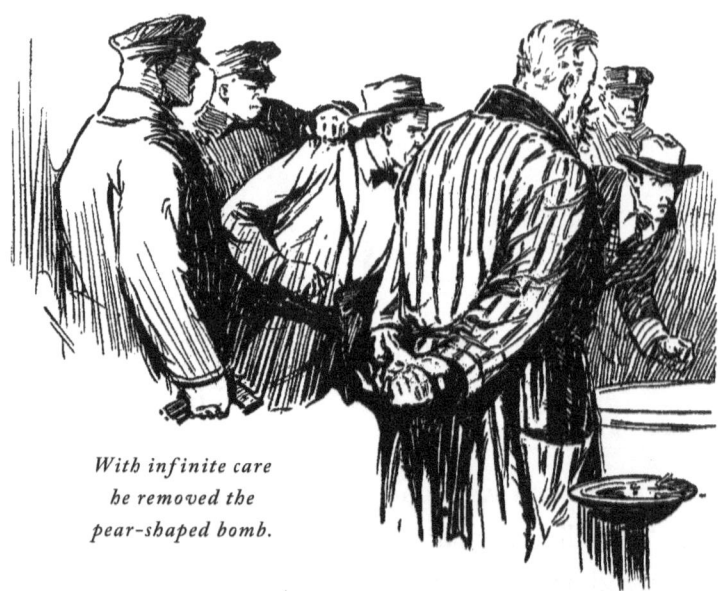

*With infinite care
he removed the
pear-shaped bomb.*

uptown power station. He has no importance in the affair other than that priority.

He sat in a very brilliantly lighted office with a huge instrument board before him, on which were vast numbers of dials. A recording ammeter ticked away at his left, tracing a graph of current-consumption for one-half of the whole city. A master voltmeter and a visual master ammeter were just before his eyes.

There were windows on two sides of the room. Through them he could look out over the sleeping city. Long rows of unwinking street lights glittered in deserted avenues. The forms of the East River bridges were outlined in lines of fire. The city was silent and still, sleeping heavily. What few noises came from the empty streets seemed extraordinarily loud.

The man with the green eyeshade opened a window and took grateful breaths of the cool morning air. He was in

his shirt sleeves, with his vest unbuttoned. It was hot in the office, with that peculiarly dry and stuffy heat with which we Americans fill our office buildings.

From far below, in the vast halls of the power station, there came a constant subdued, contented humming. Turbine-driven dynamos purred softly, making the electric current which supplied alike the street lamps and the buildings of half the city.

FROM THE OTHER windows he could see toward the east, over the sprawling bulk of Brooklyn toward the sea. There was a faint, pale-grayish glow in the sky. False dawn. Stars began to dim against its brightness. Gradually, very gradually, the dark shapes of buildings began to take form? There were no colors in the sky as yet, merely a subdued gray radiance. But a paler reflection of that pale gray light made rectangular shapes out of irregular bulks.

From the windows of the operating office the city ceased to be a pattern of glittering lights against the dark.

It acquired a third dimension. Perspectives developed, and it was possible to discover that this dim, ungainly shape was nearer or farther away than that one.

The man with the green eyeshade—his name does not matter—lowered the window and went back to his seat. It was his task to forecast the demand of the city for power, and to see to it that there were always humming steel monster dynamos in readiness to supply that force.

An easy task, ordinarily. Framed upon the wall at his left, a typical graph of the city's consumption of electricity showed the normal use of current. From six to eight at night, when people dined and electric signs flared, and all dwellings were lighted up, the demand was at its peak. Then more lights burned. More cooking devices functioned. More current was consumed by all the contrivances of an electrified civilization.

The downtown power station had a lesser peak at this hour, but its greatest load came when electrically-driven power devices of lofts and factories were operating. Uptown, the peak load came from homes.

The man in the operating office rested his hand conveniently near a certain switch. It would signal for the cutting off of certain dynamos, assigned to run the street lighting system. He waited for those lights to be extinguished. He did not look out the window for his information, but at his master ammeter. When that needle flickered back to the normal indication for this hour, the dynamos below would cease to run until needed again. Most of the monster machines were idle now, anyhow.

Presently there would come a slow creeping upward, when a myriad early risers turned on lights for their dressing. The master ammeter would record that activity. And then ten thousand electric toasters would perform their function, beginning with half an hour after sunrise, and from then on would come the steady increase in the amount of current used, until ten o'clock would see the last electric dish-washing device turned off; and the normal load of elevators, curling irons, and other trivia would require only two giant generators to run until the noon hour approached.

The man with the green eyeshade waited. The needle held steady. The street lights had not been turned off. Presently there was a slow climb upward. A myriad early risers, wakened by their alarm clocks, had turned on their lights. Time passed slowly. The load increased again. Electric toasters were functioning, and eggs were being boiled.

The man in the operating office of the uptown power station could follow the activities of a city by watching a single giant dial. But he was frowning a little. The load was increasing. There was no drop. His eyes sought a clock at hand. Just the time for sunrise. The load continued to increase.

FROWNING, HE SHIFTED his hand and swung another switch. A hitherto silent, idle monster below began to hum contentedly. Watching the dial, presently he threw another switch. Still another began to purr, down in the echoful open space where metal monsters lay quiescent.

A telephone rang beside him. He spoke impatiently.

"I don't know. That's what the load calls for." He lifted his eyes and searched a row of circuit ammeters. "No. Everything's all right. If you have to start up another boiler, better go ahead."

A few minutes later, frowning more markedly than before, he lifted the instrument and called himself.

"Get three extra boilers ready. I'm going to need them unless the load falls off."

He watched his instruments in frowning, concentrated attention. He was entirely too busy to glance out of the window. Twice he looked at a clock and at the graph on the wall. Three times the normal demand for power at this time. Now four times.

He called for more boilers to supply steam. Discipline in the power plant is as strict, of course, as in any naval vessel. Orders are obeyed. More and more of the metal monsters whirred and whined and purred themselves into a contented humming.

Eight o'clock. The man with the green eyeshade bit at his nails. Then he looked out of the window. Three seconds of incredulous gazing, and he picked up the telephone instrument.

"Prepare for peak loading," he said curtly. "There's an eclipse or something. It's still dark outdoors."

And from then on he glanced at the windows as often as at his instruments. It was dark outside. At eight o'clock in the morning the street lights of New York were glittering jewels set in rows. The East River bridges were limned in lines of glowing lights. Puzzled people began to appear upon the streets. Store fronts were lighted. Windows in apartments and in private homes began to glow in vivid small rectangles.

At half past eight the man in the green eyeshade raised the window and stared shakenly upward. The sky was a dull, dead, velvety black. No stars were visible. No trace of illumination; no faintest ray of light came down from above. The city lived and moved and had its being in what would have been an entirely normal fashion—for night-time. Nothing at all had happened. Nothing whatever had occurred. The only oddity that could be discovered anywhere was simply the fact that on that morning the sun had not risen.

2

A WORLD IN DARKNESS

NOT EVERYWHERE DID the phenomenon of darkness make its appearance so quietly. In London a bright sunshiny morning had been in being. The streets were filled with traffic. Children played in Kensington Gardens. Small tugs puffed importantly up and down the rather inadequate Thames.

In the houses of Parliament an impassioned debate was going on upon the subject of the manorial rights surviving in the village of Muttle Deeping, West Harborough, Hants. At the palace, a popular member of the royal family was in the act of entering a motor car to lay his fourth cornerstone for the week. London was, it is clear, in the middle of a normal, sunshiny morning.

Then the sky flickered, and all at once it was night. The sky was a dead, jet black. For a moment the city was stunned, before motor car headlights flamed into being. Two minutes later electric light bulbs began to glow in buildings. They dimmed, however, as the drain upon the power houses grew far more swiftly than the dynamos could be prepared to meet the load.

It was half an hour before the street lamps began to glow dully, and over an hour and a half before the city was illuminated as in a normal night, by which time the first and natural explanation of an eclipse in being was patently untrue. No eclipse ever lasted so long. And panic swept over London and all England.

In Budapest the darkness fell at high noon. In Madrid at eleven. At Stamboul—Constantinople—the sky was blotted out while myriads of the faithful bowed in prayer. In Calcutta the colors of the sunset were wiped out by an instantaneous curtain of utter darkness.

At Flagstaff, Arizona, an astronomer was peering patiently through a giant telescope at the planet Mars when the planet and all the stars beyond abruptly seemed to cease to be. He thought the telescope had met with some accident. Even later, when from the outside of the observatory the whole sky was seen to be blotted out, he still thought the obscuration due to an extremely heavy bank of clouds. But he puzzled bewilderedly over the suddenness of their forming.

Professor Schaaf was probably the first man in the whole world to evaluate the phenomenon at its true value. As May the fifth was the wedding day of his bosom friend Hines, Schaaf had spent the previous night at his flat, to listen patiently to the advantages of matrimony. He had shooed Hines benevolently to bed at two in the morning, and had slept peacefully himself. But at seven Schaaf was awake and found it dark outside.

The scientist looked at his watch and blinked, and listened to its ticking. He got up and stared out over the city, illuminated as if at midnight and already stirring. He saw the bright ribbon of an elevated train, several blocks away. He could see that it was filled with people.

He went to the telephone and called the apartment telephone operator. The Negro's voice came up gladly:

"Ya-as, suh, Professuh Schaaf! Seben o'clock. But, professuh! Ah wish yo'd tell me 'bout dishere eclipse. Hit's dark outside, suh. How long's the eclipse goin' to last, suh? Sev'l of the tenants done asked me a'ready, suh."

Schaaf grunted, and turned around to squint out of the windows again.

"Der deffil! Hm… Giff me der Meteorological Bureau. Find der number and call me back. I find out."

He padded to a window in carpet slippers. He heard Hines breathing evenly and regularly in the next room. Schaaf raised a window and stared up at the sky. An even, velvety black. No variation anywhere. As black as ink-blacker. Blacker than the darkness of an eclipse, because even during the moments of totality the stars can be seen. And starlight even upon a thick blanket of clouds would give more light than this.

Schaaf put down the window, blinking. He stood quite still, a disreputable figure in dressing gown and slippers, with his luxuriant blond beard uncombed. And suddenly his eyes opened very wide, and he began to swear softly to himself.

HE WENT BACK to the telephone.

"Der Meteorological Bureau? Professor Albert Schaaf speaking. Will you giff me der *bolometer* reading of der moment?… Der bolometer reading! Der amount of heat being radiated to der earth from der sky! Yes!"

He fumed and fretted while the telephone receiver was silent. Then he became intent.

"Yes… Hm… That is larger than a night reading, *hein?*…

What would be der reading during der moments of totality of an eclipse?…"

He shook his head impatiently. "Nefer mind der corrections for latitude. Abbroximate! Giff me der figures!"

Again he fumed nervously.

"Fery well. Thank you. Abbroximately one-fourth der normal amount of heat is being radiated to der earth from der sky. Which is too much for an eclipse, and fery much too much for night-time. I thank you. I thought I was cuckoo in der head."

He hung up the receiver and swore classic German profanity while he jiggled the hook.

"Der *verdammt* deffil!" he said bitterly; then, into the telephone: "Get police headquarters at once. Hurry!"

He scowled at the universe, represented by a section of Hines's library wall, until a voice answered.

"Hello!" he said savagely into the transmitter. "This is der Herr Professor Albert Schaaf. You know me?"

A prompt affirmative came over the wire. In those few circles where Schaaf was unknown on his own account— few indeed after his notable part in battling the scientific fiend Preston—he was known as a friend of Police Inspector Hines, who had directed those fights.

"Now listen carefully. I am in Hines's apartment. He is still asleep. I haff not wakened him because he is going to need sleep before this thing is finished. But I giff an order in his name. Send some police at once to giff adequate protection to Miss Kathryn Bush, who is to marry Inspector Hines to-day. I haff reason to think she is in danger. Send them at once, and send plenty of them! You understand?"

A grunt of astonishment at the other end of the wire. Then the incisive voice of a man of action.

"Good!" said Schaaf, nodding into the telephone transmitter. "Fery good. And then if you haff more men to spare, send them up to watch ofer Hines and me. We need them. And speed is der essence of der contract."

The incisive voice asked a question.

"Think!" said Schaaf sardonically. "Look out of der window and think, if you can, of one man who makes a specialty of raising hell with der heafens, and who has no fondness for Hines and me. That is der answer. Good-by!"

He hung up decisively, drummed nervously on his knee, and called Kathryn Bush. She was not only Hines's fiancée, she was a very capable newspaper woman, and Schaaf alternately scolded and flattered her outrageously. He liked Kathryn very much, and since Hines was going to marry somebody, Schaaf approved his choice.

Her voice came clearly, hurried and uneasy.

"Hello! What is it?"

"Miss Bush," began Schaaf apologetically, "I am sorry that I am not Hines, but—"

"I'm leaving now," said Kathryn in a strained voice. "How is he, Professor Schaaf? Is he conscious yet?"

Sweat stood out suddenly on Schaaf's forehead.

"*Gott in Himmel!*" he said unsteadily. "I am just in time! Miss Bush! What kind of message haff you got? Hines is all right. There is nothing wrong. What haff you heard?"

Her voice—doubtful and desperately anxious—came over the wire, "Your note said there'd been an explosion and you both were hurt—"

"It is a forgery!" snapped Schaaf. "For der lofe of Gott,

do not leafe your apartment! Call to der police! Raise der deffil! But stay where you are! Did you not look out of der window?"

There was a little pause, and he heard her gasp of amazement.

"I—I was awakened by the message," she said unsteadily, "and I didn't think of anything.... It's Preston, isn't it?"

"Der bolometer-reading has his name on it," said Schaaf grimly. "I haff telephoned der police to go to your house at once. I haff not waked up Hines, because I just found out what has happened. It must be der Heaviside Layer gone cuckoo. Stay where you are!"

"I will. I—I'm glad you telephoned."

"And so am I," said Schaaf from his heart. "You will telephone, Miss Bush, efery few minutes until der police come? They are on der way, but it may be minutes yet before you are safe. I am going to wake up Hines now."

"A-all right," said Kathryn. "Don't be afraid for me."

He heard the click of her receiver on its hook. And Schaaf wiped great droplets of sweat from his face.

"That deffil," he said unsteadily. "Oh, that damned deffil!"

HE WENT PADDING into Hines's bedroom and shook the sleeping man. Outside, the world was dark save for a multitude of electric bulbs, which pierced the darkness with the effect of magic. Elevated trains were roaring all over the city, now. The people of the cities of the Atlantic coastline took the sun's absence with a quite astounding calmness. They classed the darkness as that of an eclipse, and thousands of offices opened, and hundreds of factories began their work with nearly full forces of workers on hand, though the telephone switchboards were nearly swamped with vain demands on the newspaper offices and weather bureau for information they did not have.

In his bedroom, Hines sat up and blinked, and was wide awake. He grinned at Schaaf.

"Good morning! This is my wedding day, isn't it?"

"I haff my doubts," said Schaaf soberly. "Hines, damned near der worst has happened. Breston is on der job again."

Hines was on his feet in seconds. "Kathryn—?"

"Is all right," said Schaaf. "I telephoned her minutes ago. She is all right and she is going to stay all right. Look out of der window and then at der clock."

Hines stared blankly. Brightly lighted streets. Brilliantly illuminated stores. Elevated trains like streamers of fire, moving along distant steel trestles. Eight o'clock in the morning, and the sky was black with an utter, unrelieved blackness.

"But—it's night!" said Hines blankly.

"Verdamm!" said Schaaf impatiently. "Of course it is night! Night in der morning." He dropped into one of the wholly incongruous slang phrases that adorned his speech. "You are darned tooting it is night, Hines! Der sun did not rise this morning."

"The—sun—did—not—rise—this morning," said Hines slowly. "I—see."

The telephone rang shrilly. Hines started, and moved to answer it, while Schaaf stared out at the incredible darkness that lay upon the world, hours after daylight should have appeared.

His identification of the darkness with a man named Preston was not an accident, of course. There was just one man in the world who could cause meteorological disturbances on a large scale, and the three previous disturbances of Preston's creation had been somewhat like this.

It was one of Schaaf's bitternesses that he had unwittingly helped in the development of the apparatus which had done so much harm. More than a year before, he had done some highly abstruse technical research for an electrophysicist named Preston. Schaaf's share had been the determination of the mass and dimensions of the ionized bodies in atmospheric air.

He had done that work, not guessing the devilish application to be made of it, for his fare back to his native Germany, since there seemed to be no room for a theoretic physicist in the United States. But before he sailed, he had been drafted by his present friend Hines to combat the danger his measurements had enabled Preston to create.

Using Schaaf's figures in his basic calculations, Preston had developed a way to make the air opaque, black, as horribly black as the ocean's deepest abyss. And he had done it. To be sure, heretofore he had confined his blackness to the surface of the earth, but that dull, dead, velvety sky overhead was like nothing as much as the darkness Preston produced.

Schaaf did not know what Preston had done now, or how he had done it, but that Preston was responsible he was sure.

THERE WAS A sudden blaring of horns down in the street. Minutes later, the clang of the elevator door outside the apartment. Then the doorbell.

Schaaf opened the door cautiously, with Hines's service revolver in the pocket of his dressing-gown pointed and ready. There were men in uniform in the hall, with only two figures in civilian clothes, one of whom carried a tripod and camera. Schaaf fixed those two with a distinctly unpleasant expression.

"Grab those two persons, please," he said shortly, "and bring them inside here. Inspector Hines will talk in a fery few seconds."

Hines hung up, smiling grimly, as they all crowded within. He nodded.

"That was Kathryn," he said briefly.

"Thanks, Schaaf!"

The words said little. The tone said a great deal. Schaaf rumbled in his beard and indicated the spattering civilians. One of them was snarling.

Hines regarded them with a grim meditativeness.

"Who are these two men?" he asked softly.

"Lookin' for you, sir," said a sergeant of police, woodenly. "When Professor Schaaf called up for a detail to come up at once, sir, he said you were in danger. And these men were just asking for you at the switchboard downstairs, sir, and they tried to bolt—"

"I'm a reporter for the *Messenger*," snapped one of the two angrily, "and this man is one of our staff photographers. There's some talk that Preston's back of the sun not rising, and we came here to ask—"

Hines nodded pleasantly.

"Ah!" he said softly. "But reporters don't talk like that. If you were really a reporter you'd say, 'I'm from the *Messenger*' or maybe that you were 'on the *Messenger*,' but never that you were a reporter 'for the *Messenger*.' Never! Search 'em, sergeant!"

A search of the suddenly blaspheming man disclosed

a pair of heavy automatics and no newspaper credentials whatever. The supposed photographer yielded the same, with a pair of brass knuckles as additional armament.

Hines smiled.

"It looks as if you two men came from Preston. You may be interested to hear that the attempt to kidnap Miss Bush has failed, and the taxi driver who waited below for her has been pinched. He's going to talk. Are you two going to tell what you know?"

The pseudo-reporter snarled and shut his lips tightly. He stared meaningly at the other man. The other man shook his head. Hines watched the by-play.

"Sergeant, I seem to remember that you were on the bomb squad once. That camera seems to be unusually heavy. Suppose you open it up-carefully?"

The sergeant lifted the camera, turned it this way and that, and began to use a penknife. He handled the thing gingerly after the first two or three incisions. Minutes later, with a grunt of satisfaction, he laid down a pear-shaped bomb upon the table. Dangling from it there was the exposure device, which here evidently functioned as a means of setting it off.

THE TWO MEN in civilian clothes regarded the thing in gray-faced stupefaction. Hines looked at them. One of them tried to speak, and could not.

"You see," said Hines shortly, "it's a bomb. If you'd pulled the trigger, it would have blown us all to bits. But especially you. If I know Preston, he told you it was some kind of gun. Eh?"

The photographer croaked, abandoning all pose of innocence: "He tol' us it was a trick machine gun, an' if we sprayed y' wit' it—"

"At a guess," said Hines dryly, "it's combined high explosive and poison gas. That would seem logical. If I wasn't killed by the explosion, the gas would get me. You two men would be finished either way. A much better bet than a machine gun… How much were you to get for standing behind this thing and setting it off?"

The pseudo-reporter cursed horribly.

"Ten grand, damn his soul!" he raged. "And him sending us to bump ourselves off—"

"I'll give you ten grand," said Hines evenly, "for the dope on where to find him. Ten grand, and immunity."

"All I know," said the photographer hoarsely, "is he give us five grand ahead o' time an' said we'd get the rest if we croaked yuh. We don't know where he's at. We seen him yesterday in Brooklyn."

"Right," said Hines. "Tell me where and when you saw him, and you go clear."

The two men gave an address, and, to a second question, the time of their talk. Hines went to the telephone and asked for a number.

"All right, sergeant," he said impatiently, while he waited. "Turn 'em loose. And you two men remember there's ten grand in it for you if you get him. There's that much for anybody that gets him. And you'll get well taken care of if you tip off the man who gets him. Clear out!"

The two men stumbled to the door, too much shaken by the knowledge that they had been intended to blow themselves to bits, to be incredulous about their release.

Hines got his connection, in Brooklyn. He ordered a

raid at once, with a succinct statement that Preston—who was sufficiently well known by name to the police and the nation at large—had been there the day before. He stood up.

"Why did you turn them loose?" demanded Schaaf irritably.

The doorbell rang. Hines nodded to a policeman to open it, and said dryly:

"Those two men spreading that offer and news of Preston's double crossing are a lot more useful out of jail than in… What've we got here?"

Three messenger boys had arrived simultaneously with sheafs of telegrams, radios, and cables. The extraordinary nightfall had been reasoned out in six nations as possibly an extension of certain previous events in the United States. The cables were mostly addressed to Schaaf, and were from every variety of scientific body and government authority, reporting the sudden falling of darkness and asking if he could explain its cause or possible duration.

Schaaf opened the first of them and swore. He opened more, and swore more luridly. He was sputtering German profanity in a steady stream before he reached the end of them. He looked up, still in his dressing-gown and slippers, and with his blond beard bristling in every direction, to find the room empty of police and Hines hunched over the telephone, talking quietly.

"Better get some clothes on, Schaaf," said Hines. "Kathryn's coming over here. We're going down to my office."

Schaaf scowled at him.

"Hines," he said hopelessly, "der *verdammt* scoundrel has cofered der whole world with darkness! I know what it is, of course. Fife to fifteen miles up in der air, all of er der earth, there is a layer of ionization. It is der Heaviside Layer, which raises der deffil with wireless telegraphy. Breston has somehow managed to penetrate it, and he has filled it with an electric field which makes der air *no longer transparent*. Der whole world is in darkness, and there is no way in which we can possibly locate der sending-station. Because he has practically charged der entire roof of der world with darkness. What are we going to do?"

Hines grinned.

"I've already got him located within a couple of hundred miles," he said dryly. "Get busy finding out what he's got, and I'll find where he is, and together we'll settle him."

3

___

TO STEAL A WORLD

THE MORNING PASSED in unbroken darkness. Traffic thickened, grew dense, and thinned out again. Two million people, balked of information from the usual sources, were asking two other million people what they thought about the darkness, and the second two million were telling the first that they didn't know what to make of it, but so-and-so was going down to the office and there was no use being docked for absence.

Crowds filled the subway platforms and the elevated trains, and other crowds swarmed up and down from the rapid-transit stations and split up into infinitesimal fragments which coalesced at the entrances to office buildings, and always the topic of conversation was the extraordinary, inexplicable continuation of night.

Modern civilized man, however, pays the very minimum of attention to the natural part of his environment. There are literally hundreds of thousands of people in New York who are outdoors less than one hour in twenty-four. To those people the absence of daylight was an extremely trivial matter. Something to be puzzled about and something to ask questions about, but not especially anything to be worried about.

In the lesser cities of the United States, of course, the darkness loomed more largely. In the small towns it was a matter of immediate and overwhelming importance. In the villages it produced apprehension bordering on panic. On the farms it was stark tragedy. But on the whole the matter was taken with a surprising calmness. If it was a precarious sort of composure, likely to break into mob hysteria at any moment, it was nevertheless composure.

But the darkness held for hour after hour, unbroken and menacing. Ten o'clock arrived. Half past ten. Eleven. The sky remained a jetty black. The temperature of the air fell below the daunting chill which normally fills the small hours before dawn.

People in the offices and factories had worked almost gayly at first, taking the use of artificial light in daytime as a sort of adventure. But as time went on and the unwontedly protracted night continued, little groups gathered at windows, staring out uneasily.

The interchange of questions about the darkness ceased to be jocular. The adventure became serious. Concern deepened to apprehension. More and more offices were quietly closed for the day. More and more factories announced a holiday. A stream of homeward-bound folk began to crowd the elevated trains and subways.

The newspaper extras were late in getting out, and Hines, cooperating and conferring with the Washington authorities, was responsible. He had put police on guard at the publishing offices, and would not let one copy of the newspapers leave the publishing plants until he had made provision for the public reaction.

The subway and elevated lines needed to be prepared

for a monster homeward rush. Traffic squads needed to be reenforced. The reserves of the police department posted themselves, at strategic points, the elevated and subway lines prepared for a jam, and the newspapers were unleashed.

All over the city a chorus of voices was upraised, crying extra editions. In ten thousand office buildings the elevators became jammed with folk going down to buy them. And the subway tunnels roared and rumbled with empty trains rushing down town to carry back the mob that within minutes would be fighting for places.

The newspapers were much alike, though Kathryn Bush's story in the *Star* was naturally the one which gave the fullest account. All the papers, however, had reasonably complete accounts of the phenomenon. This was no time to play favorites. And nearly all of them printed Schaaf's explanation in full. He had lectured for nearly half an hour in Hines's office at police headquarters, and his explanation—though given so promptly—still holds good.

"LAST YEAR," **SAID** Schaaf, "there was a sudden flood of darkness on Fifth Afenue, and there were many robberies. Hines and myself, we discofered that a deffil named Breston had done it. He had learned that under der influence of certain fery short Hertzian wafes, der air ceases to be transparent. Actually, it was der phenomenon of der fluorescence of der ionized bodies in der atmosphere, when they absorbed all der fisible colors of light and emitted infisible ones instead.

"Der essential thing is that der air is opaque, there is no light. Now, three times, so far, those short short wafes haff been used. Once on Fifth Afenue. Once der whole city was made dark. Some few months ago Breston created a storm in der Catskill Mountains by means of der fact that when der air is no longer transparent it absorbs der heat of der sun, becomes hot, and rises in huge folumes."

All this, of course, was ancient history. Everybody knew it. The Storm That Had to be Stopped was one of the most distressing catastrophes in the history of the United States.

"Now, at der time of der Storm," Schaaf went on bitterly, "when we got to der sending-station which sent out der short short wafes, we blew it to pieces and der storm Stopped. But der apparatus for making those short short wafes had had thermit and explosifes placed about it, so that it was destroyed. Breston did that. Also we found der body of a man, burned with der explosifes and der thermit. Der newspapers printed that it was the body of Breston. We hoped it was so. But later infestigation profed that it was not. Breston is fife feet three inches tall. Der dead body was fife feet nine inches tall.

"For months past, Inspector Hines has been defoting all his time to a search for Breston. And I haff worked on der problem of combating der short wafes. *Himmel!* How I haff worked! But in both cases, Breston has so far kept ahead of us. This morning's darkness is of Breston's contrifance. But we haff licked him three times before, we will lick him again, and anything that he says to der contrary is banana oil!"

SO FAR, SCHAAF was quoted verbatim. But the rest of his lecture was expanded in most of the papers, because Schaaf's mixture of technical terms and slang was confusing. The essence of his explanation, though, was very simple.

To make the earth's whole atmosphere opaque would

have required millions of billions of horse-power. But far above the surface of the earth the Heaviside Layer in the atmosphere seemed as if made for Preston's purposes. From five to fifteen miles up there is an abrupt change in the characteristics of the air. At that height there is a layer of highly ionized air, markedly electrically conducting, which spreads over the whole earth. Schaaf likened it to a roof of conducting metal over the whole earth.

It was clear that if the short short waves of Preston's discovery could be introduced into that conducting layer of the atmosphere, they would spread out over the whole earth with but little loss of power. Five thousand horse-power would do it.

"Der thing we do not yet understand," said Schaaf, "is how Breston manages to introduce his short short-wafes into der Heaviside Layer. We will find it out, fery shortly. Breston cannot bring der darkness down to der surface of der earth, because he can haff power enough to darken only a small part of it, and der moment he does that we locate him, and when we locate him we kill him. And sooner or later we locate him anyhow!"

His expressed optimism was not altogether unfeigned, of course. He had the desperate certitude of a man who simply dares not admit the possibility of failure. At the moment that the newspapers were blazoning his announcement on their front pages, Schaaf was actually in something close to despair.

LONG, EXPLORATIVE FINGERS of light were poking upward toward the sky, from warships anchored in the harbor. Half a dozen giant ships of the Atlantic Fleet were in port. Army tanks had been loaned Hines to destroy

Preston's storm-making apparatus, and all the resources of the government, of course, would be used to restore sunlight to the world again.

The harbor was smoothly rippling, almost oily on its surface. Long lights glimmered on its waves. Then, suddenly, from the flagship of the fleet there came three or four staccato detonations. Seconds later there were thin crackling explosions high overhead. The searchlights shot back and forth, searching the roof over the world.

A little later, three or four more explosions. After a longer interval, brittle detonations high above. The searchlights moved restlessly over the ebon ceiling of the earth. And still again came the sharp sound of an anti-aircraft gun firing at an empty sky.

The searchlights followed a thin thread of whitish vapor upward. It stretched like a kite-string toward the sky. It was the trail of tracer-smoke left by the anti-aircraft shell.

Blinkers began to operate on the ships. A man on shore spoke crisply into a telephone.

Schaaf got the message, frowning bitterly in his despair. "Yes. I haff it. Thank you."

He was in Hines's office, waiting for the information. An anti-aircraft gun had fired time-fused shells to burst at progressively greater heights. The shell which burst at an elevation of forty-two thousand feet had been unseen, because its cloud of smoke had been formed inside the now opaque Heaviside Layer of the atmosphere. The layer of darkness which kept the whole world deep in night was eight miles above the surface.

"What can we do, Hines?" demanded Schaaf in despair. "Can we send an afiator up eight miles to do intricate obserfations with delicate apparatus? We cannot. Then how are we going to locate der point of dissemination of der *verdammt* darkness-producing wafes?"

Hines held up his hand, spoke quietly into a telephone. He was deathly pale, but Schaaf was too excited to notice it.

"We're coming along pretty well," said Hines grimly, "except that you've still got to find out more about Preston's weapons. I think I know, roughly, where he is."

Schaaf sat up and blinked.

"It's been apparent from the first that when we do locate Preston we have everything in our favor. We have an army we can fling against him, on land. We have aircraft to attack him by air. We can send the shells from fourteen inch guns against him from the sea. He knows all that."

Schaaf ran his fingers through his beard. "Shoot der works," he said harassedly.

"The President received a letter from him telling what his demands are going to be. Other governments have got similar letters. He's fighting the whole world, and he knows it. What weapons has he got?"

"Darkness," said Schaaf bitterly, "and storms, and a total lack of humanity."

"And we have all the other weapons. Where can he defend himself, with the weapons he has, if we do locate him?"

Schaaf scratched his chin, underneath his beard.

"Wherefer he is. Tell me, Hines."

"If he's on an island," said Hines, "he can't be attacked by an army. If he can blind any ship within twenty or thirty miles by making all the atmosphere—not only the Heaviside Layer—opaque to light, no ship can navigate to that island. And if he cuts the darkness on the rest of the world, he can make a storm that will sink any ship or wreck any aircraft in the world."

"He is on an island!" said Schaaf instantly. "Of course he is on an island! But where?"

"HE GAVE HIMSELF away," said Hines grimly. "He talked to his assassins, in Brooklyn, just fourteen hours before the darkness went on. And he wouldn't trust anybody else to work an affair the size of this, so he's at his darkness plant. At most he's not more than twelve hours from New York. More probably only ten. And the last eleven of those hours were night hours, and there are no night-flying passenger air lines out of the metropolitan district now. He traveled by train or boat or motor car. Averaging, he's not more than four hundred miles from New York if he made the longest part of his journey by train or car. He's probably not less than two hundred, for reasons of discretion. Here's a map. Draw the two circles—two hundred miles and four hundred miles away. We can block off the land between the circles. He isn't there. We can block off the area where there are no islands. If he needs to make a storm, he'll want to be on an island, not a steamer."

Schaaf looked at the area that was left.

"Der Maine coast!"

"Of course," said Hines. "And now remember he wants an island well out at sea so storms can sweep clear around it, and one that's fairly isolated, so he could have built his plant without attracting attention."

Schaaf scrutinized the map with painstaking care.

"Hm. This little speck looks promising, Hines."

Hines said grimly, "The police of New England have

been questioning fishermen. I mentioned that island especially. Only one man has been near it recently. He was ordered off by guards who told him a rich man had bought it and was making a summer home on it. And so I've checked up, and it hasn't been sold, and the present owner knows nothing about guards there. And also, it isn't a rum-runner's rendezvous. What does that add up to?"

"Plenty!" said Schaaf exuberantly. "I take off der hat. I make der grand salaam! Now we go there and haff a *Schrecklichkeit* party; wait until night, because we do not want to haff him start a storm. And we line up der Nafy, and they take der sights, and there is a signal, and *bam, pow, biff,* and he is blooey! Blown off der map!"

Hines looked at Schaaf. And for the first time Schaaf saw how pale his friend was. His face was like a mask. He reached over his desk and tossed Schaaf a little envelope.

"I was to be married to-day," said Hines steadily. "Preston's men tried to kidnap Kathryn this morning, just as they tried to blow the two of us to bits. We beat the assassins, and Kathryn, thanks to you, Schaaf, escaped the trap that was set for her. We've been busy ever since. She wrote the account for the extra edition of the *Star.* We postponed our wedding as a matter of course."

Schaaf said suddenly, "Gott! Hines, you look like der deffil!"

"You blocked one attempt to kidnap Kathryn," repeated Hines evenly. "She went to the office of the *Star.* And another attempt was made three hours ago. The one thing she didn't expect was another attempt to kidnap her, made in exactly the same fashion as the first. This time it succeeded. Kathryn's disappeared. And I had a telegram from his man, sent from here in New York, saying that he's taking her direct to his headquarters. So she'll be killed if we kill Preston."

Hines moistened his lips and said with difficulty, "The—thing that makes it bad is that we were to have been married to-day."

4

THE LONGEST NIGHT IN HISTORY

THE LIGHTS OF the city glowed in long, long rows. The whiter arclights on the Jersey side of the Hudson glittered more palely, but all lights shone bright, in the longest night in history. The gigantic electric signs flamed their advertising slogans for the world to admire at three o'clock in the afternoon. The Hudson River day boat came downstream as a glittering mass of lights. Her searchlight shot out and she docked by its rays. There was a deep-toned roaring on the surface of the river. Another. A third. A fourth motor added its roaring hum to the din. Then the four roaring noises swept swiftly across the harbor waves and lifted suddenly, and rose into the darkness that overlay the world. Tiny navigation lights flashed on, and drifted across the empty black sky where sun or moon or stars should have been. They headed out toward Kong Island Sound and vanished.

The city, left behind, went valorously on about its business. At three in the afternoon of the day that the sun did not rise, New York was perhaps typical of the whole civilized world. The more savage territories of the planet were sunk in panic, and pagan gods were passionately besought to give back the sun to the world again. In China the

shrines were filled with the sounds of gongs and firecrack-
ers. In Soviet Siberia long-neglected chapels resounded
to cries of *"Hospodi pomilui!"* Everywhere that men had
temples, those temples were swarming masses of terror-
stricken suppliants, pleading for the sun to come back
again.

But New York was more typical of the more scientifically
minded Occident. In one sense the terror was more acute,
because New York had had bitter and repeated experience
of Preston and his works. But Hines and Schaaf had said
there was no more danger, that Preston had done his worst.

New York had learned, by now, that they knew what
they were talking about. Therefore, while there was not
complete confidence in their ability to beat Preston again,
there was a definite knowledge of the cause of the darkness and a definite idea that the source of the darkness
was being attacked. So that New York was frightened but
hopeful; terrified, but not panic-stricken because of its
belief in Hines and Schaaf.

People in New York, too, had no clear idea of the magni-
tude of the disaster that impended. As long as artificial
light could be used, the average New Yorker considered
the matter a nuisance and a cause for alarm, but no immediately dangerous matter.

He read his newspapers avidly, and the statements issued
by various scientists consulted by the newspapers struck
him as melodramatic in the same way that his newspaper
headlines were always melodramatic. But he considered
them quite as remote from his own life as his morning
torch-fiend narratives.

The darkness was, however, a serious matter enough.

Leaving aside the matter of illumination from the sun, the earth was receiving only one-fourth its normal daily supply of solar heat. The layer of darkness intercepted the rest. True, the part of the earth that should have been dark was losing less than its usual nightly amount of heat by radiation into interstellar space, but matters were bad enough anyhow.

The equator was receiving no more heat from the sun than southern Greenland normally receives. New York was receiving less than is normal at the north pole itself. Only the fact that the stored up warmth of the earth's surface layers was being lost very slowly, prevented an immediate drop to below zero temperatures.

But by three o'clock in the afternoon, when the four seaplanes took off for a search of the Maine coast, the official thermometer in the Meteorological Bureau of New York City showed forty-four degrees Fahrenheit-twelve degrees above freezing. The nearness of the ocean with its vast supplies of stored heat had prevented a greater drop.

Inland, the temperature fall was greater yet. A heavy snow was falling in Cleveland. In Butte, Montana, zero had actually been reached. It was not at all difficult to compute a progressive temperature loss which would average twenty degrees a day after the first twenty-four hours, and in one week would make the normally temperate zones uninhabitable and permit of glacier formation in the Panama Canal Zone.

In the face of such figures as this, estimates that two weeks' darkness would destroy all planted crops and cause inescapable famine, seemed hardly worth worrying about. Agricultural experts were pointing out that unless Preston was defeated or his terms met, the world would starve to death. Sunlight is essential to vegetable growth, on which all life depends. But such fears, as a few physicists recognized grimly, were quite needless. Long before that catastrophe came about, mankind would not need to worry about planted crops. Long before the world went hungry, it would have frozen to death.

SCHAAF WAS SUNK in a bitter gloom as the four planes roared northward. Big planes, they were. Three Navy bombers, carrying flares and bombs and radio, and the multi-passenger flying transport which carried Hines and Schaaf and an impressive array of apparatus for measurements and photography.

The glow against the black sky, which was New York, faded away against the horizon. Only, there was no horizon. Little pin-pricks of light showed beneath the speeding ships. There were three men in the transport beside Hines and Schaaf. The pilot and his relief, and a radio operator who spoke from time to time to the pilot.

Schaaf saw Hines looking at him and said gloomily, "We are doing radio nafigation. I haff nefer been so helpless; I know more about Breston's apparatus than anybody else in der world—and I do not know der beginning of it! How does he get his wafes into der Heaviside Layer? How does he do it?"

Hines shrugged. His face was a mask, dead white and quite expressionless.

"They must have got Kathryn through," he said irrelevantly. "I had a cordon out that I didn't think a fly could break through. Every road, every bypath covered. There was a destroyer fleet out of Boston, too, to pick up any launch. But they got her through. I don't know how."

Schaaf said helplessly.

"What are we going to do, Hines? Tell me!"

Hines spoke tonelessly, without expression.

"Preston found out his power by accident. At first, I suppose, he merely thought of getting rich by helping out in robberies. But then he found he could manipulate the stock market by turning on the dark. He tried that, and found he could make storms. And now—you know his terms for making the sun shine again?"

"They haff not been made public," growled Schaaf, "and I haff been busy."

"He demands the submission of all the nations of the earth. He is to be Emperor of Earth—or he'll let the earth freeze until the survivors make him their emperor." Hines shrugged. "He has some involved conditions. Every living man to swear allegiance. Some trick arrangement by which he'll always have a corps of his gangsters about a darkness transmitter somewhere, to keep the world cowed… Of course nobody is thinking of accepting his terms while there's a chance to fight. But there isn't much time."

"If he is on that Metinic Island," growled Schaaf, "we can mass artillery and ships and blow der whole damned thing to bits."

Hines fumbled for a cigar and smiled drearily. "Isn't it funny? Kathryn and I were to have been married to-day, and I'm massing artillery to blow Preston to bits—and she'll be blown to bits with him."

Schaaf swallowed something.

"Hines! *Gott,* Hines, I am sorry!"

"Don't be," said Hines. "I'm going to be on that island when it's destroyed by shell fire. So don't be sorry for me."

THE PLANES FLEW steadily on through the darkness. Snow swirled about them for a while, and ceased. This was the afternoon of May the fifth. On the earth below, people were gazing hopelessly up at the sky of ebony. All over the world there was despair, as varied in its expression as the people who expressed it.

In Alabama, farmers moved along their cornfield rows with lanterns, watching the young shoots turning black with frost. There was frost as far south as Havana. In the western mountains, dry land farmers motored to the edges of mountain streams that had begun to flow freely. Now they were trickles again, flowing ever more slowly beneath a thickening shell of ice.

Men cursed the black sky that would not let the sun's warmth through. There was beach ice on the Great Lakes. A borax prospector in Death Valley saw by a thick miner's candle that there was a deposit of hoar frost even in that unbelievable place.

Everywhere human beings began to realize that darkness was not the worst of the evils upon them. The world was growing colder and ever colder beneath its sky of black. It was a dark world whose inky obscurity was broken only by the tiny yellow flames where yet hoping or desperately enduring people comforted themselves by the light it seemed would never come down from the sky again.

But the wild things had no comfort. Those creatures of the night which prey on others, at first moved freely. Bats soared in their erratic fashion until the increasing cold set them hunting their caves again. Owls swept abroad on noiseless wings. And some—not many—of the four-footed animals crawled or crept or slithered upon their private businesses.

But the other things lay hidden. Songbirds crouched in their nests while the night hung on interminably and the air grew icy. Little nestlings roused and chirped querulously from hunger. But night still remained. The age-old instincts, bred of terror, held the old birds still, though their young ones starved. And besides, to have left the nests after the cold increased would be to let the featherless young ones freeze.

There were very many small, bewildered tragedies in woods and forests and jungles while the darkness held.

FOUR PLANES ROARED on, ever northward, in their quest of the island where Preston had his stronghold. Gradually, the three bombers dropped down toward the earth. Gradually, the transport plane climbed. And then a signal came by radio. Schaaf grew tense and watchful. Hines grew grim and still, staring at the world of darkness all below. And then, quite suddenly, there was a vast, blinding glare below. A bomber had dropped a flare.

The sky above remained like ebony. The sea remained like ink. But there was a line of surf upon the sea, and an enormous glare beneath a swaying parachute, and three huge bombing planes in silhouette against a world all black and white.

Hines stared downward through powerful binoculars, focusing them quite calmly oh the land beyond the surf.

"I see a man—two men, running," he said steadily.

The first ball of fire was dropping swiftly. A second bloomed suddenly, farther on. An island was made clearly visible. An irregular, jagged shape, outlined by surf, with here and there a streak of white sand. Schaaf put his glasses to his eyes, and the earth seemed to leap toward him. Low, squat structures of a curiously ungainly form. A bowl-shaped apparatus ten feet or more across, made of wires which glittered in the unbearable light. And one other, incredible thing....

Schaaf blinked, and swore, and then shouted.

"I haff it!"

From the center of the island a column of solid, jetty black reared upward toward the sky. It was opaque, solid-seeming, and utterly black. It looked like the drooping tentacle of some colossal waterspout, anchored and moored. It looked like a throbbing hose through which darkness was being pumped upward to discolor the sky.

Schaaf babbled.

"Four-centimeter wafes! He has got der four-centimeter wafes! Oh, der clefer scoundrel! Der *verdammt* defer scoundrel!"

On the island three men were running toward the bowl-shaped apparatus of wires. A third flare blazed vividly. In the big ship seven thousand feet up the aircraft camera clicked steadily, exposing plates and changing them and exposing more. The radio operator was working his key feverishly.

The three bombing planes circled and soared over the island. A fourth flare filled the world with light. And suddenly one of the monster flying things down below wheeled in its flight and dived savagely.

"Difing for der blackness-beam!" panted Schaaf. "Difing—"

Three men were working frantically about the bowl-shaped apparatus on the ground. The giant bomber showed clearly for an instant, as if poised before its suicidal dash against the apparently solid column of blackness reaching upward to the sky. It shot into that blackness—

The sky split open!

From horizon to horizon lurid flames flashed into being. The sea and the island and all the world was lit by an unbearable, a terrific glare. It seemed as if all the world were being destroyed in one vast explosion, the steam and fumes of which had already mounted colossally toward the zenith.

BUT THERE WAS no blast of sound. The sky closed once more. There was utter silence save for the loud droning of the motors outside the cabin of the big plane. Far below, three magnesium flares glittered brightly.

"Gawd!" said the radio operator, awed. "What was that?"

Hines said dryly: "That was daylight, my friend. The sunlight and clouds. That was what we expect to see for twelve hours every day."

Schaaf was muttering, while he rubbed his light-dazed eyes: "There was four thousand kilowatts in that beam. What happened?"

He peered down again. There was a sudden flaring upward of lurid yellow flames. The bomber that had dived into the darkness-beam had crashed, now, and was burning fiercely on a narrow beach.

"Get der other ships away!" snapped Schaaf Suddenly. "Recall them! And we haff to go like der deffil! Quick!"

But he was too late. The bowl-shaped contrivance of glittering wires moved suddenly. A beam of blackness shot out from it. That blackness swept, upward and enveloped a burning flare. The flare went out. The beam of darkness swept on, and the flare was a dripping, swiftly falling mass of tiny yellow sparks. The beam swung sharply to one of the two remaining bombers. The plane dived and dodged, but the darkness caught it, enveloped it. The bomber dropped crazily out of the blackness; spitting sparks and burning. It crashed into the sea.

The third bomber was racing for safety. The beam shot toward it, and when it careened wildly to escape, expanded widely. It became an apparently solid object a hundred yards across. It closed over the bomber, and there was a terrific explosion. When the beam died away there was no falling, burning wreck. There was only a rain of small particles of débris.

"Go like der deffil!" snapped Schaaf. "Cut off der motors and glide! We haff to carry der news back. And for der lofe of Gott, do not use der radio! He will pick it up and we are geflooey!"

5

FIGHTING BACK

HINES SAT AT a telephone in Portland, and things began to move. He called Boston, and long, lean, greyhound-like ships with many funnels slipped their moorings and slid smoothly out to sea. Three cruisers raised steam and went after them. And there was vast activity in the Navy yard, and presently an old harbor-defense monitor went staggering gamely after the more modern ships.

He called New York, and trains were shunted swiftly here and there, and there were shouted orders and the rattling of accouterments and much profanity; then flatcars with squat, ungainly-wheeled shapes upon them rolled out of the city bound northward. They traveled at the speed of the fastest express trains, and passenger flyers were sidetracked to let them pass.

Hines called here and there, and everywhere there were swift and deadly preparations for action. At Newport, two battalions of Marines entrained with an astounding celerity. At other scattered cities other fighting men and fighting machines made ready. Three howitzer batteries were bumping at top speed over the rails to Maine. Two twelve-inch guns with railroad mountings formed a racing special train with cars of shells and their gun crews.

All the preparations were Hines's doing, and he explained his orders as he gave them in the manner of a man who does not expect to survive their carrying out. Metinic Island was no more than six miles from an accessible part of the mainland. Artillery will range that distance easily. Within two hours after Hines's return from the reconnoissance flight in which three bombing planes were lost, artillery officers had reached the future firing-point by plane and were marking out gun-emplacements and swearing at the inadequacy of the local maps.

Hines's plan was to mass artillery in such quantity and with such a supply of ammunition that Preston's headquarters could be smothered under a rain of explosives. One field gun to ten yards of target can keep that target under an adequate barrage fire. No man can live in the open under such a hail of death. But in addition there would be the warships. Four super-dreadnaughts, three cruisers, and a monitor would pound the island. Three hours before dawn there would be over twenty guns of twelve and fourteen-inch caliber trained upon the island, and upward of thirty eight-inch rifles to assist.

Nothing should be able to live on the surface or beneath it, however deep the dugouts Preston might have prepared. Hines was grimly calculating that within three minutes of the opening of fire every square foot of earth upon the island should have been plowed up by explosives. And Kathryn was there. She must be.

It looked perfect, however, from the standpoint of destruction. The resources of one regional department of the Army would be at hand before dawn. The Navy would have its ships at hand with shotted guns. The air would be alive with flying craft. A signal; a blast of cannon-fire; a terrific, long-continued battering, and Metinic Island should disappear forever.

IT DID LOOK perfect. Too perfect, considering that Preston knew what to expect now. Schaaf paced nervously back and forth as Hines gave his orders.

"He has something up his sleefe, Hines," he said irritably. "He has taken plenty from der cuffs, but he has something more."

Hines relaxed deliberately, with an effort.

"What has he got?"

"He has four-centimeter wafes," said Schaaf desperately. "They explain nearly eferything. It was calculated a year and a half ago that der death-ray of der imaginatif nofelists is theoretically impossible. But if a man makes Hertzian wafes of four centimeters frequency, he has der world by der tail. All der armies haff been trying to make them, because it can be proofed by mathematics that in der path of a beam of four-centimeter wafes def air will be a conductor der same as metal. Breston has them. He has sent a beam of them straight up to der Heaviside Layer. And his short wafes that make der air opaque, they trafel along der four-centimeter beam until they hit der Layer. There they spread out. So much is simple. Der bomber that was destroyed when we went to look simply difed through a beam of four-centimeter wafes that was carrying four thousand kilowatts of Breston's prifate short short wafes up to der Heaviside Layer. It is no wonder it crashed!

"Der thing that destroyed der other bombers is just as ample. A beam of der same conducting wafes, with darkness in it so they could see to aim it, and high-frequency current shot into it at der critical moment. A plane in a beam of those four-centimeter wafes is just like a plane touching a power-transmission line. If der frequency is high enough, there is no need of a ground wire to electrocute efery man on board. Der whole plane starts sparking, it bursts into flame and der bombs explode. That is what he has used!"

"I wonder," said Hines drearily, "if he can use it on the artillery?"

Schaaf shrugged. He resumed his impatient pacing up and down the room.

"But he has something else up der sleefe. I know he has something else up der sleefe. It is too easy! Much too easy!"

The clocks announced seven o'clock. Eight. Nine o'clock. Reports began to come in. Artillery units had arrived, were digging in. A battery of field guns was ready to fire.

Nine thirty: Two guns of a howitzer section were ready to fire. One naval gun on a railroad mounting was in position.

Ten: All the howitzers were ready to fire. The cruisers were in position and the battleships were coming up. Destroyers had ventured into the dense mass of darkness that hung about the island. The darkness was nearly a circle, six miles across. One of the destroyers came scuttling out with flames pouring from it. It reached the clear air and was aflame from end to end. It floated, a lurid torch, while its crew was taken off. It blew up and sank at eleven ten precisely.

At eleven thirty the basket-mast of a battle cruiser glowed red, halfway up its height, and its separate steel rods bent and buckled, and then cooled off again, leaving the fighting-top careened crazily over at right angles and far out over the ship's side.

"Breston is trying to fight," said Schaaf shortly. "He is swinging der beam of four-centimeter wafes around and shooting all der juice he can supply into it. It happened to hit der fighting-mast. The beam is infisible now. Since he cannot see what he is aiming at, he does not want anybody else to see der beam. It is infisible death, that beam."

HINES SMILED QUEERLY. He picked up a telephone and spoke almost softly into it.

"All ready for me?... Very well. It's understood that zero hour is 3 A.M. if the darkness is not cut before then. If it is cut, bolometer readings are to be taken and action judged by their indications. All ships and guns are to stand by in any event until the island is occupied. Very well. Good luck!"

He stood up and held out his hand to Schaaf.

"I'm going to the island, Schaaf. Good-by."

Schaaf scowled at him.

"Of all der double-barreled, triple-distilled idiots I efer saw," he said bitterly, "you are der worst! Hines, you are a *verdammt* fool! You are going to der island—"

Hines shrugged.

"It's a form of suicide," he said evenly. "I know it. But that devil has got Kathryn there. I've arranged for him to be blown off the earth. She'll be blown up with him. We were to have been married this morning. So I—well, I'm going to be there, too."

Schaaf swore explosively in guttural German.

"That is not what I am talking about!" he snapped. "That is lunacy, yes! But der magnificent imbecility is that you think I am going to let Breston's short-wafe outfit be blown to bits without getting a look at it! There is a place reserfed for me in der boat that is going to der island. Try and keep me out of it!"

Hines looked steadily at Schaaf for nearly half a minute. Then he smiled.

"You're a damned liar, Schaaf. You're going because—"

"Shut up!" snapped Schaaf again. He drew himself up to his full six feet and something of whiskered blondness. "Hines, I am a damned liar, yes! And you are a damned fool! So that makes two of us going out to be fery unpleasantly bumped off, and if you try to talk silly sentiment I will poke you in der eye. Come on!"

6

THE ISLAND OF DARKNESS

A DESTROYER TOOK the pair northward, flinging itself madly over the dark, dark sea. After the lights of Portland vanished behind them there was a period when the solid deck beneath seemed the only object in existence. There was no sky, no sun, no horizon. There was no land.

There was only an invisible bulk beneath them which quivered insanely, and a wind blowing from the oblivion before them to the oblivion behind. There was no up, no down. One grew giddy from the sheer absence of anything by which to orient oneself. The utter loneliness of the dark was terrifying, because not even the sea could be seen. Even in some imagined spaceship, isolated in empty space, there would be stars for comfort. Here there was only nothingness.

When a yellow light glowed far away and seemed like a star, it was actually a lamp in a farmhouse window overlooking the sea. And in that farmhouse the sense of isolation was so great as to induce hysteria. The folk in the farmhouse were experiencing exactly the sensations of people on a tiny fragment of earth set floating free in a cosmos containing nothing else—nothing! Not even other worlds unthinkably remote.

It was a loneliness, a desolation, that clutched at the throat. All through the world that same despair was descending. In the cities it was less appalling, but on ships that steamed over invisible seas, and in lighthouses that were always isolated and now became small hells, and in tiny mountain cabins, and small hamlets and places innumerable, the dread of the dark grew and grew.

Some people went insane, and many grew hysterical. It is a matter of record that folk went solemnly out of their villages and set the woods about them on fire so that the flames and firelit smoke would give them something to look at other than the awful blackness which lay over the world. It was a curious aftermath of the darkness that the use of illuminants at night was multiplied many times.

But on the destroyer these things were unknown. It swept on northward, horribly alone, until presently lights appeared to the left, and searchlights stabbed futilely upward, and there was a confused droning tumult over the land. The whole air force of the Army and Navy was being massed for action, together with the ships of a naval division and the artillery of an army corps.

Then the destroyer slackened speed, and went on into a bay where bonfires burned brightly, and its engines stopped and its anchor-chain clanged thunderously as it ran out. A thirty-foot cutter came alongside, moving by oars, and made fast to the landing-ladder of the destroyer. It waited.

"Efficiency," said Hines dryly. "No time lost, Schaaf. These men are volunteers for our forlorn hope. You know why I want to be on the island, but I'm able to have the zero hour held off only because the government wants to get hold of Preston's apparatus if it can. As a military weapon. We're going to try to take the island by storm."

"Der idea," observed Schaaf grimly, "is a lot of hooey."

Hines said nothing. He led the way down to the boat.

OARS DIPPED. THE cutter pulled away. A navy launch swarmed up officiously and flung a line. Half a minute later the launch was speeding for the blackness of the open sea and the cutter went tearing through the water after it, squatted down astern until it seemed the waves should come in over the gunwale.

They could see little as the two boats moved, of course, but Hines stared up at the dark shore line. Guns were massed and massing, there. Waiting and ready along a four-mile front. At one single word a storm of steel would spring from the hungry muzzles. A hurtling, screaming hail of death would leap upward and forward through the darkness. Six miles away it would descend.

Four miles of guns, packed as closely together as they could be brought up by straining locomotives and racing, swearing men. Four miles of guns concentrating on a little more than one mile of target, with the heaviest guns of the fleet to blast away what little of the island the shore artillery left.

There was no wind save that made by the movement of the towing launch, but that was bitter. The men on the seats of the cutter huddled down into their greatcoats, taking it easy. A flash light signaled off to seaward.

"We're passing between some islands," said Hines evenly. "They'll cast off when we're well on our way. The oars are muffled. If we can land on the damned island secretly, so much the better."

Five minutes, and the launch on ahead was slowing up. The men in the cutter bestirred themselves. A man in the bow tossed the towline overboard. The oars stretched out again. The launch swept around and went purring softly back into the darkness.

The cutter, without a word of command, began to move with the rhythmic pulsatory effect of a rowed boat toward the utter blackness of the open sea.

"Who's in command here?" demanded Hines.

"I am," said a voice. A flash light glowed through cupped fingers. A clean-shaved and rather anxious young ensign's face could be made out.

"Shoot der works," said Schaaf amiably. "What haff you done?"

"I've a pair of microphones overboard," explained the young officer nervously, "of the sort used for listening for submarines. They'll give us the line on two launches that are working submerged sounders for us. I can get the angles from both of them to make a course for the island even if we are blinded. And besides, we'll be able to hear the waves on the beach when we get near."

"Clefer," said Schaaf. "Fery good."

"And my men are all in linemen's boots and rubber. They're armed with—er—the regular mopping-up equipment."

"Which is?" said Schaaf encouragingly.

"Why—er—grenades, automatic pistols, and automatic shotguns throwing nine extra-sized buckshots to a shell. Also we've a couple of Lewis guns with us. We have twenty men."

"I can think of nothing you haff left out for a fine party but der beer," said Schaaf. "You haff done excellently, sir."

Oars rose and fell in a ghostlike silence. There was no splashing. Hines had ordered a boat propelled by oars because any motor-driven craft would be heard approaching the island. Hines had no hope of leaving that spot of land, but he did want to land on it alive. He fumbled for a cigar and lit it. The light of his match was the only glow of illumination in all the world.

They were far enough from shore and low enough in the water to make any possible light invisible. The sky was wholly black. The water was wholly black. Ahead and behind and to the right hand and the left there was no relief from the abysmal blackness anywhere.

Hines's cigar, small as was its gleam, provided a literal illumination by which the farthest man in the bow of the boat saw the face of his seat-mate faintly pinkened.

"If that darkness—" began the ensign.

He stopped. He was watching Hines's cigar fascinatedly. It had been a dull-red coal, brightening to what seemed a vivid incandescence when Hines puffed on it. Now it seemed to have gone out, and revived very, very faintly at each puffing. A moment later it seemed no longer to exist. **"WE'RE IN THE** darkness now," said Hines dryly.

His tone was entirely matter-of-fact, which was wise; for the men at the oars had been watching the glow of his cigar. It was the only spot of light in the universe. And when it went out, the effect was horrible.

"How do der microphones work?" asked Schaaf interestedly.

"I have the line," said the ensign unsteadily. "We're a shade under three miles from the island."

The boat went on silently. About the island Preston had brought darkness down to earth over a circular space some six miles across.

The cutter rose and fell, and rose and fell, and the three men in the stem felt the rhythmic pulling of the oars. Every man felt the opacity of the air weighing upon him, pressing upon him.

All the world had been dark enough anyhow, but to feel that by no possible device could a light be made to shine was queerly horrible. A man felt as if he were buried alive. He had an almost hysterical impulse to beat at the darkness with his hands, to thrust it away from him.

"I hear the surf on the beach in the headphones," said the ensign, a long time later.

"You should," said Schaaf placidly.

Hines then spoke shortly.

"We land and form a line. By the way, we want to land at the southernmost tip of the island. I know the lay of the land, roughly. We are to be entirely silent, passing signals by touching each other in the blackness. There are probably charged wires about the island. If we run into lines of wire, we will short-circuit them with gun-barrels to the earth, and then cut them. When Preston's instruments show a short-circuit, he will probably cut the darkness to see about it. We go ahead then. Mop up the island. There is one woman here. Be careful not to hurt her. But this is one time to fight hard! If we don't kill Preston, he'll kill us!"

The ensign said-steadily this time— "You men heard that. Those are your orders."

There was a little gurgling noise ahead, a washing, splashing sound. It ran a long distance in a straight line across the bow of the boat. The rudder squeaked, and the boat's course shifted until the sound was abeam. The oars worked monotonously. Presently the washing sound seemed to come to an end and to go away in the distance. The rudder squeaked again. They went on their former course once more.

"If you put your ear to the gun-wale," said the ensign in a voice that was barely a whisper, "you'll hear a queer humming, sir. The hull picks up the sound from the water. I've been hearing it in the microphones for some time. It sounds like engines, sir."

"Dynamos," said Schaaf in as low a tone. "Der dynamos and der Diesel engines that make der juice."

"I'm heading in for the beach," whispered the ensign. "Easy, men! Get ready to beach her, up forward."

The word passed to the bow in murmurs. The washing of waves became louder and louder. The booming of small breakers on sand grew more distinct. Hines visualized the southern end of the island as he had seen it from the air and tried to guess at the spot from the fact that they were headed for a sandy beach. He nodded to himself.

The boat checked with a grating sound. There was the little lifting feel of men leaping out to ease it ashore.

"And now," said Schaaf grimly, "*Gott strafe* Breston!"

THEY DISEMBARKED AS blind men, feeling the foaming small breakers beating utterly unseen about their rubber-booted legs. They fumbled at each other to form a skir-mish-line. At a low word from Hines they moved on.

It was a slow, a stumbling, an infinitely cautious party of

the blind. Every man's eyes were wide and staring, through sheer instinctive effort to catch some glimmer of the light that in nature is nowhere quite absent. But here, the very air was opaque.

The blackness was oppressive past conception. A man felt as if he were buried alive, as if the darkness pressed upon him, as if a shifting stuff pressed upon his breast and would presently stop his breathing.

A tiny clatter, off in the darkness. The line halted. A message passed along its length in a murmur.

"A wire about a foot off the ground. It isn't charged."

"Step over it and go on," ordered Hines. "At any alarm, fling yourselves flat on the ground and wait."

The line moved on again. Hines had cracked the crystal from a watch-compass and by the feel of its needle led the way. He, also, came upon that uncharged wire, stretched upon stakes no more than a foot above ground. It gave a little as he touched it. He passed over it.

Then, quite suddenly, a man screamed, down at the end of the line. A weapon went off thunderously in the blackness. One of the two Lewis guns roared itself empty. There was the clatter of men flinging themselves to the earth. Then silence.

Hines pressed his jaw's tightly together. Instinctively he peered about, though his eyes could convey no possible sensation to his brain. There was only blackness and stillness.

Presently he became aware of the surf drumming away behind him. Then he heard the faintest possible humming noise overhead. At the same time a pungent odor stung his nostrils. He heard Schaaf exclaim softly, swearing under his breath.

Some one came writhing along the ground, counting the prone figures he passed.

"Inspector Hines!"

The faint humming noise passed toward the right. It died away.

"Here," said Hines quietly.

The ensign's voice panted.

"We've lost three men. Stone dead. Electrocuted."

Schaaf's voice came from astonishingly near by.

"Der four-centimeter beam," he said grimly. "They heard us. Perhaps der low wires were burglar-alarms. Breston passed der beam of four-centimeter wafes all about, with der high-tension current in it. Those three men were struck by it. It was like being struck by a life wire with ten thousand volts in it. I smelled ozone just now. My nose stings yet with it. Der beam passed humming ofer our heads."

The ensign asked nervously: "What do we do now, sir?"

"Lie still," said Hines coldly. "They'll get curious presently."

The ensign crawled away. Darkness. Blackness. The sound of the surf behind them. Time seemed endless, waiting. One had a ghastly feeling that it had been an hour or more, two hours—that it was time for the massed guns, six miles away, to open fire. One's ears strained for the whistling sound of that first flight of projectiles from four miles of guns.

Gradually an infinitely faint rumbling noise made itself felt. It was felt as much as heard. The sound came through the earth. The dynamos and the monstrous generators in

Preston's underground dugouts, making the power that had darkened the world.

WITHOUT A TRACE of flickering, the darkness broke. With startling clarity the line of prone men could see. An unbearable glare smote upon their eyes, but despite it they saw.

The darkness had vanished from before their eyes. They seemed to be in a monstrous cavern whose walls were angular masses of jetty black. A great magnesium flare was burning on the ground. It lighted up three clumsy concrete structures three-quarters sunk in the ground. There were men standing near those structures. Three of them stood by a bowl-shaped thing of wires. They were looking—all the men were looking—at the line of prone riflemen. The darkness seemed to have been lifted for the precise purpose of permitting Preston's aids to look.

From half a dozen tripods some six feet or so across darkness poured out in wide, fanlike beams. Those beams united overhead to form a roof of darkness, seemingly supported by the inverted pyramids of black. They united to shut off the rest of the world. They blended almost at the edge of the surf to cut off all vision upon the water. Hines and Schaaf and the volunteers gazed for exactly three seconds the length of a colossal cavern in which lights could glow, but which was roofed and walled with opacity.

Three seconds; while a man could breathe in and out and in again. Then from all along the line of prone men gunfire flashed at the exact instant that darkness fell upon them again. The remaining Lewis gun blared into nothingness, emptying its drum of cartridges. The automatic shotguns bellowed their magazines empty.

Somewhere off in the darkness a man shrieked, and there were shoutings, and then a deadly, snarling voice cried out. Something was roaring horribly, off there in the new-fallen blackness. A spark was leaping a colossal gap with the tearing thunderous rasp that only a current up in the thousands of volts will make.

"Scatter!" snapped Hines. "They've sighted that beam on us!"

He leaped to his feet and bolted ahead. Some one pounded along beside him, though the presence of the other man was felt rather than heard, and of course nothing at all could be seen. Up ahead the sparking sound cut off sharply, leaving Hines's ears ringing with the sudden silence.

It seemed as if some wire—perhaps the high-tension wire to the four-centimeter beam—had been cut by a bullet, and now a switch was thrown. Through the ringing in his ears Hines heard the snarling voice ahead of him shout an order. He blundered on and tripped over something. The smell of scorched rubber rose from his boots.

He struck savagely at the thing with his gun-barrel, and somehow the darkness about him seemed to change. It was probably a beam darkness-transmitter, which he had smashed. But in an intangible cavern whose walls were opacity there was no great difference.

He went racing on, straining his yet-ringing ears for sounds, and crashed headlong into concrete. He gave a cry of satisfaction and began to fumble his way feverishly along its length. The man who had run beside him, panting, grunted with satisfaction as he in turn felt the concrete.

It was Schaaf. He mumbled to himself and Hines

caught, *"verdammt,"* and *"Schrecklichkeit"* and other much less repeatable words.

A door! Hines fumbled at his belt and found one single grenade.

"A steel door, Schaaf!" he panted. "I'm setting off a grenade before it. Get back around the corner!"

He deposited the little globe of iron, jerked out the pin, and fled.

The earth shook and a blast of sound which was like a blow on the chest smote them—for all that they were around the corner of the concrete. Then Hines flung himself forward again, rasping his fingers on the rough concrete and choking on the fumes of the explosive.

The door was blown away, blasted from its frame. No glimmer of illumination came through the awful darkness that was everywhere, but Hines stepped boldly through the opening with his automatic shotgun held ready for the instant light should reach him.

The curious feeling of a metal floor under his foot. Then emptiness!

He went hurtling downward, falling into bright and blinding light. He struck something with his shoulder in the act of falling, and it wrenched his muscles cruelly but partly broke the drop. He wound up with a crash on concrete, all of fifteen feet down, and lay still for an instant, dazed.

HE HAD A vague impression of a room that was sunk deep in the ground. There were masses of glittering glass, and many lights, and a humming noise filled all the air with a monotonous drone. Hines realized indistinctly that the curious squat structures on the island were merely the roofs of dugouts, dug down to safety below the surface of the earth. Then he heard a peculiar tearing, spitting sound near by.

His eyes focused dazedly on his shotgun, lying on the floor a little distance off. It was smoking strangely. Sparks were darting from it into the stone floor. It began abruptly to glow a dull red. Suddenly it exploded luridly. Every shell in its magazine went off in a single blast which was not disastrous solely because the red hot metal offered so little resistance to the expanding gases. They tore it apart almost like so much dough.

Somebody or other was racing down the steel steps Hines had tumbled from. Huge hands swept Hines from the floor. He smelled burning rubber. He knew that it was Schaaf who tore his automatic pistol out of his belt and flung it away. He knew, also, that it was Schaaf who leaped with him to one side of the room. He had a dizzy impression of glowing tubes of glass all about him.

Then a snarling, arrogant voice said in insolent satisfaction:

"Police Inspector Hines, I believe, and my former assistant, Professor Schaaf. Very well met! I've wanted to have you two men killed for a long time."

7

THE MAN WHO MURDERED LIGHT

HINES'S AUTOMATIC PISTOL tore itself to pieces as the shells in its butt went off all at once. Its fragments on the concrete floor glowed dully red, then slowly cooled off when they ceased to emit sparks.

Hines staggered to his feet and found himself penned in behind a monster bank of vacuum tubes which glowed redly. The glass of the tubes was inordinately thick. These tubes would not break by concussion, nor by however determined a blow of a man's fist—Preston had learned, from his debacle in the Storm.

Hines was conscious of them, and of things below them which might have been gigantic transformers of the type used in radio. But as his brain cleared from the crack on the concrete floor, his whole attention was taken up by the facts which it was immediately necessary for him to face.

Schaaf was beside him, crouching a little to have his whole body behind the banks of vacuum tubes. Schaaf was snarling a little, and his blue eyes were glinting fire. He seemed to be unarmed as well as Hines, and he was gazing across the deep-sunk room with an expression of concentrated malevolence.

Preston was there, the man Hines had seen exactly once,

and for half a minute only, but whom he had been hunting for months. He was standing by a small platform which itself was next to a wide door through which the humming noise came. Preston's hand was on a small thing which looked rather like a searchlight, except that instead of a mirror for a reflector it had a sort of grid of glistening wires. There were two switches on its top.

Preston was small and dapper, and wore a neat Vandyke beard trimmed to an accurate point. He looked like a highly civilized man, even alongside the nattily attired pair of followers who lounged always within feet of him.

They were gangsters, those two, from impeccably tailored clothing to impossibly expensive haberdashery in vivid color.

Preston seemed precisely the pattern of the professional man—until one noticed his eyes. They were blank and hard and triumphant, precisely the eyes of a madman with paranoiac delusions of grandeur. They were insolent and scornful and very, very arrogant eyes. They were the eyes of a man who has persuaded himself that he is invested with supreme authority, and who derides and despises the mere worms of humans within his gaze. Unfortunately, Preston's ideas of his own powers were not delusions. They were facts.

He smiled at them, and his smile was filled with the same vanity-inspired scorn.

"I assure you, Schaaf," he said in a metallic voice that made one long to kick him, "I assure you that your being alive now is due to my forbearance."

Schaaf spoke, his voice purring with rage. He spoke in

German, and the words crackled. At the end he added wrathfully:

"And if you don't understand der names I called you, you are a lot of banana oil!"

He turned to Hines, growling, and Hines knew somehow that Schaaf was inspecting the contrivances, the elaborate hook-ups, the involved array of apparatus with a desperately concentrated attention, working frantically to understand their operation.

Hines's head was clearing swiftly, and he looked about, and went sick with a helpless rage at the same time that his pulses pumped with fury. He looked at Preston with eyes like flames. Preston had had Kathryn kidnaped. Preston had—

"You saw what happened to your weapons," said Preston, smiling unpleasantly. "I'm letting you live because it amuses me to watch you. I have—" he looked at a wrist watch— "I have more than half an hour before Inspector Hines's artillery blows this island out of the water. And I am inclined to let you two beg your lives. I won't give them to you, but I'll listen."

"Beg, der deffil!" snapped Schaaf. "Preston, you are der most complete idiot in der history of der human race! With der brains I reluctantly admit you possess, you could haff been a benefactor of mankind! And now we haff to kill you!—Where is Miss Bush?"

Preston threw back his head to laugh. His two guards regarded the two men behind the vacuum tubes with a wary, indifferent alertness. They were killers, hired to do murder to order. They regarded Schaaf and Hines as the professional killer always does regard his prospective victims.

"She's here," said Preston sardonically. "She's here! Quite a pretty girl, too. And safe—so far!"

Hines's teeth ground together. Face to face with Preston, a consummation for which he had hoped and worked for months. And helpless. Preston had destroyed his weapons with that little searchlight-like thing.

"It is lucky for you that she is safe," snapped Schaaf. "Breston, you *verdammt* fool, do you realize that you are licked before you start?"

SWEAT WAS STANDING out on Schaaf's face. He stood tense in every muscle, and Hines had a queer impression that Schaaf was all brain, that every particle of him was racing madly to absorb the meaning of the wires, the tubes, the switches, the connections in this diabolical control room. He seemed to feel Schaaf working desperately to piece together the meaning of every appliance and how it worked.

"Licked?" Preston laughed, the mirthless, scornful laugh of the paranoiac. "You are living by my pleasure, because it amuses me to watch—"

"That is true to a certain extent only," said Schaaf. He spoke with a measured calmness in which only Hines could detect the false note. "I tell you why. I haff solfed your apparatus! Before I left der mainland to come here, I had explained to my assistants der entire method of all your defices. I tell you you are licked, and I proof it. Der darkness wafes I have made myself. And moreofer, I haff made der four-centimeter wafes that make der air conducting and enable you to throw a beam of radiation that is like a life wire charged with electricity, wherefer you will. And der people on der mainland haff der apparatus too!"

Hines's eyes flickered. Schaaf was bluffing. It was a monumental sort of bluff, and the one thing that might work—if Schaaf could carry it out. Schaaf was bluffing for both their lives, now, and Kathryn's to boot.

"I tell you how you and I make der four-centimeter wafes," said Schaaf, grimly. "Der vacuum tube as at present designed cannot possibly go below a quarter of a meter, and then der wafe is not a pure sine wafe. I know! But you haff four-centimeter wafes, and smaller. Yes! And der word of how you do them is going all ofer der cifilized world right now. Because you can take six tubes, each one emitting wafes of one-fourth meter length, and so adjust them that der separate wafes of der separate tubes come four centimeters after each other, gifing you a beam of der death rays. *Hein?*"

He grinned savagely at Preston, though sweat stood out on his forehead. And Preston snarled.

"You can carry der process farther," said Schaaf in a judicial tone. Hines, listening, marveled at the assurance with which Schaaf was stating, as definite facts, his hurried deductions from the apparatus about them. "By der use of a sufficient number of tubes, you can make wafes of any length you choose, merely by der superimposition of one wafe-outline upon another. Der United States Gofernment is now turning out this apparatus in quantity!"

He waved his hands about the room. "Der darkness wafes are made in that way. Der conducting beam is made in that way. Eferything you haff is made in that way. And we haff eferything you haff efer thought of, with ten times der power you haff, and a hundred times der brains! You are licked, Breston! Hines and I, we came to this island because you are der damnedest scoundrel in forty nations. You haff Miss Bush here. Giff her back and we giff you half an hour's start. No more! You are licked! We make der bargain! Turn ofer Miss Bush, unharmed. Turn off der darkness. We giff you half an hour to escape in. That is efery damned thing we will giff you. And then we come after you, and I, personally, choke you by der neck until I kill you!"

PRESTON WAS LIVID. Hines's pulse leaped in savage satisfaction. Schaaf had worked out the whole thing from sight of Preston's outfit. His bluff was working. Preston did believe the whole world was equipped to fight him with his own weapons.

But his madman's eyes flamed with the crazy rage of shattered vanity.

"Everything I've got?" he snarled. "This too? Tell me how this is done!"

He flung a switch on the top of the tiny projector. There was a sudden vivid glow at a table against-the wall some fifteen feet from Hines. A long, serried ray of tubes leaped into light. Utter silence fell.

"Look at that metal!" raged Preston. "Look at it!"

He pointed a shaking hand at the fragments of Hines's two weapons on the concrete floor. And they turned suddenly white—snow white. Then they became wet. A liquid trickled from them and dripped to the concrete, where it bubbled furiously and formed a thick white mist that spread out over the floor. Preston flung back his switch and as the bank of tubes went out, he laughed in shrill, insolent, vanity mad triumph-because Schaaf's cheeks had become drained of every particle of blood.

"That's what I'm going to use on Hines's artillery!" boasted Preston hysterically. "This little projector is all I need! All!"

Schaaf clenched his hands more tightly still.

"*Gott!*" he muttered thickly. "*Gott!*"

"You didn't work out that one, eh?" demanded Preston arrogantly. "Now I'll tell you: that's the same thing as all the rest! Fluorescence! Causing one type of energy to be changed to another! Under my four-centimeter waves, the air becomes fluorescent. But these waves work on iron!

"Where these waves strike, the surface of the iron becomes fluorescent. It absorbs heat from the air and from its own interior! It turns heat to short radio waves, and every particle of iron in the beam of these waves, no matter how far away it is, radiates away every particle of energy it possesses? It sinks to absolute zero! Four hundred and sixty-two degrees below zero Fahrenheit!

"You saw air liquefy in contact with the iron that was red hot a moment ago. What's going to happen to the men on your battleships when every particle of iron or steel drops to the temperature of liquid air? What's going to happen to your guns when they're down to the temperature of liquid helium and the gun crews try to fire them? They'll fly to bits like brittle ice! Licked, am I? I'll wipe out your damned artillery with half a kilowatt in this projector! I'll sink your battleships with their crews frozen solid.

"I'll play that beam on New York and every particle of steel in the city will be brittle as ashes! I'll bring down every damned skyscraper in the town. I'll teach them a lesson they won't forget. Make my apparatus and try to work it against me? I'll—"

He was working himself into frothing rage. He was shouting. He was bellowing. His voice was a strident scream of rage, the rage of the man who has convinced himself that he is the most intelligent of all living men and then finds the distinction threatened.

"You fools!" Preston gasped. "Trying to fight *me!* Like savages with clubs going against a battleship! I'll show you! I'll show—"

Schaaf had bluffed, working out what Preston had done, after a swift survey of the apparatus about him. He'd seen Preston's transmitters and had raced his brain to the manner of their operation. He'd tried to bluff that all the world knew now how Preston had kept it sunk in night. But he hadn't known this one last trick, which was the most deadly of all. And Schaaf muttered thickly to himself with his eyes sunken in and dull. Because this last weapon was invincible.

THEN HINES LOOKED sharply upward and snapped, "All right men! Everybody in here!"

He gained two seconds only; two seconds in which Preston was looking upward, and his guards with him, toward the door into which Hines himself had stumbled. But that two seconds was enough. Before they could look down, Hines had leaped, dragging from their sockets two of the thick tubes to use as missiles.

The first one struck Preston and flung him against the projector. Hines was within a yard of Preston when he heard Schaaf cry out. But it was too late to stop then. He sank his fingers in Preston's throat as one of the guards screamed.

The projector of the freezing beam had been whirled around. A guard had felt his arm frozen to the elbow as he tried to raise his weapon. He screamed, and screamed, and Schaaf went into action frantically, flinging the huge vacuum tubes about and crashing them until the second guard was helpless and the freezing beam was off.

But Hines paid no attention. He forgot that he should be getting a bullet in the back of his head at any instant. Preston was squirming, under him, getting at something in his pocket. There was a sickeningly muffled explosion in the middle of the battling pair of men. Another.

Preston seemed literally to go mad. Frothing at the mouth, he tried to sink his teeth in Hines. He fought crazily, insanely, with maniacal strength. Hines forgot that there was anything in the world but this one single man he hated. He forgot everything—

And then Schaaf was pulling him to his feet, crying:

"We haff fife minutes, Hines! Fife minutes only! Find Miss Bush!"

8

ZERO HOUR

THE TWO OF them came above ground with Kathryn, and only two minutes to spare. The ensign and ten men were about to assail a squat concrete structure after the orthodox fashion of warfare when Hines gasped, "Get your men! Get 'em to the boat! We killed Preston but not his men! Zero hour's two minutes off!"

The air upon the island itself was no longer opaque. Schaaf's berserk rage among the vacuum tubes had cut that off. But the column of darkness leading to an utterly black sky still held steady. Somewhere in the extraordinarily clear air a rocket shot up, very far away.

The ensign's whistle shrilled madly. Hines, Schaaf, Kathryn, and a dozen men raced for the boat. Other men loomed up, panting, and flung themselves through the night. Once a man tripped over a low wire and four men fell on top of him. There was a long drawn out, deliberate whining sound in the air. It was growing louder. It rose to a shriek and passed overhead and went off deafeningly a quarter of a mile away. The four fallen men were up in the fractional part of a split second at that sound.

Into the boat in desperate, panting haste. Shoving off.

They had been rowing a pitifully short time when little

licking flames became visible on the skyline toward shore. Somewhere in the upper darkness there was a hail of steel and high explosive hurtling toward the island.

Something shrieked and splashed overboard not a dozen yards away. The drumming noise of a barrage began, and held for nearly a second, and then the sound of exploding shells was not like a barrage at all. It was like one long, continuous explosion, punctuated with monstrous blasts of sound which could be nothing less than twelve inch shells exploding.

The men at the oars pulled like madmen. The air was full of the shrieking of steel missiles, and the island behind them was lost in a mass of darting flames like marsh fire. Things fell into the sea on all sides with monstrous splashings, and the cutter pitched crazily, and more shells screamed and whistled and howled, and lambent flames of death and destruction played over the island, with ever and again a blinding flash and an overpowering concussion where a big projectile had hit.

It seemed to Hines, holding fast to Kathryn, that they would be battered to pieces by sheer waves of sound if stray shells did not do the work. For that was a more immediate danger still. Many shells that fell short of the island ricocheted and exploded in mid-air, or splashed into the sea again on the farther side. Some fell fearfully near them. Some struck in the shallows near the shore, and those explosions sent concussions through the water that made the hull of the speeding cutter quiver and shake. They racked and twisted the little cockleshell. The monstrous waves generated by the explosions flung it crazily about, and the concussions wrenched its timbers, and the blasts of the detonating shells half-dazed those in it.

But the oarsmen pulled like madmen. The ensign shouted encouragement and orders. And slowly—so slowly—the cutter drew away from the inferno that was the island.

HINES WAS HOLDING Kathryn fiercely tight when he realized that Schaaf was shouting in his ear. They were a mile away from the island, but the din was still deafening.

"Hines!" bellowed Schaaf. "Hines! *Die Sterne!* Der stars are shining!"

The wind over the water was bitter cold, but as the cutter drew farther and ever farther away from the low-lying place that had been Preston's stronghold, all the world seemed to take on a nearly normal seeming.

Stars twinkled and glittered in the sky overhead. Far to the east a vast, partly round orb was coming up over the edge of the world. For the world had an edge again! It was the moon. And there were dusky little shadows against the stars, which would be clouds, and generally the world seemed astoundingly normal.

Later on, of course, the sun would rise, and there would be great winds rushing to meet its warm rays, and men and women and children would go mad with joy at sight of the orb they had missed for exactly one day.

Schaaf, swearing joyful Teutonic profanity, would plunge into a new task before him, of research and duplication of Preston's results, and would come out of it bleary-eyed from lack of sleep, but with apparatus which would perform every one of Preston's tricks to order.

He would hale Hines back from his honeymoon to join

with him in forming the International Weather Control Corporation, whose typhoon patrol vessels are to be found wherever bad weather threatens in the tropics, using Preston's discoveries to create half a dozen small counter-storms where a hurricane or typhoon threatens. Those same tiny storms, too, he and Hines would use to lengthen the Alaskan summer by two months and raise the winter temperature by nearly thirty degrees.

All this was yet to happen, and the possibly greater benefit of liberating an unlimited supply of power by Preston's freezing ray. Liquid air drips from every iron surface on which those rays are playing. Nowadays, that liquid air provides the power to run the monster generating stations at Manhasset, and Panama, and at Algiers. And since their success, others are being built as rapidly as the structures can be completed. It seems probable that within a relatively few years coal need no longer be mined for power, nor need nations bicker or quarrel over petroleum.

But on that morning when the ship's cutter rowed away from Metinic Island, the coast toward which it moved was flickering oddly as if heat lightning were playing there. There were lurid spoutings of fire and shattering explosions coming from the land they had left, and there were dim bulks all around the horizon, which emitted tongues of flame and unbearable thunderings. Even overhead there was noise.

It was a constant, long-continued screaming of things soaring through the air to fall upon and shatter further the already devastated earth of the island. The battleships and cruisers were literally destroying that small bit of Earth.

Where the fourteen inch shells exploded there was only empty space left, into which the salt water seeped slowly.

The cutter went on, snail-like, while destruction raged behind it Schaaf fingered his beard and made blissful explanations to the ensign, to whom his blending of abstruse technicalities and incongruous slang was nearly unintelligible. Hines relaxed slowly from his tension. He knew that Preston was dead now. He was sure of it at last. Quite, quite sure—he clenched his strong hands.

Kathryn said uneasily:

"I—I've a great story for the *Star*."

"Forget it," said Hines briefly. "We were supposed to be married yesterday, Kathryn."

"Y-yes," she admitted. "We were."

"So," said Hines, "we are going to be married to-day."

He held her hand fast.

"Y-yes," she said, after a long time. "We are… But oh, when I think what might have happened, I wish I'd never heard of Preston. I wish he never had existed."

"Shush, my dear," said Schaaf paternally. "He got you a husband. Der statement is banana oil."

ABOUT THE AUTHOR

ANYBODY WHO WANTS to pass an uncomfortable half hour needs only to sit down and try to write something about himself for "The Men Who Make the Argosy" page. I've been trying it quite that long, and it isn't easy. The trouble is that you are expected to be truthful, and yet you want to be interesting.

The second is the difficult part. Nobody will be especially thrilled, for instance, to learn that I am a Virginian; that I've got two dogs, a canary, and a duck; that I live thirty miles from a railroad by choice, because I can do up to seventy miles an hour on the roads around here without adverse comment, and more under favorable circumstances; that I've served in two armies without injury save to my self-esteem; that I nearly broke my neck in a glider away back in 1908, and just took my three daughters—aged three, six, and nine—up in a plane for the first time the other day; that I am a Democrat; that my front porch is at this moment littered up with a mess of wires and coils and gadgets to make a contrivance almost as weird as, if less spectacular than, the devices described in some of my yarns—and that it seems to work; that I am not a prohibitionist; that I love to write serials, and hate to read 'em; that I have been a writer for fourteen years, and that it is still hard work; or that my most cherished ambition is to sleep late in the mornings.

But that's about the best I can do to fill up this space, though I'd like to make it exciting. I sold one of my first stories to *Argosy* just about the time I began to shave. I shall hope to keep it up at least until I have long white whiskers. Meanwhile… Well, the latest is "The Sleep Gas."